Praise for the

Dark Elves 1: Taken

"Mykles is not afraid to push the envelope in order to create a story that captivates the reader."

— Rho, *A Romance Review*

"Ms. Mykles as woven a deliciously erotic fantasy with *Dark Elves 1: Taken*. I was hot and bothered by the first chapter!"

— Luisa, *Cupids Library Reviews*

"Full of smoldering passion *Dark Elves 1: Taken* will tempt and fascinate the reader into being a character in this book."

— Sheryl, *eCataRomance Reviews*

Dark Elves 2: Mastered

"*Dark Elves 2: Mastered* is a riveting fantasy tale that will snatch you from the very first page and keep your eyes glued to every word."

— Mireya Orsini, *Just Erotic Romance Reviews*

"I was positively giddy when I learned that the continuation of the *Dark Elves* series was being published."

— Miaka Chase, *The Romance Studio*

"From beginning to end, *Dark Elves 2: Mastered* is a sensual tale set to a world that will deliver the reader passionate delights."

— Dawn, *Love Romances*

LooseId®

ISBN 978-1-59632-671-2
DARK ELVES: TAKEN
Copyright © 2008 by Jet Mykles

Cover Art by Anne Cain
Cover Design by April Martinez

Publisher acknowledges the author and copyright holder of the individual works, as follows:
DARK ELVES 1: TAKEN Copyright © March 2005 by Jet Mykles
DARK ELVES 2: MASTERED Copyright © June 2005 by Jet Mykles

Printed in the U.S.A. by
Lightning Source, Inc.
1246 Heil Quaker Blvd
La Vergne TN 37086
www.lightningsource.com

Contents

Dark Elves 1: Taken
1

Dark Elves 2: Mastered
147

DARK ELVES 1: TAKEN

Chapter One

Even in the early evening noise of the tavern, Diana's silence was deafening. Gala sat beside her, nursing an ale gone flat. Waiting.

"I'm going after him," Diana finally announced, standing.

Gala shot to her feet, her hand darting out to take Diana's wrist. "You can't!" she protested, even though she knew it was hopeless. Diana had *that* look on her face.

Diana's fine, dark brows lowered. "I can. And I will."

"But you've heard the stories about the mountains," Gala insisted, following as Diana stormed toward the stairs that led up to their rented room.

"Bah! That's just what they are. Stories. I'll agree that passing over the mountains is probably a hard trek, but they've not even been gone a day! We can catch them, get my money back, then come back here."

Gala wasn't so sure. Although they were new to the area, she and Diana had heard tale after tale of both the Rhaen Mountains and the Dark Forest. The mountains, it was said, were impassable save by a very few caravans owned by masters who'd traveled the route countless times. But even they were often beset by natural forces, and people almost always disappeared through travel misfortunes.

The stories about the Dark Forest were more sinister. Those included tales of entire bands entering the depths of the forest and simply disappearing, then the bones of some of the victims showing up neatly arranged toward the safer outskirts of the forest. Neatly arranged so that it was sure no animal could have accomplished it. And the bones, from what anyone could tell, were always those of the male victims. Female victims were never seen nor heard from again. Rescue parties sent after those missing either never returned or returned with wild stories of black phantoms and sinister magic.

But Gala had known Diana since childhood and had traveled with her as her only companion for the past five springs. She was the untrained healer, the pickpocket, the negotiator. While Diana was the fighter, the instigator, the lure. Together, they'd managed to get enough odd jobs to stay alive as they continually wandered.

The previous night, Diana had been cheated, her money stolen, and the culprit had taken off in the morning -- while Diana was passed out cold -- with one of the mountain caravans. It had taken Diana most of the day to recover from the thief's blow to her head, but once she'd recovered, her anger flared. And Diana's anger, once sparked, did not die easily.

Diana hefted her bag, quiver, and unstrung bow and faced Gala across the tiny room they'd shared. "I know you don't like this idea," she said, visibly trying to rein in her anger. "You don't have to go with me. I can be back by tomorrow night."

Resolute, Gala shook her head. "Where you go, I go. We've been through worse before."

Even angry, Diana had to smile. But it was brief. Then she was out the door.

* * *

The track was easy enough to follow. The thief, in fact, had been the one to tell them what they now knew of the caravans that crossed the mountains. There were only two tracks that any caravan would take, both wide enough to fit the typical merchants' wagons. The High Road was actually faster, but more treacherous, as it went over one of the tall mountains. The Low Road added weeks to a trek, but it was safer, even if it skirted the edges of the Dark Forest throughout most of the journey.

"Camp is held on the road, as well," Gala recalled the charming man telling them. "No one's allowed to step foot off the road."

"Why not?" Diana had asked, already intrigued by him.

"Too dangerous. Anyone who loses sight of the road never returns."

Diana had laughed. "Never?"

Gala recalled the oddly serious look in the man's sparkling blue eyes. "Never."

Gala, for one, believed him.

Although the twisted oaks and soaring elms that lined the path were gorgeous, there was a sinister cast to them. With true night fast approaching, Gala became certain that eyes were upon them. Diana was mostly silent, still smarting on the back of her skull where the thief had struck her. What words she did utter either had to do with their travel or with the questionable parentage of the thief they now tailed down the Low Road. The forest closed in around them. Sunlight was left behind. Evidence of plenty of wildlife grew around them.

"These people are insane," Diana said suddenly, gesturing toward a covey of quail that scurried boldly across the road. "This place is a wealth of game."

Gala stirred at the change of subject, but only nodded. She adjusted her seat in the saddle, yawning to shed the apathy caused by the gentle roll of her horse's gait.

"Where's this 'dark danger' we were warned of?" Diana scoffed as the last vestiges of sunlight disappeared and plunged them into thick, gray twilight. Even so, Gala saw her friend's hand drift toward the sword at her belt.

"Should we make camp?" Gala asked, spurring her mount to walk abreast of Diana's.

"No. Let's keep going. The caravan will be making camp soon. We should catch them before daybreak."

Gala nodded, her eyes darting from shadow to shadow. Night had fallen on them abruptly, and only the scant moonlight provided illumination to the path ahead of them. To either side was inky darkness.

They rode in silence for a time.

"It's warm," Gala realized.

Diana took a moment to judge, idly rubbing a hand against her chest. "It's got to be the trees," she stated. "No breeze."

Gala nodded, but continued to look about. Why was she flushed? Of a sudden, her tunic was either far too tight or her breasts had swelled. The saddle between her legs grew increasingly uncomfortable as she realized she felt…aroused?

"Diana," she murmured, finally convinced that what she felt was not natural.

Diana gasped, and Gala whirled to face the same direction. Oddly, her hand didn't fall to the hilt of her shortsword. Nor did their horses balk. Both mounts came to a calm halt beneath their riders. But both riders were distracted from that oddity by the figure that appeared before them.

"Appeared" was an apt term, as the dark figure seemed to materialize from the inky shadow of a particularly large oak which overhung the road. The tall figure was completely contained within a voluminous, hooded black robe. Two spots of glowing red were all that pierced the darkness within the hood.

Red?

Gala and Diana sat their mounts, riveted. Gala licked suddenly dry lips, aware her breathing had quickened, as the figure raised black hands to the clasp of the hood, just below where a chin should be. In one beautiful, fluid movement, the robe parted and slid to the ground.

Both women gasped.

A man stood before them. A man unlike any either had ever encountered before. Tall and muscular, he resembled the perfect specimen of a lean, human male, but the skin that was stretched taut over chiseled muscle was pure, gleaming black, like the surface of a moonlit pond. The two points of red which had glowed from within the hood proved to be the irises of his eyes, eyes that held them captive from beneath stark white lashes. Snowy white hair fell straight and gleaming over his shoulders and down his back, held back by two braids at his temples and what looked to be one behind his head. Strange white designs, like tattoos, emblazoned his chest and belly, as well as his forehead.

Vaguely, Gala wondered that she saw such detail, until she found that she was now standing just a few feet before the man. How had she gotten there? When had she dismounted, and how had she crossed the short distance to him without being aware of it? Diana stood beside her as well, she noted out of the corner of her eyes. Only the corner, because she could not tear her gaze from this man with his gleaming onyx skin and delicately pointed ears. An elf? She'd never heard of dark-skinned elves, let alone those with skin the hue of the blackest night. She stood now before him, taking the hand that he extended. All the while, her gaze was fastened to his, even when his focus was on Diana. He was so amazingly beautiful! A piece of the most mystical moonlit night made flesh.

His hand was warm as it encircled hers and drew her close. The top of her head was about on level with his shoulder, putting her mouth right in line with the black, puckered nipple to which his hand was gently guiding her lips. She parted them willingly and lapped at his flesh, her hands raised to flatten against his belly and side. His skin tasted like cool spring water and hot cinnamon spice, a heady, strange combination that saturated her tongue and slid down her throat. Her own moan vibrated in her throat as she sucked harder.

She felt lips on her forehead, a sweet caress. Then the

hand on the back of her neck pressed until she realized she was meant to kneel. She did, her body sliding sensuously down his until she reached her knees and her eyes were level with his cock. Thick and proudly erect, it thrust at her. She lapped at her own lips, still tasting his nipple, and wrapped her hand around his beautiful organ. She'd never before thought the male form particularly awe-inspiring, but this creature's entire body was a gift from the gods. She slid her hand down the shaft, finding it was, curiously, already slick to the touch, easily sliding through her grasp. Although Gala had never performed such an act with her few other lovers, she opened her mouth and guided that fleshy tool past her lips.

Diana saw Gala from the corner of her eye. A part of her mind suggested that this should stop. But the beautiful black man's hand was caressing her face. She turned to catch his gaze, riveted on her despite Gala's ministrations to his sex. Murmuring something she didn't understand, he gently pried her lips apart with his thumb, then eased the thick digit into the wet recess of her mouth.

Obediently, she suckled, lulled by his deep, resonant voice.

What was he saying?

What was she *doing!?*

But she couldn't stop. The thumb in her mouth was a small substitute for the organ in Gala's mouth, but it was curiously just as effective. Diana felt things melt low in her belly. At length, he tugged her forward until he could press her against his side. Her leg bumped Gala's shoulder, but she couldn't concentrate on that. Not when his glistening black lips were bending to take hers. His kiss was bliss. Warm as sunshine to a chilled body. Eagerly, she drank from him, sucking his tongue into her mouth before he had a chance to offer it. When he pulled from her, she protested, reaching. Smiling, he backed away. Only distantly did she know her friend stood beside her.

The intriguing creature made an abrupt, downward gesture with his hand, and suddenly everything went blank.

Another black figure peeled from the shadows of the trees, arriving in time to catch the taller woman as she slumped in spelled slumber. The sorcerer caught the smaller. The unconscious women were held tenderly as the black figures stepped off the beaten path into the thick of the forest.

Chapter Two

Obsidian hands anchored Diana to the bed as her body continued to writhe. She groaned, unable to vocalize the explosive ramp to her orgasm. His cock filled her to bursting, and still she wanted, *needed* more. On all fours, she clawed at the sheets beneath her, bunching a wad of fine linen into her mouth to staunch her screams as he twisted to a different angle and hit her in a spot she'd never known she had. Sweat covered every inch of her body but failed to cool her. Her wet hair plastered in tendrils to her neck, the sides of her face. One heavy lock fell over her eyes, but it didn't matter. She couldn't see. There might be tears in her eyes, but with every other wetness, she could no longer tell.

Her legs threatened to cramp, but still she forced them to slam her hips back against his. The pleasure was torture, but her body wouldn't allow her to stop. With a scream, she came again. Her entire body imploded, so tense her muscles shook. She collapsed to her belly, panting in an effort to get air into her lungs. For precious moments, that was all she could do, all she could think of.

Then as he withdrew, she realized to her astonishment

that she wasn't sated! Although she was sore from the inside out, her juices continued to flow, her breasts ached, and her empty cunt was still pulsing.

Desperately, she dragged a hand over her eyes, trying to pull herself from her daze. Moans reached her ears. When she could focus, it still took her precious moments of staring to decide on what she was seeing.

Gala. Her friend. Her companion. Gala lay on her back beside Diana, her smaller body nearly hidden beneath the beast with satiny black skin.

What is he? Diana had enough sense to wonder, even as she refused her hand's urge to reach out and stroke the rippling muscles on his bare back. He was shaped like a human, but she was sure he couldn't be. Even in her haze, she knew nothing with skin that color, ears that pointed, nor eyes that glowing red was human. Silky, soft white hair fell in glorious waves, curtaining his face from her and nearly hiding Gala, as well. Gala, who desperately clung to his big body as his hips slid that wonderful, monster cock in and out of her.

A sudden flip of his head tossed his white locks to the far side of his head, and that wickedly gorgeous face turned to Diana. Reason and rationality left, and she crawled on aching limbs to get close enough to press her lips to his. She didn't care that he was fucking her friend. She didn't care that her position brought her close to her friend's naked body. It didn't matter. She'd do anything to touch him again.

Without thought, she slid her hand down his back to his buttocks. Her mouth now laving at the hard muscle at the back of his shoulder, she slid her fingers down the crack of his ass until she found his balls. His groan of appreciation hit her somewhere below her navel, and she continued to fondle him as he pumped into Gala. Growling, Diana repositioned herself so that her legs straddled his hairless calf. The hard muscle there did nicely to rub her aching clit.

Gala came. Distantly, Diana knew it, but she was far more interested in her own approaching climax. She wanted him to fuck her again. How many times had he already fucked her? How many times had he brought her to climax?

Had he yet climaxed?

Thoughts shattered as she came again. This time, her weak muscles wouldn't allow her to continue riding him. She slumped into a pile beside him as he continued to ride Gala.

What was happening?

Determined, Diana backed away until she could slide in a clumsy heap to the floor. Glancing up, she saw clear red eyes watching her, but he didn't even break stride. Not even as Gala was clearly biting his neck. Hard.

Sweet god of war, she wanted him again! He smiled, and she was nearly mad with the desire to suck that succulent lower lip into her mouth. Groaning, she buried her face in the rumpled sheet. She concentrated hard on finding control, on finding her voice. Something was wrong.

She had no clue how long she sat there. The coital sounds only a few feet from her were tuned out as she sought her center.

THWACK!!

Diana's head shot up just in time to catch sight of the business end of a whip slithering off the beast's shining black back. He was kneeling now, Gala half seated, half lying before him.

THWACK!

Diana's mind was suddenly clear, and she scrambled away from the bed. Gala, her face a mask of panic, tumbled from the mattress. They scrambled to the corner and huddled together, heedless of their nudity.

The beast didn't seem to notice, frozen with a look of agony on his face.

A female voice screamed in rage. On the other end of the whip was a woman, or at least a female version of whatever the beast was. Like him, her skin was satin black and her hair shining white, but her ears were not pointed. She wore very little -- a long loincloth draped loosely over her hips, and little slippers. And she was very pregnant.

She drew back and expertly hit him with the whip; at least six feet of supple white leather hissed through the air to cut at his back. He jerked, his head thrown back, but he made no move to escape her. Nor did the whip rip his skin as it should.

"Diana...?!" Gala gasped.

But Diana had seen it too. He wasn't in pain, not if the bobbing of his erection was any indication. Before their astounded eyes, the cock that had taken them both to countless climaxes burst forth his seed as the female again let the whip go.

With a pleased groan, he crumpled to a heap on the bed.

The female snarled something in what could only be their language, then proceeded toward the bed. The girls scrambled back against the wall, eyeing the whip still uncoiled in her hand.

"We didn't know!" Gala cried.

The female frowned at them. She pointed with the whip handle. "Are you all right?" she asked in clear commonspeak.

Diana scowled, but Gala was effusive. "We didn't know he was yours. We didn't. I mean..."

"Don't be ridiculous," scoffed the female, coming to stand beside the male, who was almost purring with contentment. "I know very well what happened. You were under a spell." She kicked at the male's hand as he reached to stroke her leg. "And you don't even know yet what's happened to you."

"What's happened to us?" Diana demanded, quickly scanning the room for any sign of their clothing or weapons. Neither were evident.

"Come with me. I'll let you get washed up, get some food for you, and I'll tell you."

"We'd rather leave."

The female's clear blue eyes locked on Diana's. "You can't ever leave. They won't let you."

"To hells with that," Diana pronounced. She shot to her feet, completely forgetting the state of her body. Her legs protested and buckled. Only Gala's ready help got her to the ground without injuring her.

The female sighed and called out something in that other language. Instantly, two more of the beasts, these two far more burly than the first, appeared. The female pointed and, much to Diana's dismay, they came and picked up each of the girls. Diana wanted to fight, but there was nothing left in her. The first beast had used her body beyond exhaustion.

Chapter Three

The girls were taken to a strange little bathing room. The windowless walls were carved to look like stone and mortar, but the feel of the place was obviously underground. Everything was remarkably well kept. There was only a bit of a dank cave smell. A pool in the ground larger than any tub Diana had previously used was filled with pleasantly warm, lavender-scented water. There was no mold, no slimy walls.

"Don't get comfortable," Diana cautioned Gala as her friend was about to step into the pool. "We don't know what's happening."

Although the water was inviting beyond measure, both girls contented themselves with dipping cloths in it and using those to wipe sweat and sex juices from their skin. They avoided each other's gazes.

"Diana…" Gala started softly.

"No," Diana denied. "I don't want to talk about it. Not now. Let's get out of here first."

"But…"

"No. Please. I…can't."

She couldn't meet her friend's eyes. Each time Diana looked at her, she vividly recalled the sight of Gala's smooth skin, her pert breasts bouncing as that beast fucked her to climax and beyond.

Thankfully, Gala remained silent as they finished their washing. They wrapped their nakedness in long, light cloths left for them, as they were the only covering available aside from the drying cloths. The same two huge men awaited them when they emerged, and escorted them down a short, torchlit hall.

The room in which the female awaited them might have been a parlor in any lord's manor. Fine furniture was spread across a wood plank floor. Even the walls, which must have been more stone, were papered to look normal. Again, the lack of windows was the only hint they were belowground.

The pregnant female reclined on a lady's couch, eating with dainty fingers from a bowl perched precariously on her bulging belly.

"Welcome," she said, a touch of sarcasm in her voice. "Please, have something to eat." With a wave, she indicated a side table covered with a buffet of dishes. "I know you must be hungry."

"Where are we?" Diana demanded, grabbing Gala's arm when she would have approached the food.

The female smiled. "I'll answer all your questions as best I can, I promise. But you really should eat first."

"How do we know that the food isn't part of this spell you mentioned?"

She arched a brow at Diana. "You don't. I can only tell you that it's not. It's just normal food. The spell has already been cast, and the fucking you received sealed it." The last was said with a slight snarl.

Diana felt her blush at the blatant words, but continued to stare the female down. "What spell?"

With an irritating grin, the female shook her head. "Eat first."

"Diana, please," Gala interrupted when Diana opened her mouth to refuse. "We can't go very far on an empty stomach."

"You see?" said the female, staring into her bowl. "Your friend speaks sense."

"None of this makes sense," Diana growled. However, she released Gala and followed her to the table. Most of the food was recognizable, both by sight and smell. Rich venison roasted with small red potatoes and mushrooms dominated, but there was also a hearty stew that smelled like rabbit, as well as vegetables. That didn't negate the possibility of poison, but Diana had to concede that they were already captured. Poison didn't seem to make much sense.

Diana and Gala both made plates and took them to the pillows the female indicated on the floor before her couch. Diana wanted to protest. The positions made them seem supplicants to the lady, but for all she knew, this was the queen of these people and therefore due the respect.

Once she'd seen that they'd actually begun to eat, the female spoke up. "First, let me introduce myself. My name is Iana."

When Diana made no motion to respond, Gala supplied their names. Iana noted Diana's reaction with a wry grin, but said nothing. She addressed herself to Gala. "I don't expect you've ever heard of *raedjour*, have you?"

Silence indicated that neither girl had. Iana nodded. "No, you wouldn't have. But that's where you are, in the underground kingdom of the *raedjour*. It's quite an extensive city, actually, and goes on for miles underneath the forest and mountains."

"The *raedjour* are the mystery of the Dark Forest?" Gala asked.

"They are. As well as the dark terrors of the Rhaen Mountains. Fitting, don't you think, given the skin color?" she asked, holding out her arm to display her obsidian skin.

"The *raedjour* have been killing people in the Dark Forest for centuries?"

"Yes. But not everyone was killed. Males, usually yes. But no female has ever been slain intentionally by a *raedjour* man. Their goddess wouldn't abide it. Instead, they capture them."

Gala supplied the question Iana wanted. "Why?"

"Quite simple, actually. You see, the *raedjour* were created by their goddess -- Rhae -- as sexual consorts before the gods left the earth. She'd never expected to leave, you see, so she didn't think ahead. She only created males. When she left, she had to do something to ensure their survival. So she told them to steal human women. They already oozed sex, so there was no doubt the women would be attracted. The goddess gave them a spell to convert human women to *raedjour* so that the women could have the *raedjours'* babies."

"You were human?" Gala gasped.

The anger and sadness in Iana's proud gaze was evident

as she nodded.

"But they've been doing this for centuries. Why continue to take more women?"

"For some reason, only male children have been born."

"Ever?"

"Ever." Iana smoothed a hand over her belly. "I myself have had four sons. This will be the fifth."

"With…?"

"His name is Nalfien. He's the most powerful sorcerer among the *raedjour* at this moment. And, as *raedjour* measure such things, I'm his wife. His truemate."

"I'm so sorry," Gala bemoaned, reaching out to touch Iana's hand. "We truly didn't know…didn't mean…"

"You mean the fucking? Think nothing of it." Despite her words, it was obvious the "fucking" bothered her. "You'll find *raedjour* society quite unlike human society where sex is concerned. Even truemated *raedjour* will fuck others, both male and female. In Nalfien's situation, he fucked you to set the spell. He tells me it's necessary."

Neither Diana nor Gala could hide their shock at Iana's direct words.

"But you wanted to know about the spell," Iana continued, ignoring their reaction. "It wasn't just the spell that made you want them. As I said, their ancestors were created as consorts to a goddess. There's something about them that will naturally attract you. The spell, however, made you crazy with lust. I don't understand it all, but as far as I know, the lust distracted you so the change spell could get past your natural defenses and start the change."

"The change?" Diana demanded.

"To *raedjour.*"

"No!" Diana cried, shooting to her feet. Although her legs were still somewhat wobbly, she was able to stand.

Iana regarded her mildly. "Where do you think you're going?"

"I won't change."

"And you believe you have a say in this? You do remember the two rather large men that brought you here? They're still out there. I'm surprised they haven't barged in already."

Diana shook with rage, fists bunching and flexing. Iana continued to stare. "Wouldn't you rather sit nicely for the little time I can steal for you, and find out what is in store for you?"

"I won't."

Iana's eyes slitted. "Good. Fight them. I'm the first to hope you'll win. But I don't think you will, and you *certainly* won't if you don't know what is coming in the immediate future."

"Diana," Gala soothed, "please, sit down. Let's hear what Iana has to say."

"I can't sit," Diana muttered, beginning to pace the room.

"Please, Iana," Gala asked, "go on."

"Very well. The spell isn't very consistent. Some women change immediately; some take longer. I can tell you that becoming *raedjour* means you can no longer stand even the most mild sunlight. I know, I've tried. Even on the coldest, most overcast day, a few moments in the sun and your body heats unbearably, and the light is too bright to see a thing.

The other side of the coin is that you never get cold. The torches here are mostly for light for those who are still human -- because you also acquire night vision that would put a cat to shame.

"As for what's about to happen to you, you should brace yourselves. You know now that you're here for breeding purposes, but that's not the full extent of it. There's only one possible man who can impregnate you. Your truemate. No one knows why -- and believe me, it frustrates them no end -- but each man only seems to be fertile with one female in his lifetime."

"How do they know?" Gala asked.

"Remember I said this is a sexual society. Most, if not all, truemates have, on many occasions, fucked others, truemated or no. The rule still stands. Either they're only fertile with their truemate, or it's the truemate's presence that makes them fertile to others. As no one can really tell, it's assumed that only truemates are fertile."

"So what happens to us?"

"You'll be taken from here to the first of a long line of lovers."

"No!" Diana cried.

Iana ignored her. "You'll stay with each man for nine nights. If, at the end of that time, you're pregnant, a truematch is announced and you're his."

"*His?*" Diana demanded.

"How can they tell if you're pregnant after nine days?" Gala asked over Diana's objection.

Iana's eyes shadowed, staring at her belly. "They know."

"So they just pass us from man to man until we're pregnant?" Diana cried.

Iana nodded. "You'll have short breaks after each nine days and when your moontime comes, but even that will stop after a time. *Raedjour* cycles are different from humans."

"How long does it take?" Gala asked in a tiny voice.

"To find your truemate?" Iana clarified. "It varies. From my own experience, I lost count at forty lovers before Nalfien planted me."

"Forty!" Diana cried. "No! It won't happen. I..." She wavered on her feet, her knees again wobbly.

"Diana, are you all right?" Gala asked, immediately at her side, though she was wobbly herself.

The door opened and the first male -- the sorcerer -- walked in. "Iana," he greeted his truemate in commonspeak. "I trust you've had a nice chat with our guests?"

"You son of a skunk!" Diana spat, still struggling to stand with Gala's help. She lost the battle and fell to her hands and knees. "What have you done to me?"

"Extraordinary," she heard him murmur as he slowly approached her. "You have such strength, Diana. But don't fight the spell. It will only hurt you."

"I won't give in to you."

"That's the spirit," Iana cheered, glaring at her mate. "Fight him, Diana. Fight him with all you are!"

"Iana, that's enough," he admonished.

"This isn't happening," Diana gasped, trying to lock her arms to keep from collapsing to the floor.

"Deny all you like," Iana said, not unkindly. "But, believe me, it's happening."

That was the last Diana heard before the world went black.

Chapter Four

Diana woke in a softly lit chamber. The bed beneath her was comfortable, and the light blanket was all she needed in the warm room. Open windows were set in the wall across from her, displaying pure blackness beyond.

She glanced about the chamber to find herself alone. Sitting up, she saw that the chamber was quite a normal-looking bedchamber, complete with clothes chests and a side table set beneath a polished disk. Rising, she crossed to the window. It was barred, the space between the bars far too narrow for her to fit between. Experimentally, she tugged the bars. Solid and unmoving.

Beyond the opening, she could make out the rock of the cavern ceiling. Minerals played the part of stars in the stony sky. Below was a perfectly normal-looking courtyard surrounded on three sides by the building she was in. The fourth side was a stone wall possessed of an open but fortified gate. Although the design was more elegant than any she'd seen, the strength of the fortification was evident.

The door's lock clicked. She whirled, the fact that she was naked now apparent to her, but it was too late to do anything about it.

It was, of course, one of *them*.

He wasn't quite as stunning as the sorcerer had been. Not quite as chiseled, and none of the curious white tattoos marked his skin. Still, this one was gorgeous. He was tall, and every inch of him was carved muscle. Snug trousers hugged his thighs and soft boots covered his feet. His chest was gleaming, bare black. This one's hair flowed in a straight ivory flow from the crown of his head to the middle of his back, with a few wispy tendrils brushing his chest. His violet eyes gleamed as he viewed his treasure.

"I am Boutel," he said, taking a step toward her.

She dropped into an attack-ready crouch. "Stay away," she warned.

He raised one silky brow and took another step, but her raised fist stopped him. "You'll fight me?" he asked, surprised.

"With everything I've got," she promised. "I won't be raped."

He chuckled, bracing his hands on his lean hips. "It would hardly be rape, dear woman," he purred. "*Raedjour* do not need rape. Unless --" His eyes dropped to sultry slits. "-- that is what appeals to you."

Her eyes narrowed. "Hardly," she answered. Unbidden, she recalled her time with Nalfien. Remembered not caring that he was fucking her friend. She'd only wanted to touch him. If this man could affect her similarly, was there anything she could do?

Boutel took another step toward her. She sidled away. His gaze sharpened, a feral grin curving his black lips. The bastard was enjoying this!

He circled her, a gleaming panther stalking a defiant doe. She scowled when his hands went to the fastening of his trousers and untied the laces.

"Keep your trousers on!" she demanded.

He only laughed. "Oh, no." From the opening sprang a cock as dark as he was, and every bit as alert. There was no nest of hair at the base of that organ, nothing to relieve the expanse of onyx skin curving from groin to cock tip. The skin would be hot, like the sorcerer's. What else would be the same?

He sprang. She screamed, realizing she'd let herself be distracted by his cock. He caught her arm and twisted, forcing her back to him. She tried to kick at him, but he eluded her, shoving one leg in between hers. The bed was too close behind her -- before her, now -- and he quite easily tumbled them onto it.

She screamed again, bucking underneath him, but he only held her until she calmed. His long hair tickled her left cheek. Spitefully, she bit it.

He laughed outright, infuriating her. Worse, the proximity of his body filled her attention. Carved muscle pressed against her back. His arms pressed against her sides as he held her wrists tightly. He shifted, the new position snugging his cock into the crack of her ass. Groaning, she buried her face in the bed beneath her, shocked at how hard it was not to press back against him.

"Yes," he purred, his breath a caress to her temple. She shuddered when his lips found a tender spot behind her ear. His tongue trailed along the shell of her ear until he could use it to guide her lobe into his mouth. "I promise you only pleasure. We're bred for this."

"Give it to some other woman," she demanded, very little conviction in her voice.

Gently, he bit down. "You're my woman for the next nine days," he said around her earlobe.

She bucked, and they both groaned as the movement fit him more snugly against her. His hands clenched around her wrists. His lips dropped to her neck, gently nibbling her nape. "Relax, Diana," he soothed, retreating enough that his lips reached the curve of her shoulder and his cock eased down until it nudged at her moistened entrance. Warm. So warm. And did she feel a light sheen of oil rubbing from his skin to hers? Not just his cock, but his chest and arms. And it smelled divine! Had he oiled his body before coming to her? She wiggled again, but that only succeeded in wetting the tip of his cock in her juices.

"So sweet," he murmured, his breath melting the bones of her spine. By tilting his hips, he eased more of his shaft through her juices. The blunt head rasped against her clit, and she gasped.

Her wrists fell free when he released them to better angle himself. *Run!* She ordered herself, but her body wouldn't obey. Filled with his odd, spicy scent, covered by his body, her traitorous muscles were tensed and ready, her very womb drooling at the prospect of his entrance.

His fingers traced a path down her back, lingering over the swell of her buttocks. She refused to hear his murmured words, clenching her eyes shut as his caresses heated her skin. Made a token struggle when his hands grasped her thighs to haul her up into a more accessible position, but he easily subdued her. Then she was positioned.

Then he was inside.

Groaning, she clasped the bedclothes to either side of her face, pressing the sheets to her face to mute the sound he pushed from her as he tunneled endlessly inside.

"Ah, yes," he cried, seated to the hilt. He paused, letting her inner walls adjust to him. Grip him. "You see, Diana."

I see that I'm under a spell that makes... Ah! Gods! He was pulling out, the friction sending shivers to her toes.

And in. Slowly. So she could feel every glorious inch. She moaned.

"Life with us can be so good," he crooned, pulling out. He did it twice more, slowly sinking the sword deep into her heart.

Then, abruptly, he slammed in. She gasped. The sudden move was enough to snap her just a bit from her haze. With a cry, she lurched forward, struggling to escape the sensuous weave that ensnared her.

Startled, he lost his hold on her. She tumbled head over heels from the bed, scrambling on all fours to the farthest corner of the room.

"Diana!"

She heard him behind her and whirled. "You will *not* take me that easily!" she declared, ignoring that he *had*, in fact, done just that.

Standing before her, his cock was just at her eye-level, poking out of the trousers he still wore, and just out of her reach. Bobbing before him, it gleamed even more than before, wet now with her cream. Unconsciously, she licked her lips.

He frowned down at her. "Nalfien said you'd be

reluctant," he grumbled. "But why?"

"I don't want this," she snarled.

"You did just a moment ago. What's changed?"

"I don't know you," she answered, reflex. She had to keep him talking. Or was it that she had to distract herself?

He dropped to a crouch before her, close but not so close that she couldn't breathe. He smiled. "I'm doing my best to let you know me. Intimately."

She ground her teeth, clutching her arms uselessly about her knees. "Smug bastard. I don't *want* to know you."

He cocked his head to the side, hair tumbling over his shoulder. "Must I restrain you?"

Her eyes went wide. It must be the spell. Why else did the picture of his strapping her down make her heart race?

He grinned. "I think you'd like that."

She shook her head frantically. "No."

"Oh, yes."

He rose gracefully and turned toward a chest across the small room from her. Trembling with need, Diana used the warm -- warm? -- stone walls to gain her feet. There were only a few lit candles in the room. No fireplace. No firepit. How were the walls warm?

She had no time to contemplate further. Boutel had taken what he needed from the chest. Rope. Soft and silky, by the look of it, but thick and solid, as well. Grinning, he wound much of its length around both of his hands.

She trembled, forcing herself to believe it was fury and not lust which did this to her muscles. She watched his advance, knowing it was hopeless. He stood half a head taller than she and was twice as wide. She'd heard that elves were delicate creatures with bones as light as a bird's. Obviously, these dark elves were not of that species. Unless the bird were an eagle or a roc.

She darted aside at the last possible moment, not knowing where to go, only knowing that she had to fight rather than submit. He chased her, laughing. They darted about the room. She hurled a candelabra at him, horrified when he caught it and -- it seemed -- extinguished the flames with a look.

When he finally caught her, pinned between the wall and his body, she wasn't sure he hadn't been toying with her. Nor was she sure why she was running. Their scuffle in the warm room sprouted sweat on her naked skin. The heated air was dripping with the scent of him, and she was crazed with lust the instant his chest hit her back.

Grappling, snarling, although she no longer knew why, she finally struggled against the ropes alone. His cock was a searing brand each time it grazed her lower back or buttocks, and her only coherent thought was to deny herself the demand that he fuck her. She wanted it. He likely knew she wanted it. She wouldn't *say* it!

Once she was securely tied, he picked her up and tossed her on the bed. She rolled onto her back, lying on her trussed arms. The position and the crisscross of ropes he'd bound her with presented her breasts as a blatant lure. Her splayed legs were an open invitation.

An invitation he did not ignore. Without giving her any time to muster an escape, he fell on her, thrusting into her pussy in one hard glide. The primal sound that emitted from her throat was somewhere between a scream and a groan.

Even the painful wrenching of her arms couldn't dampen the searing pleasure of his sex pummeling hers. He braced himself above her, elbows to either side of her shoulders, fists tight in her hair. His mouth descended on hers, and she kissed him without thought of denial. His tongue was another necessary penetration.

Her first orgasm was loud and violent, only his heavy weight pinning them to the bed as her strong body bucked and writhed. Her second orgasm found her legs locked about his hips, her heels digging into the soft skin just below his buttocks as she used them to press him inside. Her third orgasm found her mewling, the sensations just as strong but her body depleted beyond fight. She missed his release through the never-ending trembling of her own. She was unconscious before he ever pulled out.

Chapter Five

Moons later...

Long before the door opened, Nalfien set aside the scroll he was reading. He sat quietly in the large chair, facing the door as Gala peeked around the heavy wood.

"Enter, child," he greeted her look of apprehension.

She scurried in, closing the door behind her. He took the opportunity to admire her sleek, soft body, only partially hidden beneath the filmy silk wrap that fastened at one shoulder and draped her torso. Her long, wavy blonde hair was a bit lighter than it had been when he'd taken her from the forest, a sign that she would be one to change rapidly once she found her truemate.

She leaned back against the door, her hands behind her. Nervous. He wondered what the cause was. Yes, he could have read her mind, but he tried not to intrude on the thoughts of others unless it was strictly necessary.

He held out a hand, encouraging her to approach. "What ails you, child?"

She frowned as she closed the distance between them. "I'm not a child," she insisted.

"Very well." He took her hand and guided her to sit on the padded stool at his feet.

The two of them had developed an odd bond in her past few moons with the *raedjour*. On each of her days between lovers, she asked incessant questions. Entranced by her curiosity, he felt compelled to answer. She was sharp, this one, easily missed behind her veil of quiet. Her down-turned eyes saw more than many who looked at a problem straight on. Because of that, because of her incessant curiosity, he'd quartered her near his own rooms and granted her permission to visit him between lovers.

He waited, watching her fidget, until she asked her questions.

"Why haven't I found my truemate?" she finally asked.

Ah, so that was it. "Unfortunately, my dear, it's not a predictable occurrence. Some women never find their truemate."

"What happens to them?"

"They are given quarters of their own in a place that's come to be known as the brothel. There they are cared for until the end of their days."

She nodded, riveted by her own hands making creases in the flimsy wrap she wore, rather than raising her gaze to his. "Can a person tell if they've found their truemate? Or do only you sorcerers know?"

He smoothed his hand over her thigh, just above her knee. Being *raedjour*, it was difficult for him to be near bare flesh without caressing. He did it without thought. "We confirm the truematch, but some are aware of the truematch before we tell them."

She raised her eyes, but made it only to the tattoo blazoned across his chest, a symbol of Rhae's favor. "How do they know? How did you know? With Iana."

He smiled, allowing his thoughts to drift as he spoke. "I knew by the touch of her. The taste of her. She was home. She was mine."

"Why didn't you know initially?"

"Initially?"

"Don't you lay the initial spell on all women?"

"Ah. No. Most, but not all. At the time, I was seeing Hyle -- one of my apprentices -- through his initial passage into becoming a spellcaster. I was occupied for moons. During that time, Rhicard filled my place."

Gala nodded absently. Rhicard was the only sorcerer she'd met other than Nalfien.

Nalfien placed a finger below her chin and raised her face to his. "What troubles you, Gala?"

Her clear blue eyes brimmed with confusion. "I feel something I don't understand," she finally admitted.

"What do you feel?"

"A tingling. Arousal." She closed her eyes, turning inward. "A warmth like I've never felt before."

He smiled. "That could be a sign of a truematch."

"I don't see how," she said, scowling prettily.

"Whyever not?" he asked, trying to recall who her last match was. And why hadn't she been planted?

Her eyes reopened, focusing on him. "Because I feel this around you."

He blinked, shocked. "That's quite impossible," he

declared before he could think.

She shook her head, grabbing his wrist when the movement dislodged his fingers from her chin. "It's true. I feel this only in your presence. I crave your touch."

Disgruntled, he sat back in the chair, eyeing her warily. To do her credit, he carefully checked his own emotions. Nothing. Nothing above the fondness he'd come to feel for her. Certainly not the hot flashes of lust or the simmering tenderness he felt in Iana's presence.

Gala leaned forward, hands braced on his thighs. "Is it possible for you to have two truemates?"

He shook his head. "Not to my knowledge. Not in any history I've known."

A moment of panic took his heart. Many times he'd wished for a more pliable mate. Although she'd been his truemate for quite some time, Iana had yet to lose her human ways, her human spites, her human jealousies. Many of the tasks he performed sparked her more ugly traits. It was then she brought out the weapons. He closed his eyes as lust overtook him at the thought of her whip biting into his skin. No, despite her faults -- or perhaps *because* of them -- Iana was his own truematch.

Gala's hands slid farther up his thighs, and her determined little fingers undid the knot that held together the wrap about his waist.

"Gala, what are you doing?"

"Please," she begged, sinking to her knees as her tiny hands clasped his erection. "It feels so good."

Yes, it does, he thought as he groaned when her hot mouth sank onto his cock. Although he knew he should stop her, Nalfien tangled his hands in her curly locks and guided her mouth as she suckled him. It had been so long since he'd allowed another woman to take him willingly, outside of the initial charm. Iana rarely pleasured him like this.

Gala had learned a thing or two from her list of lovers. Nalfien let his head sink back to rest on the chair while she pleasured him with her tongue, lips, and hands. He didn't stop her, not even when he allowed himself to climax in her mouth. To his surprise, she swallowed it all. He actually had to pull her away from his limp organ as she tried to bring it back to life. She would know from experience with his kind that it would not take much stimulation to do so.

"This will stop here," he declared, pushing her gently away.

"But what about what I feel?"

"We'll discuss that."

She shook her head, trying to get closer. "Fuck me first."

"No."

"You did the first night."

"And only the first night. Iana is my truemate. You do remember her whip?"

She winced. "I remember."

"I'm not the only one she uses it on."

She blinked big blue eyes at him. "I could never use a whip on you."

That effectively quelled his lust. He could smile now, could touch her. "But, child, that is what I need."

Her eyes went bigger in shock. Then she fell back to her knees. "I don't understand."

He stood, retying the wrap about his waist. "Remain here a moment." He walked across the room, ostensibly to retrieve a mug of wine for her. He also mentally summoned Hyle. Of all of Nalfien's apprentices, only Hyle and Savous excelled at solving riddles. Savous was best at truth and history. Hyle was adept at magical puzzles. Of any of them, he was best to help find a solution to Gala's problem.

Gala nursed the wine Nalfien gave her, staring into the watered depths rather than watch him roam the room. She didn't need to watch him. She could feel him. She'd been so certain he was the one. She didn't know what was happening to her.

Suddenly, an odd burning flared low in her belly, an arousal sharper and more intense than she'd ever encountered. Confused, she looked up just as the door opened.

The man who entered captivated her. He was quite short for a *raedjour*, probably not much taller than she. Diana would certainly be taller than he. Within the loose opening of the short silk robe he wore, a tattoo similar to Nalfien's flared across his chest. Having asked Nalfien, she knew that particular pattern was a mark of a sorcerer. Although his blazing red eyes were a more blatant clue. His flaxen hair hung heavy and straight to the middle of his back, secured to his head by two braids that began at his temples and joined together at the back of his neck. He was clearly young, not having grown into the sharpness of the older man.

"Hyle," Nalfien greeted. "May I introduce you to…Gala." The pause due to the fact that Gala had dropped her mug, spilling the remnants of her drink on the stone floor.

The apprentice turned his attention to her. His features were soft, nearly feminine, and his rounded, glowing red eyes did not have that upward tilt which made some of the *raedjour* look evil. The eyes rounded further in shock when he saw the intensity of her gaze.

Or perhaps he felt it too? Did his skin tingle? Were his insides melting? Did he have to hold stock-still or else fling himself at her?

"Hyle," she breathed, clutching her wrap so hard that she dislodged it from her shoulder. His eyes dropped to her bared breast, and she could not have mistaken his hunger.

It took him two tries before he could say, "Master, I..." But he paused, unable to tear his gaze from her flesh.

She beamed and took that first step. The first poured into another until she was pressed against him, breast to chest, groin to groin, gathering handfuls of that glorious hair. A look of panic overrode his hunger, but his hands settled on her hips as though they belonged.

They *did* belong!

Unable to wait longer, Gala yanked his face down, pressing those soft lips to hers. They shared a groan. It was he who opened his mouth to her questing tongue.

Nalfien's chuckle gave her pause, and she reluctantly pulled away from making a meal of Hyle's mouth. The apprentice blinked down at her, barely able to focus.

"M-master?" he questioned, still unable to take his gaze from Gala's adoring eyes.

"Gala, would it be safe to assume the feelings you mentioned have intensified?"

Her smile hurt her face it was so large. "Oh, yes."

"What do you feel?"

"Hot. Beautiful. Safe." She frowned at Hyle. "Impatient."

Nalfien chuckled. "Ah, yes. Well, I would ask that you be patient with Hyle. He's not yet had the pleasure of being with a woman."

That helped Hyle to break their shared gaze. He tried to pull away, embarrassed, but she locked her arms around his neck to prevent his escape. She turned her head to face an amused Nalfien. "Never?"

"Hyle is young. He's also quite a serious student. He has…foregone the pleasure of women in favor of his studies."

"Hmm." Gala turned back to the beautiful man, who was indeed not much taller than she. Softly, she kissed his jaw, trailed her lips back to his ear. "We'll put a stop to that."

Startled, Hyle jumped back. It was enough to dislodge Gala's grip. "What…what's happening?" Gala let him escape, but tracked him with an intense stare as he put Nalfien's large chair between them.

"I called you here to help me divine an answer to why Gala had feelings for me as a truemate, although I'm already truemated. It seems, however, that you've provided the answer with your very existence."

"What do you mean?"

"I would be very surprised indeed if you were not Gala's truemate."

Hyle's panic clearly grew at the sight of Gala's predatory smile. "How can she be my mate?" he asked. "I've not lain with her."

Gala made a happy, purring sound that made Nalfien laugh. "I think Gala would be most happy to rectify that situation."

"B-but, this isn't how it happens! How can she know?"

Curious herself, Gala turned to see Nalfien's reaction -- which consisted of a shrug. "One can only guess. Some feel the bond with their truemate quite intensely. Some do not. As to why Gala felt these things toward me, I can only speculate that it would be our close association." He smiled at Gala's questioning look. "Hyle is not only one of my apprentices, he is also my son."

Gala accepted this initially, although she couldn't help feeling a tad embarrassed at wanting the son when a short time previous she'd begged the father to fuck her.

"Yes," Nalfien was continuing, nonplussed. "I have a strong suspicion about this. Gala seems sensitive to magic, which could also be the cause of her attraction to me." He smiled at Hyle's aghast look. "But this is quite fortunate. Who knows when we would have put you on the list of her lovers?"

"Could he be next?" she asked.

"Most certainly."

"Master!"

"Yes?"

"I have work to do."

Nalfien shook his head. "Hyle, of all my apprentices, you are the most studious and the hardest worker. I appreciate that I can rely on you. But there is nothing -- nothing! -- more important than a truematch. You agree?"

Hyle eyed Gala warily. "Yes."

"And if we think there is a truematch, all rules would bend to assure it, yes?"

"Yes."

"It's done, then. Gala, would you mind forgoing your day of rest?"

She answered with a smile and a shake of her head.

"I thought not. Hyle, you should take Gala to your quarters now."

He opened his mouth in what looked like the beginning of a protest, but then his gaze locked with Gala's. She put all she felt into her eyes, all warmth and promise. "As you say, master" was what came out of his mouth.

She beamed, remaining where she stood as he rounded the chair. Tentatively, he held out his hand to her and she took it. Heat flared between them. He jumped. She shivered.

She silently followed him from the room, heedless of Nalfien's fond gaze. Hyle hesitated once outside the door. "You should, um..." He gestured at the wrap, which exposed her breast.

She grinned at his embarrassment. Of all the *raedjour* she'd met, she'd yet to see any embarrassed. It was adorable! Her heart swelled as she fixed the wrap, then took his hand again.

It was a short walk to his quarters. Obviously, he was to be near-at-hand for Nalfien. His rooms weren't sumptuous, nor were they tidy. She saw immediately that he tended to leave items wherever he happened to set them, rather in their proper places.

Mumbling something in their purring language, he moved to release her hand, reaching for the nearest pile of clutter. She tugged back, making him face her. "Leave it," she murmured, sliding her free hand up his chest, his neck, until she could tangle her fingers in the hair at the back of his head.

"Gala," he breathed, staring at her in wonderment.

She smiled, gently guiding his lips to hers. She taught him to kiss her, coaxing his tongue from his mouth and into hers. He caught on quickly and, with a ragged groan, released her hand so he had both of his free to fill with her back and buttocks. She didn't protest; rather, she worked with him to press their bodies as close as possible.

She broke the kiss with a gasp, dropping her head back. His wonderfully strong arms held her effortlessly. He bent his neck to nuzzle the soft shallow behind her ear.

"Either you've done this before, or you're a very quick learner," she teased.

He chuckled softly, a sound which warmed her already boiling blood. "Kissing? This I've done before."

"Oh." Of course. Nalfien had pointed out to her during one of their discussions that in a society where women were scarce, sexual relations between males were inevitable. It had taken her some time to come to terms with this, but she believed she had. "You've just never been with a woman before?"

"No." His lips were doing marvelous things to her earlobe.

A horrible thought occurred to her. "You are...*old* enough for this, aren't you, Hyle?"

Again the chuckle. "Yes. I've just never --" He shrugged. "-- really wanted to. I don't socialize much."

She relaxed, distracting herself by combing her fingers through his glorious hair. She found the braid at the back and began to unlace it. As he nibbled her neck and shoulder, she freed the hair and pulled some forward to drape over his shoulders. Her shoulders. She quivered, wanting to wrap herself in that warm silk and roll around in it.

"Hyle."

"Gala?"

"Do you have a bed?"

That earned her a full laugh, which pleased her even more than the chuckle.

He carefully pulled back from her, sliding his hands down her arms until their fingers clasped. His face was a picture of joyful anticipation, his fears seemingly melted by the heat of the lust between them. Matching his smile, she followed as he walked backwards, effortlessly guiding them both into the adjoining chamber.

"Are you using magic as a guide, or are you just that familiar with this room?" she teased as they entered the darkened room.

He glanced over his shoulder and two candles in a shared holder flared to life. She started. Neither of the other sorcerers she'd met had made such an obvious show of their power. She chuckled. "Show off."

He laughed again, stopping when his knees hit the side of a simple but wide bed. She closed the small distance between them, sliding her hands into the opening of his robe. Quickly, she slid it from him, then made short work of the trousers he wore. When he was finally, fully exposed to her gaze, she was overjoyed to find him exactly as she wanted him. As he wasn't as tall as the other men, neither was his cock as long. But this suited her fine because many of the others had had to compensate for organs that wouldn't fit fully in her pussy. His gleaming black organ was thick, however, as she discovered when she encircled it with her hand. She trembled at the thought of the friction it would cause thrusting deep inside her.

He groaned, clutching her shoulders a moment for support. She smiled, leaning forward to nip at his shoulder as she pumped his cock to release some of the natural juices the *raedjour* exuded -- another thing she had learned of them. Created originally for sex, the *raedjour* males exuded a lubricant that covered their bodies in a light, oily sheen that would gather and gain in necessary places when they were aroused.

When she could stand it no longer, she pushed him gently. Obediently, he fell onto the bed, scooting back at her insistence until he lay prone before her. She licked her lips as she studied him, allowing him to see the pleasure she took just at the sight of him. She stripped off her wrap for him, glorying in the simmering warmth in his eyes as he studied her in turn. She smiled. He matched it.

She knelt on the bed at his feet, bending to plant a kiss on his ankle. Taking her time, she kissed her way up his calf, his knee, the inside of his thigh until she could nuzzle her nose in the bend where thigh met groin. She breathed in the warm, musky scent of him, lapping gently at the tender skin of his balls, sucking them slowly into her mouth. Her actions brought his cock to full, bobbing attention, so she trailed the big, throbbing vein up the bottom of the shaft until she could use her lips to pull the plum-sized head into her mouth.

"Ah, Gala!" he shuddered, clutching the bedclothes.

She wrapped her hand around the shaft and devoured him, lapping up the tasty lubricant and happily swallowing the drops of seed that seeped from the head. But soon she couldn't stand it any longer. Promising herself she would suck him to completion sometime soon, she withdrew her mouth and climbed his body, trailing kisses as she had along his legs. By the time she reached his face, he was desperate. His hands were buried in her long, wavy hair, pulling her mouth to his. She allowed it for precious moments as she braced over him with one locked arm and pumped his cock with her free hand. Finally she broke from his kiss to position herself. She no longer had the time or the patience to tease. She needed him inside her. Now! He placed his hands at her hips to help steady her as she raised herself, aimed his cock, then blissfully impaled herself on it.

Her climax -- much to her surprise -- was immediate and intense. She braced over him, her body quaking. Beneath her, Hyle cried out as her clutching channel pulled out his own orgasm. It was a moment of totality, the moment they became one, with no doubts in either's mind.

She collapsed atop him, desperately trying to breathe. He hugged her to him, struggling with his own breath. Finally, she laughed. "I'm sorry, Hyle. I couldn't hold back."

She felt him shake his head as he squeezed her. "Please, no apologies. I couldn't either." He stroked her back, ending with a fond squeeze to her buttocks. "I've never felt anything like that."

She laughed again. "Normally it takes a while longer so you can enjoy it."

"Mmm." He nudged her buttocks, moving her groin just enough for her to realize that he was hardening again. "Perhaps we could try again?"

Gladly, she snuggled against him. "Oh, please. Let's."

Chapter Six

Klack! Klack! Whoosh! K-klack!

From his balcony vantage above the combatants, Commander Salin grunted, crossing powerful arms over his chest. "You should have given her a read blade."

Nalfien scowled. "We shouldn't have given her a weapon at all."

Krael, Salin's second-in-command, laughed. "How else were you going to tire her out? Fucking wasn't working."

The sorcerer grumbled, but the sound was ignored by the two warriors engrossed in the fight below. The small arena was one of many set aside for weapons-training for young or inexperienced *raedjour*. This one, with the soft sand floor, provided both a padding and a footwork hindrance. A hindrance which did not detract from the fighting ability of the woman below.

Her opponent was her latest lover. Garn was winning the match, but she wasn't making it easy for him. If she'd had a true blade and knew how to use it properly against the tough *raedjour* hide, the match might have been on more level footing.

"Is he playing with her, or did he just miss that opening?" Krael mused.

"He'd best be playing with her," Salin grumbled. "Perhaps he requires more practice."

Krael nodded, absently brushing back his long white hair. "I'll see to that."

Salin nodded, but his focus didn't waver from the match. Truthfully, he cared little about Garn's abilities. Over the cycles, Garn had proven himself a capable warrior time and time again. It was the woman who had Salin's rapt attention. Although laboring under the handicap of a dulled wooden blade, the sand floor, and scant leathers evocative of sex more than combat, she handled herself beautifully. He would wager she'd had some weapons-training, but the majority of her skill was through hard-won experience. Rage spilled in a scream from her lips as she ducked Garn's attack and managed to bring up her blade to slice him across the back. Salin wanted to bark at her to shut her mouth and thrust instead of cut, but he held his tongue.

Truthfully, his reaction to the match surprised him. Women were rare to the *raedjour*, but as commander, Salin seldom wanted for female company. There were enough women who had lost a truemate, or had never found one, who had abundant sexual needs. There were even two or three who had been trained in weapons in their human lives and continued the practice once among the *raedjour*. But for some reason, this one intrigued him. Her anger beat against him like a warm breeze, wild and directionless. She lashed out at her captors as easy targets, but he didn't think they were the true cause of her anger. Just the latest cause.

He moved forward to brace his arms on the balcony

railing. Below, the woman turned, faltered. Garn nabbed her about the waist and took her heavily to the sand. The practice blades were flung asunder.

Beside Salin, Krael purred as Garn swiftly ripped aside the useless scraps of leather that had barely covered the woman's sex. Both commander and second inhaled deeply, their keen senses easily picking up the heady aroma of her arousal. "Like it or not, Nalfien," Krael mused, "*this* is what gets this particular woman."

"So it would seem."

As they casually discussed her, Garn had freed his cock. Salin watched carefully, gratified to note that despite her sneer, the woman -- Diana, yes, that was her name -- surrounded him with both legs and arms and violently welcomed him into her body.

Diana couldn't think. Sand crept under the hem of the ridiculously short excuse for a bodice and invaded the crack of her ass. Her lungs labored mightily to get enough air. And every nerve twitched and tingled, desperate to get that long length of black cock as deeply embedded in her pussy as possible.

She didn't know why they'd allowed her weapons. It must have been her first lover -- Boutel? -- who told them that she'd used every moveable item in the rooms against him during their time together. After that, she'd been introduced to this sandy arena and given a selection of dulled weapons. She couldn't win the matches. She knew that. Not when the adrenaline from the fight combined with whatever they'd done to her to spike her arousal to feverish pitches -- until, by the end of the battle, she'd fuck anything that moved. The long, hard grips of the practice weapons had even caught her eye on occasion!

And this match was worse. For some reason, they had an audience. And that audience included a man unlike any other she'd seen. How did she know he was different? He was dressed well, in what little he wore. Trousers and an embroidered sash as a belt were all she had glimpsed. The trousers looked well made and the belt flashed with gold embroidery. But his scant garb wasn't it -- the long-haired man beside him, with the exploding star pattern tattooed on his face, was dressed in the same manner. Was it his hair? It was far shorter than any other man's she'd met among the *raedjour* thus far. Cropped just above his sharp jawline, it was a riot of white-gray curls with one long lock obscuring one eye.

No. She didn't know what it was, and she was frustrated she couldn't make out more detail from her place in the arena below the balcony from which he watched. But his presence had distracted her, enraged her, and, unfortunately, aroused her.

She clutched at the hair of the one who fucked her now. She couldn't even remember his name. Couldn't recall if she'd ever asked it. And all she was aware of was the eyes of the other watching. She tried to roll her present lover onto his back, wanting to show herself off to this other man, but the huge lunk held her down. Growling, she scratched at his back, but that, of course, only spurred him on.

Frustrated, she turned her head and gasped. *He* had moved forward, muscled arms braced on the balcony railing, eyes locked on her. Her gaze filled with him, with what she could see of the chiseled features and eyes that glowed a soft red. His small grin was devastating. Her mind's eye filled with the image of that huge body in the place of the one atop her, of those lean hips pounding a matching, beautiful cock at the very entrance of her womb.

The image set her off. She exploded with a scream, tearing at the tough black skin of her lover's back. He cried out, rearing up to brace his upper half on his forearms, giving him a better angle to pound her mercilessly. But she asked no mercy. She clutched the sandy ground, straining to match his rhythm as she closed her eyes and replaced him mentally with the other.

"How many of us has she had?" Salin asked, still entranced as Garn slowed through Diana's second orgasm. He saw the fine tremor that went through the man's back and knew the effort it cost him not to come. *Showing off for his commander,* Salin thought.

"Fifteen," said Nalfien. "All, but the first, from Krael's recommendations."

Salin nodded. His second had recommended the men because Salin had been...what? He couldn't recall now.

"Is she like this with all of them?" Krael asked for him. He was Salin's second for a reason, often supplying necessary information or asking pertinent questions while Salin put together the pieces.

"As far as I know," Nalfien admitted, stepping to the railing beside Salin. "I've not watched any before this."

"She's called the 'hellcat' for good reason," Salin mused.

Krael snorted. "She needs to be put in her place."

Salin smiled, aware of his lieutenant's preference for

submissive women. Salin, however, craved a good fight.

"Yes," Nalfien sighed. "She's destined for the brothel if she doesn't find a truematch."

For some odd reason, that statement set Salin's blood boiling. He imagined this hellcat among the women of the brothel, continuing to welcome men to her bed until she either stumbled on her truemate or she died.

Below, Garn began to pump again. The woman below him moaned, clearly exhausted but, just as clearly, still aroused. Garn fumbled at the lacing of her bodice, loosening it just enough to free one plump breast.

"I want her," Salin declared as his man latched onto what looked to be a succulent nipple.

Behind him, Krael and Nalfien shared a glance. Although aware of it, Salin ignored it.

"Indeed?" asked Nalfien.

"Indeed."

"And why, may I ask?"

The question was benign, but the history between the commander and the sorcerer gave it deeper meaning. Long ago, in Salin's youth, Nalfien had tried to convince Salin to become his apprentice. Once, Nalfien might have helped Salin fan the flames of the magic threaded within him. But Salin had refused. He'd chosen instead to follow in his father's footsteps, to become a warrior to beat all. In this, he had succeeded admirably. But the rejection remained between them, compounded by the fact that Salin's younger brother, Radin, was one of Nalfien's most talented apprentices.

Salin straightened, tearing his gaze from the intriguing

woman with an amazing amount of effort. He met Nalfien's red gaze. "Because I do."

Nalfien's lips twitched, but he didn't smile. "I already have a list of men for her after Garn. Supplied by your own lieutenant."

Beside him, Krael stilled, familiar with the tension between the men.

"I know that." Salin gazed down his nose at the sorcerer. "What do I have to do to be next with her?"

Nalfien took a long moment to study the younger man. Truth be known, he admired Salin. Like his father, he was a natural leader with a certain aplomb that made his men proud to follow him. Like his brother, he had a mischievous streak, which got him into trouble as often as it produced brilliant ideas.

At length, Nalfien smiled. "Consider it done, Commander," he said.

Salin scowled. Behind him, Krael's head swung around in shock at the easy capitulation. "No demands? No favors?" Salin asked.

Nalfien's smile grew. "It might be that I could call on a favor sometime in the future."

Salin growled, one black lip curling up to nearly touch his pointed nose. "I don't like owing you, Nalfien."

The sorcerer cocked his head to the side. "I could certainly put you at the end of the list." It was his right. Only one person had power above Nalfien where the human women were concerned, and that was the king himself.

"I could ask Valanth," Salin suggested.

Nalfien shrugged at the mention of the king. It was well known that he and the monarch were not on particularly favorable terms. It was also well known that, as one of the king's personal guards, Salin was. "You most certainly could, Commander. But as his majesty is in commune with Rhae for at least another fortnight..." He let his voice trail off. The king, when in commune with their goddess, could be unavailable for moons at a time.

Many a man under Salin's command wanted his chance at the hellcat. She posed an interesting challenge. Salin didn't want to wait until he could force Nalfien's hand through the king. In truth, he didn't want to involve the king at all, for Valanth might decide to try her himself, and women were always *different* once had by the king.

Salin pondered a long moment. Below, Diana's body rumbled in a groan that snatched low in his spine and made his cock twitch. The decision was made. "Done. I'll owe you a favor."

Nalfien nodded. "I'm honored, Commander."

Chapter Seven

This time, two of the hulking guards took her to another set of rooms. They left the rooms in which she'd stayed during her day between men, and strode down the long, brightly lit hallway. At the other end of this hall and through a bare stone courtyard was the small arena where she had sparred with her latest lovers. But her guards took her deeper into what she could only describe as a tower. Although such a term, underneath the stone sky, seemed strange.

Occasionally, young men scurried past on errands. It seemed they did most of the drudge work in *raedjour* society, acting as servants to the older men. All men, young and old, spared hungry glances for Diana in her spare, silken wrap and soft leather boots. She pretended to ignore them, also ignoring the tightness of her nipples and the dampness of her crotch. She was getting good at it.

They traveled up two flights of winding stairs and down a carpeted hallway to a solid door emblazoned with a sinister weblike design. One of the guards knocked. A moment later, a young man opened the door, his sleek white hair pulled back into a tail. Diana tried valiantly not to ogle the youthful muscles of the arms that extended from his open leather vest.

The youth stepped back, bowing slightly. The guards entered, then led her quickly through a sparse, though well-appointed, main room to a second door. This one they opened, pushed her through, then closed the door behind her.

"And good afternoon to you," Diana grumbled as the lock *snicked.* "Or morning. Or night." She rolled her eyes. She didn't have any idea what time of day it was any longer. In this underground kingdom, it was always blackest night.

She glared about the room. Her ire drained somewhat as she got a good look at the furnishings. This latest man had to be more privileged than those she'd seen to date. The bedchamber, to start, was nearly twice the size of the two rooms she'd been given during her time with the *raedjour.* Wall sconces with real candles rather than torches lit the room, along with a cheery fire in a carved fireplace. Expensive woven rugs were scattered across a smooth, clean stone floor. Four clothes chests were lined along one wall. A table near the door was spread with what smelled like a delicious meal, all covered with linen cloths or enclosed in shining pewter tureens. A padded platform, which she assumed posed as a bed, dominated one wall, piled with pillows and silky furs. No blankets. Not that they were needed, as the room's temperature was quite comfortable.

Misgivings crept up Diana's spine. To date, the room in which she and Gala had talked with Iana on that first, fateful night was the finest she had ever seen. She didn't know what to feel or do.

Off to the side, nearly obscured by ornate folding screens, she saw contraptions that boiled the misgivings from her mind. A standing X had obvious purpose, with stout chains dangling from rings at both the top and bottom ends of the X. A small, benchlike contraption sat next to it, with rings and chains similarly dangling in strategic places. Suspicious, Diana went back to the bed and lifted one of the furs to get a look at the side of the bed. Yes. There were rings set into that, as well.

She scowled. Every one of the *raedjour* to which she'd been given had bound her at one point or another, usually when they were weary of physically holding her down. She was not prepared to admit how she had enjoyed it. How wonderful it had been to unleash all of her anger, to rant, to curse, and yet still be taken.

No. She wouldn't admit that.

The door's lock sounded and the heavy wood swung in soundlessly. She turned only her head and schooled her face into a dismissive sneer, prepared to begin the next battle.

In walked...*him!*

She froze, the instinctive reaction of prey to predator. Her eyes went wide as he cleared the threshold then calmly closed and locked the door behind him.

He was even more amazing up close. From the balcony, he'd looked magnificent. Up close, he was sinister beauty in motion. He was taller than any *raedjour* she'd met, easily over seven feet if she had to guess, and every inch of it was honed muscle. Buttery-soft, black leather boots draped his feet, marking the end of legs that went up forever within loose linen trousers. An embroidered silk sash wound about an impossibly slim waist. His bare, sculpted abdomen emerged from that sash, fanning out to a hugely broad chest. The same sinister web design she'd seen on the outer door of the suite was emblazoned in one of those curious white tattoos across his pectoral muscles. Bulging arms rippled as he crossed them casually over his chest. His long neck held up a face of wicked pleasures, promised by the full curve of his black lips and the rakish tilt to snowy white brows. His white hair was cut much shorter than any man she'd seen among the *raedjour*, the riotous white-gray curls barely reaching his chin. One thick forelock fell over his right eye but failed to conceal the burning dark red of the iris.

Red. Power. She'd learned a bit during her time with the *raedjour*, and one tidbit was that the more red the eyes, the more magical power they had. Nalfien's eyes actually glowed bright red. One of his apprentices whom she'd seen was clearly red. But this man's eyes smoldered like a banked fire waiting to erupt.

He waited, perusing her every bit as obviously as she did him. He had to be some sort of lord, however the *raedjour* measured such things. The rooms, she could only conclude, were his, along with the sumptuous trappings.

He finally spoke. "Diana."

She shivered. The deep pitch vibrated in her womb, causing something to break and melt in her groin.

"I am Salin," he introduced himself, nodding his head. "Welcome to my home."

She sneered. "This is not my choice."

He shrugged, a slight tilt of his head. "True. But perhaps we can make it pleasant."

"I don't think so."

"Don't you?" he asked, unconcerned. He stepped toward the food table and lifted a tureen cover. "Are you hungry? Thirsty?"

"No."

All the same, he went to a nearby table and picked up a bottle of the light wine they drank in place of water. "Do you need to use the facilities?" he asked, gesturing toward a partially open door she guessed led to a private privy.

She stopped her immediate denial, realizing that it probably wasn't a bad idea. "Yes."

With a nod, he indicated she should proceed.

She skirted the bed platform and stepped into the cool privy room, shutting the door behind her. Once inside, she took a moment to catch her breath and try to still her beating heart. She had to be quiet. Their hearing was better than any creature she'd yet to encounter or hear tale of.

She washed her face with the cool water than ran in a constant stream from a hole in the wall into a basin with a drain, and pulled her hair into a tail. She froze at the sight of herself in the mirrored disk on the wall. Was it the poor lighting of the room, or was her hair a lighter shade of brown? Sweet Mother of us all, was she changing?

More to escape that fact than anything, she exited the room.

He sat on what looked to be a comfortable covered chair with a low back. One long leg was draped over the side, and she stifled a groan, for the position snugged his dark trousers in just the right way to show an impressive bulge between his thighs.

He smiled, which told her that her reaction had been visible. Bristling, she stomped to the table and poured herself some wine. He was silent as she finished it.

Wasn't he going to *say* anything? *Do* anything? All of

her previous lovers had begun sex play immediately, eager to shove their cocks into any available orifice.

When she turned to face him again, she caught him in another slow perusal of her nearly naked body. She'd grown accustomed to such looks in the past weeks and could not understand why *his* look was tactile. Could he touch her with magic alone?

Finally, he rose. "Are you well rested?"

She shrugged. "As well as can be expected for a prisoner."

His gaze grew unaccountably sharp. "Have you been treated poorly?"

"What do you call being bound, manhandled, and raped repeatedly?"

"Raped?" he inquired mildly.

"I was taken against my will."

The small smile took her breath. "Against your will? Was your body not wet with your own sweet juices and prepared for the invasion? Were there occasions when you didn't ask for more?"

Scowling, she turned from him, unable to think coherently as she drank in the sight of him. "The spell made me want them."

"No, Diana. The spell wore off long ago."

"Then something made me want them. I've never been such a... I've never wanted men like that."

"Hmm. You had also not been among the *raedjour*. You've been told we were created for a goddess's own pleasure."

"Yes!" she hissed.

He chuckled. "Most women would see this as a benefit."

"I am not most women."

"On that, I agree."

She whirled to face him, face hot and body even hotter.

He crossed the room to another table. Reaching under it, he withdrew a sheathed sword. Her breath caught as he turned to face her. She knew that sword. It was hers!

Deftly, he drew the blade, brandishing it in the light. Sized for her, it looked ridiculously small in his broad hand. He cut the air twice, then nodded as he resheathed the blade. "A serviceable weapon. You selected it?"

She knew he was a trained warrior just from the ease with which he held the blade. She nodded.

"Well done. I would imagine that it would have been costly up above."

She frowned. "How would you know that?"

He grinned. "We're birthed by humans, recall. Most become loving mothers and teachers. We learn quite a bit about your world, despite our absence from it. How do you think we all learn commonspeak?"

"How convenient."

"No. But we manage."

To her shock, he suddenly tossed the sheathed sword to her. She caught it with barely a thought, her hand instantly on the grip. He nodded his approval.

He was unarmed, dressed only in boots, trousers and a

sash.

His grin widened. "Draw it."

Her sense of honor warred with her need to attack. "You're unarmed."

His eyes hooded, increasing their resemblance to banked coals. "Am I?"

She paused. Most skilled fighters carried concealed weapons. It shouldn't surprise her that this one would.

"Draw it," he prompted again.

Still she hesitated. "Why?"

One silky eyebrow arched. "To use, of course."

"I'm obviously not of your caliber."

That seemed to anger him. "That stops you? Even the best of us makes mistakes. You could get lucky."

"I'm nearly naked." She spread her hand down her thigh, over the silky wrap.

"I noticed."

"I can't very well fight when I'm naked."

He frowned. "And why not? What does it matter how you are dressed? Your enemies will rarely wait for an opportune moment to attack."

She bristled, hearing the voices of her father and brothers in his tone. They'd scoffed at her for wanting to learn to use a sword, but when they'd finally given in, their tutelage had been long and frustrating.

"It wouldn't do me any good to try and fight," she stated. "You're a head taller than me and twice as broad." She didn't know why she was reluctant to fight this one. With the others, given any type of weapon, even blunted, she'd erupted like an angry cougar. But now, with her own sharpened weapon, she was uneasy.

All smoldering lust drained from his eyes as he straightened to his full, considerable height and mirrored her stance. "Pitiful," he scoffed. "I had thought you had more fire than this."

"Don't you dare patronize me!" she spat, clutching the wrapped leather of her sword's hilt. "It's not my ability that I see lacking -- it's my advantage."

"And do you only fight when you're at an advantage? How is it you're still alive?"

"There's no possible way I could win."

"Ah." He glared, and she would bet he was truly angry. "Then you deserve to be fucked like the victim you are."

Screaming, she drew. Her upper cut sliced through thin air as he moved, quicker than a cat, to the side. She managed to redirect the sword, but one big hand caught her wrist in a solid lock, jarring her arm to a halt. Grunting, she tried to kick at him, only to tangle her leg with his. In a simple move, he brought his foot back and tumbled her to the rug, her sword in his hand.

She braced herself, knowing he could kill her easily, but also knowing that killing her was not what he intended. She stared up the incredible length of his body to his smiling face. Expertly, he turned her sword and extended it hilt-first to her. Growling, she snatched it, irritated when he released it with nary a cut.

"Again?" he asked mildly, stepping back without offering to help her to her feet.

She cut at his feet, certain she could have injured a man

who was less quick than this one. But he only laughed, jumping over the blade.

She climbed into a crouch, thinking. She knew this was an act, a device to wear her out. She'd learned that any exertion caused the *raedjour* to ooze more of that lubricating oil from their skin.

"Is it the oil on your skin?" she asked almost conversationally as they circled each other.

He quirked a smile. "Oil?"

"The oil you sweat. That's what causes the attraction, isn't it?"

His smile warmed. "That's part of it."

"What's the other part? A spell?"

She lunged. He dodged, batting away the sword with his bare hand. "Can it not be natural sexual attraction?"

"Nothing about your race is natural."

Cut. Duck. Slice. Parry. *Whoosh!* He caught her arm as she extended it a wee bit too much, and used her own momentum to yank her past him. His fingers caught in her wrap and loosened the knot at her shoulder. When she turned back to face him, the cloth draped low enough to expose one breast. His interest flared, and she used the split second to attack. He recovered almost immediately, but the hesitation was enough that she did manage to slice across his belly.

She froze, staring in frustrated amazement. The blade was sharp, the cut was solid, but she left no more than a surface scratch on that gleaming obsidian hide. She knew that her own nails couldn't draw blood, but she'd been sure a sword could cut them open.

He grinned at her consternation, drawing a long finger along the line that would have opened a human man's bowels. "Thrust, don't slice," he advised calmly.

Still reeling, she lost her ready stance and simply stared up at him in amazement. "Are you *all* like that?"

He nodded. "You will be also after the change."

Her nostrils flared over her snort. "I won't change."

"You'll change."

Her anger rose again and she attacked. They played their game for quite some time, crossing the room, rolling over the bed platform, knocking over the food table. The damage to his possessions did not seem to bother him at all. He took delight in their sparring, even providing helpful suggestions. Which only enraged her further.

And it was a game. If she hadn't guessed it before, she knew it now. Although he was now careful of the thrusts, he continued to evade and best her at every turn. Very soon, he divested her of her wrap so that she fought naked, save for the soft, low boots that covered her feet.

She was tiring, her lungs laboring, her blood pumping. More and more, he caught her in almost embraces, causing her back to slide against the hard planes of his chest, or her breasts to crush against him. Finally, in one such embrace, he twisted the blade from her hand and tossed it aside.

"Enough," he declared, releasing her with a push that sent her sprawling backwards onto the bed platform.

She remained prone, breathing hard as she locked gazes with him. She'd felt the erection tenting his trousers. Felt it and wanted it desperately, although she wouldn't voice that aloud.

But he remained standing between her spread thighs, hands on his lean hips as he caressed her naked flesh with his eyes.

"Do you want me to fuck you?" he asked.

She blinked, surprised by the question. Her other lovers had all waited until she was hot and ready, but none of them had *asked*.

"No," she heard herself lie.

He smiled, nodded, and stepped back. "So be it."

Her jaw dropped when he turned toward the door. He paused only to scoop up her blade and scabbard, sheathing the sword as he left.

He spared a final glance as he stood in the open door. She remained in the position he'd left her, too shocked to move. "I'll send Jarak to clean the mess later. Sleep well, my sweet."

And he was gone.

Chapter Eight

Diana woke from an exhausted sleep when a young man entered the room with a tray. He must have already been in while she was sleeping, as the mess from the previous night was gone. The tray he carried supported a light repast that the *raedjour* seemed to favor earlier in their "day."

She watched silently from within the pile of pillows and furs. He was the same youth who had answered the door when the guards had escorted her to Salin's rooms, so he must be Salin's personal servant. His hair was long and straight, bound with a simple leather thong at the base of a graceful neck. His leather vest was tied loosely over his bare chest, and his leather trousers lovingly hugged muscles that might one day be as pronounced as his master's.

"Are you all built like stallions?" She sighed.

He jumped and spun to face her. Thankfully, he had already set the tray and its contents on the table. "Lady," he said, nodding his head in respect. "I hadn't realized you were awake."

She sat up, conscious of her nudity but allowing the supple fur blanket to fall about her waist. True to form, his gaze sank to her breasts, but she gave him full credit for rapidly dragging it back up to her face.

"Are you a servant?" she asked boldly.

He nodded. "I'm Commander Salin's squire, yes."

She narrowed her gaze. "May I ask how old you are?"

A ghost of a smile made him look even younger. If his skin weren't pitch black, she would swear he was blushing. "One hundred eighty-seven cycles, lady."

She blinked. "Excuse me?"

He smiled. "Humans don't age as we do. We age about ten times slower than you."

"How do you know so much about... Oh, right. Human mothers."

He smiled, turning back to the tray to lay out the meal as her mind spun.

"My," she sighed, allowing her eyes to stray over his well-shaped backside. "I'd heard there were other races like that; I'd just never..." She frowned. "How old is...Commander Salin?"

"I'm not sure exactly, but I know he's over five hundred."

Diana sat in stunned silence. Taking that silence to mean she was done talking, the young man finished arranging the tray and bid her a good night as he exited the room.

She'd heard of other beings, yes. Elves and merfolk were said to live longer than humans. But she'd never personally met any. Until now, it seemed. The length of life astounded her. Her grandmother was the oldest living human Diana had ever known, and at eighty years she was a mere babe compared to the young man Diana had just spoken with.

Overwhelmed, Diana sank back into the furs. What did this all mean? Why would such a long-lived race need humans to procreate? How could a magical race not have other means to reproduce? These were not new questions to her, but she'd yet to find suitable answers.

Frowning, she rose and went to the tray. As she ate, her mind turned to less philosophical topics. Why hadn't Salin fucked her? She knew he thought it his right. They all did. Why had he hesitated? There had been one man who'd preferred, it seemed, to see his seed spurt onto her belly rather than inside her cunt, but even he would sometimes slide it inside her. Why hadn't the commander?

Commander. Yes, that definitely sounded important. She wondered what the term meant to them. Did he command an army? If so, how large? Just how many *raedjour* were there?

She was unable to answer the question before she finished eating. She wandered the spacious room a bit. Finally bored, she curled up in the mound of pillows and furs on the bed platform and slept away the rest of the day.

* * *

When she woke, he was there. He sprawled in the covered chair again, watching her as he idly masturbated. He was naked! Her gaze riveted to the gorgeous length he caressed. Sleek and long, it was alive in his hand. The one eye stared and wept at the sight of her.

She raised her gaze to meet his. Sheer lust pulsed in the red beneath his seemingly sleepy lids. Slowly, he smiled. "Good evening, sweet. Are you sore from our exercise last night?"

She was, but she wouldn't admit it. She said nothing.

He cocked his head questioningly to the side, then shrugged. Like a big, lazy cat, he pushed from his seat. On his way toward her, he scooped up a pair of wrist and ankle restraints lying on the table beside him.

At the sight of that, she scrambled from the pillows, a cry of protest on her lips. Lightning quick, he was on her. She bit and clawed to no avail as he hauled her to the padded bench at the side of the room. Straddling her belly, he made short work of buckling the restraints around each wrist then attaching them to the chains secured to loops on the sides of the bench. She cursed him, struggling to ignore the teasing caress of his hairless balls, hot and soft against her belly. She tried also to ignore the bobbing erection that occasionally tapped her breasts as he leaned over her. Once her wrists were secure, he quickly reversed his position, favoring her with an excellent view of his tight, black buttocks as he fought to restrain her legs. She screamed her fury, focusing it on him rather on herself. Herself because she wanted nothing more than to lick her way down the hard contours of his back until she could take a satisfying bite out of that delectable ass.

At last she was bound, and he dismounted to admire his handiwork. Sturdy leather straps encircled her wrists and ankles, each one latched to a chain. The chains were taut enough to keep her spread atop the bench.

The gleam of joy in his smoldering red eyes was unmistakable. "Comfortable?"

"Damn you!" she spat. "I don't want you in my body!"

He paused at that, rubbing at a slight scratch she'd

managed to make on his chest, just below his tattoo. "No?"

"No."

He sat beside her, sliding one hand down her belly and along the inside of her thigh. He deliberately skirted her pussy, which wept for him, despite her words.

"Are you sure of that, sweet?"

"Yes. Something makes me lust for you. I know I can't deny it. But I don't *want* you," she used emphasis to make the distinction.

He bent double, lowering his face to hers. It took amazing effort to turn her face aside and deny his kiss. Undeterred, he laid his lips in a butterfly's touch on her temple, his breath softly gusting her hair. "Doesn't the lust mean that you *do* want me, sweet?"

She pulled in a breath, furious that it shook. "No."

He understood well enough. He heaved a sigh as he dropped to her side, his face above her belly. "Pity," he mused, leaning forward to simply breathe on her sensitive skin. "Because I would love nothing more than to fuck you."

"Go ahead. I obviously can't stop you."

He ignored her, intrigued by the way her skin twitched beneath his warm breath. She bit back a groan when he touched his tongue to her skin, sampling her. "Tasty," he murmured, taking another lick. For what seemed like forever, all he did was lick her belly, nibbling her curves and gently sucking at her trembling skin. He went no higher than the tender skin underneath her breasts and no lower than the line of her groin just below her belly.

At length, he moved, positioning himself between her legs, then he repeated the wonderful torture to every inch of her legs, paying particular attention to the crease between leg and groin without touching any sensitive, wet tissues. He even suckled each of her toes, forcing her to fight a groan as she envisioned that hot mouth suckling other, more sensitive portions of her anatomy.

She was a trembling mess by the time he climbed her body to lavish attention on her arms. She stared at the wall behind her head, willing herself not to feel it. Willing her body not to respond. It was impossible. Her skin was hypersensitive, and his strange attentions made her aware of erogenous zones she hadn't realized she had.

Braced on all fours above her, with the fierceness of his erection keeping his cock out of contact with her, he lapped and licked at her chest above her breasts, then worked his way up her neck. He dallied at the curve of her jaw and spent great amounts of time behind both of her ears. He returned to her neck, choosing a sensitive spot to suck. Hard. To her abject humiliation, she actually came, a softly punctuated climax that left her wanting more.

"Mmm," he purred, lifting his head so he could look down at her face.

Flushed, she turned glazed eyes up at him, lips parted.

"Do you want me to fuck you, sweet?" he asked as he had the previous night, nipping at her stubborn chin.

"No," the answer came on a sigh that spoke the exact opposite. She was even a bit surprised to hear it herself.

With a groan, he straightened and climbed off her. She tamped down the disappointment in her belly when he released her bonds and, like the previous night, made for the door.

He turned when he reached it to throw her a saucy smile, then he was gone.

No sooner had the lock clicked than two of Diana's fingers were tunneling into her pussy as far as they could go. No stranger to giving herself pleasure, she desperately rubbed the heel of her palm against her clit. Within seconds, she came hard against her hand, a long, rolling orgasm that had her entire body shaking.

It only helped a little. Still quaking, she lay back on the bench and closed her eyes. As if he were with her again, she could feel every tortuous lick.

* * *

Salin leaned his back against the chamber door, eyes closed as he savored the sound of the last soft moans of her orgasm. In his mind, he replaced himself with the hand he knew she used to pleasure herself, imagined the full length of his rock-hard cock imbedded in the sweet, wet depths of her body as she shook out the end of her climax. He smiled at the sweet torture, promising himself that before the nine days were through, he would feel that.

Sighing softly, he opened his eyes to see Jarak watching him. The younger man stood just inside the outer door of Salin's five-chamber suite. Jarak's blue-black gaze met his master's, then dropped to Salin's crotch suggestively before returning to Salin's face. Salin grinned, which the younger man took as a command.

"Not here." Salin stopped Jarak before he reached him. Groaning, Salin pushed from the door and crossed the main chamber to the other bedroom. Although he didn't think her ears were sharp enough to hear them from within her room, Salin didn't want to chance it. Until she was his, there were certain aspects of *raedjour* society he wasn't ready to divulge. Humans had strange notions where certain sexual practices were involved.

Salin folded into his favorite chair, facing Jarak, who knelt before him. The younger man hesitated at his master's knee.

"May I ask a question?"

"Always," Salin responded immediately. Jarak's final education was a responsibility he took seriously.

"Why don't you take her?"

Salin smiled. Leaning back in his chair, he massaged his own cock. "I could. I *want* to. But I have to wait."

Jarak watched Salin's hand, licking his lips, but obviously he was still confused. "Why?"

"If I just take her, I give her the excuse to dismiss me. Like the others."

Jarak's gaze brightened. "So, by not fucking her, you're different?"

Salin nodded, releasing his cock and scooting his hips forward a bit in a silent request. Obediently, Jarak nodded. But before he bent his head, he once again met his master's gaze. "I hope you win her," he said, an odd determination in his gaze. "She suits you."

Salin would have responded, but Jarak's head bent and his warm, dark mouth closed over the head of Salin's cock. Groaning, he dug his fingers into Jarak's sleek white hair, urging him on. Despite Salin's iron control over his body, his cock protested the taunting of the past two days. It wanted

Diana. Wanted to spear her cunt and get strangled by what it knew would be sweet, tight walls. Jarak's skilled mouth was nice, and usually more than enough for release, but even as Salin's cock tightened then spewed forth down Jarak's throat, Salin recognized neither he nor his cock were satisfied.

Now he was positive of the fact he had kept so far to himself. His latent powers sometimes gave him intuition, intuition his brother Radin warned him not to ignore. And that nagging intuition told him in no uncertain terms that the woman in the other room was his truemate.

Chapter Nine

The third day, he brought her sword back. They fought again, and she lost. This time she ended up trussed to the standing X, her arms hanging from secured chains over her shoulders and her legs spread to the two legs of the X.

"We'll get you a leather corset," he said in a rumbling voice that caressed her from inside. "Yes. Once I tame you, I'll dress you all in leather. But then it will be white, to contrast with your lovely black skin."

"You won't tame me," she assured him, glaring daggers.

He only smiled, his fingers trailing through the tight curls that protected her sex. "Sweet, you're already tamed. You just don't know it."

"Arrogant bastard," she spat. "Is that a racial trait?"

He grinned, tweaking one of her nipples. "Arrogance? No. No more so than humans." He pinched one nipple hard enough to wrench a gasp from her. "I simply have an overabundance."

"I noticed."

He chuckled, sliding his fingers underneath her breasts to caress the warm, tender skin.

She asked, suddenly allowing herself questions she'd denied before, "Where did you come from?"

"Me personally, or my race?"

"Your race."

"I thought you'd heard this story?"

"Tell me again."

"Have you heard of the goddess Rhae?"

"No."

He shrugged, still distracted by her breasts. "I didn't expect you had. She seems to only be known to us. At least by that name. It's said it was She who created us, a race of consorts."

"Consorts?" No one had used that particular term before.

He grinned, leaning forward to graze her cheek with his lips. "That's what *raedjour* means: 'Rhae's consorts.' We were created as fuck toys."

She shivered. She'd known that from Iana, but the way he said it made it all the more real. "Is that just legend?" In her travels, she and Gala had seen evidence of the gods through a number of wonders, but she'd yet to encounter a race with such direct ties to their patron deity.

"Actually, no. It's fact. At least that is what our kings have told us, and they're in direct contact to Rhae. High priests, if you will."

"They could be lying."

A flash of anger was quickly squelched. "I don't believe they are."

"So what happened?"

His hands were busy, inciting the fire in her skin with

light caresses, but he continued to appease her curiosity. "When the gods left the world, Rhae was forced to abandon us. It was then She realized She'd missed an important fact about us -- there were no women." He leaned forward again to kiss her temple, undeterred by the fact that she tried to avoid him.

"So now you kidnap and rape innocent human women?" she demanded.

He lapped at her earlobe, causing her to shiver. "You continue to use that label."

"What?"

"'Rape.' Such an ugly word."

"What label would you use?"

His mouth slid sensuously down her neck to nip softly at the top of her shoulder and the mark he'd left the previous night. "You've enjoyed what's been done to you. No pain has been given you that did not go hand-in-hand with pleasure."

"I've been tied and chained and taken against my will," she protested, rattling her bonds to make her point.

His mouth continued downward, now at the top of one breast. "And you look beautiful bound. Your eyes blazing, your body straining for release." He nipped the top of her breast. "You've enjoyed the restraint."

She had. The fact that he voiced it only upset her. She squirmed. "Fuck you!"

"In due time," he promised, finally reaching her beaded nipple. From his great height, he was bent nearly double to reach it, but he didn't seem to mind at all as his hot, black tongue swiped it.

"Besides," he continued conversationally, his breath

teasing the taut, wet nub, "we like to think we give something in return."

She gasped when he abruptly captured the hard bud and sucked hard. It took her a moment to recall her line of thought as he alternately laved and bit at the tip of her breast.

"It's not right," she finally managed to say.

"Hmmm?" he inquired, switching to her other breast.

"I don't have a choice."

"Mmm," he agreed. He spent a few glorious moments suckling before he straightened to meet her glazed gaze. He braced those long, powerful arms on the cross just above her, his huge body nearly draping her front like a cloak of darkness. "Not quite fair, I agree. But we were born with the natural instinct to procreate. As we have only the one way, we make do."

"I didn't ask for this," she insisted.

One large hand descended to lightly caress her cheek. Her chin. "I've given you the choice, sweet. Have I not asked before I've taken you? Have I not restrained myself when you've denied me?"

He had. He, alone. The others had only waited for physical signs of acceptance or submitted to her frustrated demands. This one asked permission. This one, who probably had more clout than any of the rest combined.

She avoided the question. "Will you keep me in bondage the rest of my life?" she demanded as he bent toward her breast again.

He glanced up with a devilish glint in his gaze. "Only if that's what you desire, my sweet."

"Damn!" she growled, twisting and struggling against her bonds in what she knew was a feeble attempt to keep her breast from his diabolical attentions. He chuckled and allowed her to fight, watching the bounce of her breasts, then infuriating her further by playfully juggling them.

"You're truly beautiful, Diana," he mused. "Especially so in your fury."

"Monsters, all of you," she cried, yanking at her bonds. "Perverse monsters."

He stepped away as she struggled, casually going to the table to pour himself a drink. She grudgingly noticed the huge erection which bobbed along before him. His control was astounding to deny *that*.

"Actually, you're right," he agreed amicably. "We are monsters. Created by a lusty goddess who wanted an unending string of tireless lovers and fearless guards." It sounded as though he was quoting a well-known story. But then, among the *raedjour*, it likely *was* a well-known story. "Born to the night, with skin like armor and instincts of the finest predators. Our one main weakness seems to be sunlight." He grinned as she perked at the tidbit of information. "Consider that a gift, my sweet. I've given you our one vulnerability."

"So now you can't let me go?"

A strange smile took his lips, determined yet somehow unsure. "I don't plan to ever let you go, sweet."

She watched through narrowed eyes as he returned to her, wine cup in hand. "You'll have to in six more days, won't you?" she accused. "That's the rule. Nine days, and if I'm not pregnant, you pass me on."

He wouldn't meet her gaze, his eyes trained on the wine cup as he tilted it just enough to dribble red liquid over her breasts.

"That's the rule, isn't it?" she insisted.

"That's the rule," he admitted, using two fingers of his free hand to smear wine across her sensitive skin.

"At the rate you're going, I won't be pregnant, and you'll have to let me go," she pointed out, almost cheerily. "You *do* know how babies are made, don't you?"

A full laugh erupted from his belly. Without answering her, he knelt before her, setting the cup on the floor beside him. That hot, clever tongue commenced lapping up the wine which had spilled down her belly. Not until he had suckled every drop of wine from her skin, used his lips, tongue, and teeth to explore and torture every inch of her breasts, did he straighten and force her to look at him by burying two huge hands in her hair.

"I know how babies are made," he assured her, wine-scented breath caressing her lips.

For precious moments, she didn't recall what he was talking about. He waited until her eyes focused on his, smiling at her disorientation.

"I know that I'm going to dive into that hot, wet pussy of yours and plant my seed at the very mouth of your womb. And I'm going to do it again and again until you forget that my cock isn't a permanent part of your sweet body."

She shivered, unconsciously licking her lips. "What's stopping you?" she heard herself ask.

He smiled, gently kissing her lips. "Do you want me to fuck you, sweet?" He paused over her parted lips. The denial didn't come, but neither did the request.

On a hard breath, he swept his tongue past her lips, delving the depths of her mouth to mate tongue-to-tongue. Bound by both his hands and the chains, she was helpless to deny him. Helpless, until she recalled herself. Defiantly -- ignoring the inner voice begging her to let the kiss continue -- she bit down hard on his tongue.

His cry was muffled by her mouth. His hands pulled painfully at her hair. She tasted blood.

Horrified by her own actions, she released him.

He pulled back, face averted as he worked jaw and tongue to make sure both were still intact. She swallowed and fought the gorge that threatened to rise as some of his blood slithered down her throat. His fingers remained fastened in her hair, although the painful pull was gone.

Then he turned to face her once again. A dribble of blood escaped the corner of his mouth to run down his sharp chin, so very red against his glossy blackness. She met his gaze. She expected rage. She wouldn't be surprised if he killed her now.

She didn't expect the smile.

"Did you enjoy the taste of my blood, sweet?"

"You...you *enjoyed* that?"

Carefully he licked his lips, wincing only slightly. "I wouldn't have thought it. But I can if you enjoyed it."

Her eyes went wide. "You can't be real!"

He smiled. "I told you, sweet, my race was created for sex. *All* kinds of sex. If my partner enjoys it and I'm so inclined, I can enjoy a great many things. Even pain." He leaned in closer, grazing her cheek with his lips. "And I'm inclined to enjoy anything that brings you pleasure."

She shuddered. "Get away from me."

Salin sensed that her taste of blood had effectively quelled her pleasure. Unfortunately, it hadn't done the same for him. Much of a *raedjour* male's sexual stimulation stemmed from his partner's pleasure. But although Diana's ardor had cooled, Salin's need for her kept his high.

Knowing he'd get no further reactions from her that day, he nuzzled her ear one last time before kneeling to release her ankles. She avoided his gaze when he stood to release her wrists, and he stepped back to allow her to escape him. Regretfully, he watched her curl up on the bed of furs, her back to him.

"Don't let it frighten you, sweet," he soothed as he replaced the cup he'd abandoned on the floor.

She didn't respond, curled within herself. He felt her confusion over the pulsing arousal.

"I'll send Jarak for a tub and water," he said, swiping at the blood that drizzled from his mouth. She'd cut skin, but she hadn't hurt him as badly as she likely thought. Inside and out, his race was incredibly hard to hurt. And although she had wounded him, the minor cut would be largely healed by the next day. "Would a soak in hot water please you?"

She didn't even turn. "You leaving would please me."

The words cut deeper than her teeth, but he didn't show it. Salin was nothing if not a master of concealing his emotions. "I'll send Jarak anyway. Good day, sweet."

With that, he left her. This day, it was easier to cool his ardor, so he declined Jarak's ready offer to appease him.

Instead, he did as promised and sent the boy for a tub and water. On instinct, he sent for one thing more which he thought would make his truemate happy.

Chapter Ten

Diana watched Jarak and two other young men wrestle a large brass tub into the room. They each took turns leaving the room to retrieve buckets of water from the fresh, streaming supply in the privy. Stubbornly, she didn't move from the bed platform. Her eyes strayed to the doorway initially, but one of the larger, bulkier guards stood sentinel against her escape.

When the tub was full, the youths departed. Jarak left a tray of fruits, cheese, and fragrant nut bread. Diana sulked, knowing the water was cold. Didn't they recall she didn't have their seeming immunity to temperature?

Then another man entered. At first she thought he was another youth, but then she changed her mind. He was certainly young, but there was something of experience about him that the others didn't have. He did have a soft, youthful appearance with rounded features and full, pouty lips. His long, snowy white hair was bound by two braids from his temples that combined to one long braid in the back. It was when she saw his eyes that she reassessed his age. They glowed powerful red, clear with arcane knowledge. The knowledge in his eyes was at odds with the boyish smile he gave her.

"Lady," he said, voice barely above a whisper as he nodded a greeting to her.

He then hovered his hand over the tub. Within moments, Diana saw steam rising.

"She likes it scalding, Hyle," said a familiar voice from the doorway.

Diana's head whipped around to see Gala standing by the door guard. At least, she was relatively sure it was Gala. It sounded like Gala and was *shaped* like Gala, but... "Gala?" she asked, just to be sure.

Laughing, Gala looked down at her body. "Hmm, I suppose I *do* look a little different." Her tanned skin had paled and had a distinct dark gray tone. Her sandy blonde hair was considerably paler as it fell loose about her shoulders and bare breasts. In fact, all she wore was a skimpy, shimmery wrap about her hips and sandals on her feet. The eyes that looked up and met Diana's, however, were clearly those of her lifelong friend. "It's me, Diana."

Ignoring the presence of the men, Diana scrambled from the bed platform into her friend's welcome embrace. She didn't care that she was naked and Gala was mostly naked. She didn't care that Gala had clearly become a part of this world Diana was struggling to fight against. At present, she needed the reassurance that something, someone, from her former life was there. "I'm *so* glad to see you," Diana murmured.

Gala laughed, hugging her fiercely. "And I'm glad to see you, too. I'd wanted to, but..." She shook her head. "Never mind. What's important is that the commander's given us some time together."

"Salin?"

Gala nodded. "Of course. It's his time with you and his choice to give it up. I'm so grateful to him!"

Some of Diana's excitement quelled, melting into a scowl. Gala, familiar with the look on her friend's face, chose to ignore it by turning to the young sorcerer.

"Hyle, I want you to meet my best friend." She stepped toward him, the handclasp they shared a comfortable one. "Diana, this is Hyle. My truemate."

The significance of the term froze Diana's blood. "Then you're…"

Gala nodded, her free hand dropping to caress her flat belly. "I'm pregnant."

Diana couldn't speak. She couldn't congratulate her friend, despite her obvious radiant happiness. In two sentences, Gala had further wounded any hopes Diana had harbored of escape. If she left now, she would go alone. Without her lifelong companion.

Again, knowing Diana's moods, Gala turned to Hyle. "Don't take her lack of greeting personally, my love." She kissed him tenderly on the cheek. "Thank you for the water."

Nodding his understanding, he caressed her cheek with two loving fingers, kissed her lips briefly, then, with a last nod to Diana, left. The burly guard left with him, and the lock clicked.

"That wasn't very nice," Gala chided softly, moving further into the room. "Oh! Salin's rooms are much bigger than ours!"

"*Nice?*" Diana demanded, stomping to Gala's side. "Nice? How can I be nice to one of those monsters?"

"They're not monsters," Gala said calmly, picking up one of the linen cloths and unfolding it.

"Not monsters? They abducted us. Raped us…"

"I was not raped," Gala chided. "And neither were you."

"I was taken by force."

"Because that's what excited you."

Diana shook her head. "You're not talking rationally."

"And when have you ever talked rationally?"

Diana gaped at her friend, who continued to calmly lay out bathing supplies.

"The fact of the matter is that they took us. Yes. But I've come to the realization that *someone* was going to take us eventually, Diana. If not the *raedjour*, then a team of bandits. Or maybe a guard troop too far away from home. Or maybe we'd wander onto enemy lands and be taken and sold into slavery. The life we were leading as mercenaries wasn't going to allow us a long, happy life." She faced Diana. "You should get into the water while it's still hot."

"Fuck the water."

"Gods, Diana! Do you have to fight *everything?*"

Diana gaped again. Only very rarely did Gala lose her temper, and even more rarely did she direct it at Diana.

"We're here," Gala continued, reining in her anger. "We're not going anywhere. There is a lovely bath full of hot water sitting right next to you. I know you haven't had the pleasure in a long time. Could you *for once* just fucking enjoy the little pleasures in life?!"

That sparked Diana's anger. "Who the hell do you think you are?"

"I think I'm the person who's watched you fight against any good thing that's ever been given to you. I'm the person who's watched you dismiss every good thing that you've worked hard for. I'm the person who's sick to death of following you on your hopeless quest for happiness." Gala stood back, crossing her arms over her chest. "Well, guess what, Diana. *I'm* happy. Happy here. Happy with Hyle and the *raedjour.* This is a *beautiful* place, if you'd just open your eyes to see it. And Salin..."

"I won't discuss him."

"Why not? Because he just could be your match?"

"He's not."

Gala looked as though she wanted to say more, but didn't. She stepped back. "You should take advantage of the bath while it's still hot."

Mentally battered and emotionally tired, Diana's anger dissipated. Glum, she stepped into the wonderfully hot water and carefully submerged her body. Gala was right. It had been a long time since she'd enjoyed a full, leisurely bath. Without another word, Gala pulled up one of the ornate wooden chairs and started combing through Diana's hair.

"You're happy?" Diana finally asked.

Gala dipped a cup in the water and poured it carefully over Diana's fine brown hair. "Yes."

"What's he like?"

"He's wonderful. He's not like most of the rest of them. He's quiet and thoughtful, but he's so smart. And his magic! I didn't know one being could do such things with his mind! Once he..."

Gala continued, happily chatting about little occurrences

between her and Hyle in their short time together. Even Diana had to admit -- to herself -- that her friend had never sounded happier. Tidbits about Hyle drifted into snippets about things she'd seen in the *raedjour* city. Gala declared that Diana would soon need to visit the common bathing chamber, as it was a huge cavern of natural mineral spring tubs that the *raedjour* had painstakingly carved over the centuries. She went on to describe some of the art she'd seen, and then a dancing troupe during one night's festivities. Gala went on and on, long after Diana had finished washing and had simply sat back in the tub to enjoy the lingering warmth.

Animated, Gala wandered Salin's rooms. She explained how well the *raedjour* cared for the women they captured. "We're special to them, for obvious reasons," she declared, examining the standing X to which Diana had been chained the previous day. "Every one I've met has been very careful to show me respect as Hyle's mate."

"As Hyle's mate," Diana repeated. "Not before?"

"I wasn't allowed to roam much before Hyle. As you already know, they watch you very carefully before you truemate. But they treated me very well even before that."

Diana sniffed. Gala sighed and continued to roam.

"Diana, you haven't been...*hurt*, have you?" she asked, eyeing the chains dangling from the padded bench.

"Does it matter?"

"Of course it does."

"It wouldn't change anything."

"It would. They're not allowed to hurt you, Diana. Well, unless that brings you pleasure."

Diana shuddered, vividly recalling the taste of blood and

the burn of lust in Salin's eyes.

Gala continued, now hovering at the foot of the bath. "Their pleasure is tied to ours, Diana," she explained. "Anything they can do to please us heightens their pleasure. Anything they do to hurt us, hurts them. For the time that they're with a lover, it's more than just a physical bond."

Diana frowned at the cloudy water gently lapping at her thighs. "Is that true?"

"Yes. They monitor you and compare so that every successive lover knows what pleased you before." She gestured at the bondage equipment. "Diana, they couldn't *do* any of that to you unless you enjoyed it."

Diana scowled. "It's the spell."

Gala shook her head. "Not all of it. There's a charm, yes. It's the one Nalfien used at the start. But that's only meant to distract us so that he can search our minds. See if we're capable of living with them."

That got Diana's attention. "Capable? What happens if he decided we're not capable?"

"Not many women aren't."

"But what if we *weren't?*"

Gala frowned. "I don't know."

"Of course you do."

"No, I don't. I never asked."

Diana studied her friend's face. She knew Gala too well not to see the truth of that.

"But what I was saying *before*," Gala went on, "is that the charm wears off. After that, it's just their natural appeal. They were made by a goddess…"

"Yes, yes. I know all that. Made by a goddess as fuck toys."

Diana rose from the now-cool water. Gala handed her a soft linen cloth to dry herself. Nothing more of import was said as Diana rubbed her hair dry, then combed it out. Finally, however, she sat before a polished disk, looking at her reflection. Gala sat quietly behind her on the bed platform.

"I don't want to stay here, Gala," she said.

"Why not?"

She turned to face her friend. "You'll never see the sun again."

Gala shrugged. "I've discovered beautiful things in the dark."

"You'll live in caves the rest of your life."

Gala let her gaze travel Salin's sumptuous room. "I see nothing wrong with this cave. And I can assure you that the rest of the city, while maybe not as rich, is just as beautiful."

"You'll never see your family again."

That gave Gala pause. "I will miss Trin" -- her sister -- "but then, I haven't seen her in cycles. With Mum and Da gone, that only leaves Quince, and I'm not likely to miss him."

Diana, too, didn't have any family to miss. Her beloved father had died many years ago, and her brothers were nearly strangers to her now.

Still, she shook her head. "It's not right."

Gala sighed. Glancing at the timepiece in the corner, she stood up. During her ramblings, Gala had explained that the small statue of the goddess Rhae had a magical flame in the bowl she held before her and that flame told the time by color. Yellow was midday, blue was midnight. Currently, it was a soft green.

"I have to leave," Gala said, walking toward Diana. "The commander gave us until daybreak."

Diana frowned. "I don't know why he bothered. He's only toying with me."

"Why do you say that?"

Diana stood. "I don't see how he expects to get me pregnant since he hasn't fucked me yet."

Gala's eyes went wide. "What?"

Diana shook her head. "Not once."

"I wonder why?"

"I told you. He's toying with me. They all are." She shrugged, pulling her friend into another hug. "I'll try and be glad that you found happiness, Gala. Really, I will. But I don't think there's any hope for me."

* * *

Fresh from a night of training with his men and a refreshing time in the bathing cavern, Salin returned to his suite to find Hyle in the main room. The young sorcerer was seated cross-legged on a bench by the cold fireplace, eyes open but seeing nothing. Salin knew the look. Radin wore it often enough. It meant the sorcerer was using his other senses to see, to feel. Practicing.

Even sensing Salin's presence, it took Hyle a few moments to break from his trance. It wasn't instantaneous like Radin. Hyle still had much to learn.

The young sorcerer stood, nodding his head in respect to the older man.

"Hyle," Salin greeted, dumping soiled clothes on a nearby chair for Jarak to gather and launder later. "Are the ladies still within?"

"They are."

"And what have they been talking about this night?"

Hyle frowned. "I don't know. I wasn't in the room with them."

Salin suppressed a smile. "You mean you didn't eavesdrop?"

"Well, no."

Salin shook his head, clucking his tongue. "Hyle, what are we to do with you? You've spent entirely too much time with Nalfien and Rhicard. They've made you much too *honorable!* You need to spend more time with Radin."

Hyle didn't always catch on quickly to jokes, but he did catch on. He smiled. "I'm sorry, Commander. I'll try and take after Radin a bit more."

"On second thought, don't. Or if you do, don't tell Nalfien it was my idea."

They shared a companionable laugh.

"On a serious note, Hyle, my thanks for the loan of your truemate."

Hyle shook his head. "You're welcome, Commander, but I should thank you, as well. Gala has wanted very much to see her friend."

"What is it like to be truemated, Hyle?" Salin asked casually.

The younger man's face instantly lit up, his joy obvious. "It's a true wonder, Commander."

Salin nodded, turning away lest the astute young man see the stab of jealousy. Salin wanted personal knowledge of that joy and knew instinctively that he could only have it with the stubborn woman in the next room.

The chamber door opened. Gala stepped into the outer room, Diana hovering behind her. Salin stood still, wondering if Diana would make a bid for escape. Her green-gold gaze clashed with his, but she remained leaning within the doorway, arms crossed protectively beneath her breasts. He wondered if she knew how well she fit, how right she looked in the doorway to his bedchamber.

"Commander," Gala greeted, nodding her head in due respect. "Thank you so much for allowing me time with Diana."

He took the hand she offered and stooped to raise her palm to his lips. She was such a little thing, the top of her head barely reaching his nipples. "It was my pleasure," he purred, enjoying the tendril of pleasure his kiss caused her.

The white-hot stab of jealousy he felt from across the room shocked him. Diana wouldn't know he could feel it, and couldn't have hidden it if she tried. Forgetting Gala's palm, he turned a triumphant gaze toward Diana.

Bastard! She thought, watching him treat Gala with tenderness. *Her* he'd manhandle, but *Gala* he'd treat with kindness?!

The look he shot her confirmed everything Gala had told her this night. He *could* feel her emotions. *Damn!*

Gala glanced over her shoulder at Diana, but neither Diana nor Salin acknowledged the presence of anyone else in the room. Recognizing that fact, Gala went to Hyle and led him quietly from the room.

Salin's gaze narrowed as soon as they were alone. Rhae's tits, she was gorgeous! Naked and glowing clean, her silky hair a shining blanket across her shoulders and back. Her smoldering scowl only added to the allure.

Slowly, he walked toward her. "Did you enjoy your visit?"

She swallowed, struggling to stand her ground. "Yes." Then scowled. "Thank you."

"Oh, that admission hurt. Didn't it?"

"Yes. It did," she muttered. She retreated from his advance. "Why did you do it?"

He shut the door behind them, never taking his eyes off her. "Did it please you?"

She growled, spinning on her heel to stalk to the farthest corner of the room, far away from the bondage contraptions he left to keep her company. "I don't want to hear any more about how my pleasure is your pleasure. Gala filled me in, so you don't have to go on about it."

He decided then and there that Gala deserved a gift. A boon. Anything he could do to thank her for talking to Diana. He could easily see that Diana had been thrown by her friend's acceptance of her new life. By the things Gala had said. As usual, his impulse had been right.

He glanced at the cold water of the bath. "Did the bath please you?"

"Stop it."

Smiling, he stalked her. "Do the furs on the bed please you? I chose only the finest for you."

He allowed her to slip past him, watched her firm ass as she crossed the room. "This," she said, pointing imperiously at the bondage bench, "doesn't please me." She pointed at the standing X. "This doesn't please me." She stood beside the small two-tier bench she was sure he had plans for. "I don't know what this is, but it certainly doesn't please me." She snatched the wrist and ankle straps from their resting place on the bench and jangled them at him. "These don't please me."

During her tirade, he'd come closer. She hauled back her arm to hurl the restraints across the room, but he caught her unawares from behind, curling one arm around her waist and catching her throwing wrist with the other.

"I beg to differ, sweet," he drawled, pleased that she didn't lash out. Even more pleased to feel the gentle sweep of twittering pleasure that seeped off her skin. "I think they please you very much."

"Is that what the others told you? The other men who've had me? Did they laugh? Did you compare notes?"

He wrestled the restraints from her hand while carrying her to the large bench. She squirmed, but that only served to rub her ass against his cock through his trousers, increasing the erection he already sported.

"No laughing, sweet," he assured her. "Every man who had you is thankful for the privilege and would gladly have you again."

"I'll just *bet* they would. No!"

The last was as he forced her onto the bench, this time on her belly. The curses again flared as he manhandled her into the restraints and chained her down. Rhae, she was magnificent! Fighting even though she knew she didn't have a chance, her strong body squirming deliciously against his. He could hardly wait until she turned and her strength grew with her body's new constitution!

When she was securely bound, he took his time admiring the fine curves of her back and the delectable swell of her ass. He cupped one firm globe with his palm. Instinct again, he pulled back and slapped it.

She jumped, only the bonds keeping her from flying away. "Damn it, no!"

But her body told him the truth. She was shocked, but that didn't detract from the warmth spreading through her.

"You have a beautiful ass, Diana," he told her, climbing onto the bench until he was kneeling between her spread thighs. Reverently, he caressed her cheeks again, loving how she clenched them. He smacked her other cheek.

"Salin, no!"

"Ah, I love the sound of my name from your lips, sweet. Say it again."

"No. Ah!" The last when he spanked her again.

"Say it again."

"Damn you!" Smack! "Salin!"

He groaned, lowering his face until he could draw his tongue over one edible globe. "Yes," he breathed, nibbling as she clenched again. "Again."

She stayed silent, then shrieked wordlessly when he spanked her again. She bucked and cursed, but if he didn't feel her growing arousal with his *raedjour* senses, he certainly had physical proof when he slid his fingers through the drenched folds of her sex. She gasped when his finger barely touched that sensitive nubbin at the apex of her sex.

No, not tonight. Not yet.

He returned his attention to her ass, forcing her cheeks apart to drag his tongue wetly down the warm center. She was outraged. Shocked. None of the others had taken her this way, he knew. Her anger had been too great, her resistance too strong. No other had seen the need to push the issue, content to sink into the wet depth of her cunt. But Salin was determined to make her want it. She was his, and he would take every orifice of her body and make her beg for it.

He bit her, testing how much she would take. He ignored the string of epithets that burst from her mouth and concentrated instead on the mounting pressure he sensed in her womb. On the intoxicating scent of the hot honey that oozed from her sex.

For Diana, it was a confusing struggle. Only one other had suggested the penetration of her ass, and the mere suggestion had sent her into a rage that had effectively quelled his lust. But this was different. Although Salin touched places she had previously had no desire to ever be touched by another, she felt her arousal as keenly as he.

She stopped cursing him. It didn't do any good anyway. She turned that attention inward, determined not to enjoy his attentions. But it was futile. He kept her off guard. Just as she could deny his tongue felt good, he'd switch to squeezing her ass. When she could concentrate on that, he spanked her. As her outrage grew, he'd split her cheeks and drag his tongue across surprisingly sensitive skin. This *shouldn't* feel good!

When she stopped screaming at him, he started talking. Telling her all the wicked things he'd do to her, promising her heights she'd never dreamed. Once his tongue had thoroughly wet her, his fingers started a sneaky, wiggling invasion. With all the sensation, she couldn't even be sure of what he was doing until she felt one long finger sink in.

"Salin!" she cried, but it sounded weak even to her ears.

"Don't tell me to stop, sweet," he rasped, almost begged. "Just feel, sweet. I swear to you, you'll like it."

Sweet Mother of us all, she actually believed him! Her body, heightened by two nights of arousal with no true release, trembled on a fine line between desire and denial.

Teeth bit into her ass as the finger slowly slid out, mostly. His free hand spanked her other cheek as the finger thrust slowly back in. Did he have more than two hands?! She could no longer be sure. His finger pumped slowly, gently. His tongue caressed. Palm slapped. Gods, was that another finger?

"Salin, not this way," she begged, but her voice was a husky breath. Her hips -- damn them! -- were pumping in rhythm to his thrusting fingers. It hurt, but, somehow, it also didn't.

"Oh, yes, Diana," he crooned, lips soft against the burning skin of her bottom. "You're so fucking tight."

"Salin," she cried, arching to lift her hips toward him when an errant thumb slid through her nether lips and lightly rubbed her clit. "Ah, Salin!" This was impossible! Her ardor had succumbed to other men, but never like this! What had he *done* to her?

It no longer mattered. She was lost. He'd found some switch -- hidden deep in her ass, of all places! -- that slowly drove her out of her mind. He pumped her, and she could well imagine his fingers were that gorgeous cock of his. Gods, yes! At the moment, she even wanted that massive piece deep inside her ass!

Salin pumped her harder, pushing mewls from her gasping lips. He paid careful attention to the wash of pleasure that washed through her and over him. It hurt her, yes, but she was past that now. Her body was wound tight from the pent-up desire of the past few days. She struggled now to slam back onto his fingers, and he struggled not to remove them and replace them with his cock. She wasn't ready for that. But she would be. When she was his.

When she broke, she screamed. Her body shook in an orgasm she clearly didn't expect. He bit her quaking ass and groaned, cursing himself his denial of her. His own body shook, and he had to use every bit of his centuries of training to bring it back under control.

Gently, he eased his fingers out, watching as her rosebud, red from loving abuse, contracted back on itself. He gave it one last fond kiss before pulling himself away. Diana lay limp before him, stunned silent. A part of him wanted to demand she acknowledge what had just happened, but a smarter part of him kept him silent. It wouldn't do to push her too hard.

Groaning softly, he adjusted the fit of his trousers. His cock was like to kill him before this was through. He crawled from between her thighs and quietly released her bonds.

She wouldn't look at him. Once free, she curled into a fetal kneel, arms over the back of her neck, forehead nearly on her knees.

"Humans," he cursed, feeling her confusion and guilt. "There's nothing wrong with what just happened, Diana," he told her firmly, afraid her shame would ruin what, to him, was a beautiful breakthrough.

He again considered forcing the issue, but decided against it. Though it broke his heart, he left her.

Chapter Eleven

Salin tossed in the bed he occupied in his suite's second bedchamber, unable to sleep. That little bit he'd been inside her infected him, making his blood run hotter than normal. He'd declined Jarak's offer of release. Neither the younger man's ass nor mouth was Diana's, and he certainly didn't smell like her. Feel like her.

Nine punishments of Rhae! Cursing under his breath, he rolled from the bed. Jarak roused from his own bed platform across the room, but Salin waved him back to sleep.

She was sound asleep when he entered the room, a collection of smooth curves mostly hidden by soft furs. He stood in the doorway a moment, well aware that even if she were awake, she wouldn't see him. He could see perfectly well in pitch darkness, but she wouldn't gain that ability until she turned. Until all that soft, pink flesh darkened to gleaming black.

He took a deep breath and stalked toward her. Carefully, he lifted the pelts that covered her until she lay bare before him. Yes, all that pink flesh, those soft curves, the carved muscle. He slid a hand over the rounded curve of her hip, dipping it around her thigh to pull gently until he rolled her onto her back. She sighed but didn't waken, one hand curled delicately by her softly pouting lips.

Unable to resist, he lowered himself to his belly, stretched out between her welcoming thighs. In her sleep, she was so much that she didn't allow herself to be when awake. Soft. Welcoming. Endearing. In an oddly possessive moment for one of his race, he hoped he was the only one to ever see this side of her.

She was warm and fragrant, vestiges of what he'd scented earlier. Spreading his hands underneath her splayed thighs, he kissed the tender skin where her hip became her leg. Ran his tongue down the crease between groin and leg until he could just nip the undercurve of her bottom. Taking his time, he nibbled her flesh, tormenting himself by avoiding her sex, all the while breathing deeply of her edible aroma. He circled her sex, nipping lightly at the crisp curls on her mons. She sighed, unconsciously angling her hips to give him better access. He smiled, skirting the little nubbin of nerves that peeped from under its protective hood, to reach the fleshy lips below. His body actually trembled at his first, true taste of her. He rolled her flavor on his tongue like fine wine, slowly savoring every nuance. Carefully, slowly, he suckled the lips of her sex, drinking her in.

She sighed again, sliding one leg up until her calf rested on his back, her thigh on his shoulder. He welcomed the pillow for his cheek as he angled his head to slide his tongue into her channel. He played there, exploring her folds and crevices with his tongue until he felt the impatient buck of her hips.

Smiling, he took her subconscious hint. Up he licked,

spreading her, until he found that hard nub and pressed firmly. She gasped, her hips rocking. Groaning softly, he sucked her clit into his mouth, nursing, teasing it with his tongue and teeth.

Orgasm woke Diana from a hazy dream of colors in darkness. She opened her eyes, and the complete lack of light did nothing to increase her sight. But she felt him. As the tremors in her body subsided, she felt his arms wrapped around her thighs, hands relaxed on her belly. His mouth -- oh, his mouth! That was locked deliciously on her cunt, sucking her back into another...

Her back arched, her thighs struggling to close on the intense sensation. He growled, altering his hold so that those strong arms and hands kept her splayed as he continued to devour her.

"Salin," she begged, reaching down to clutch his silky hair. Only she wasn't sure what she begged, since she didn't seem to be pulling him away so much as trapping him where he was.

He growled again, sinking his tongue as deep as it would go into her channel, nodding so that his nose pressed, rubbed her clit.

"Ah, wait," she cried, writhing beneath him. She knew it was him. The others had done this. Other men -- all *raedjour*, none human -- had made her squirm, but she *knew* it was him. She knew the hot muscles beneath her calves belonged to the tall, arrogant commander.

"Salin!" she screamed as her entire body undulated with agonizing pleasure.

He refused to give her any time to breathe, pausing only long enough to take a breath of his own before angling his head another way. This time he sucked her clit into his mouth and unwound one arm from her thighs so that he could sink two -- three? -- fingers into her clutching channel. She cried out, pounding his back, nearly doubling herself in half to clutch at his shoulders. But again, she didn't seem to be pushing so much as pulling. Pulling him to her, pulling him into her.

They fought like this forever, it seemed. She fought not to feel, not to soar, and he fought to make her quiver and scream. She was losing. Worse, she couldn't really bring herself to care.

Finally, she lost all strength. He'd depleted her to a trembling mass of muscle and wet tissues. She fell back to the furs, arms akimbo and legs splayed. Breathing hard, eyes closed, she could only lie at his mercy.

His attentions grew tender once again, acceding to the fact that there was just no more orgasm in her. Smiling in the dark, he lapped up her juices, kissed the inside of each warm thigh, then pulled away. She expected a comment, a confirmation of triumph, but none was forthcoming. He crawled up her body and used his strong hands to roll her limp body to the side. He used a few moments to arrange her body into the warm curve of his, her buttocks nestled against his belly, his rock-hard cock trapped between her thighs.

She awaited his nightly question. The one he'd not asked earlier. Briefly, she considered if she'd deny him again, despite her present exhaustion. When it didn't come, she yawned and settled, not quite snuggling into his embrace.

"This means nothing." It was all the protest she could muster.

She felt the small breath of a chuckle near her ear just before he kissed her temple. "Of course not."

Chapter Twelve

When she woke, he was gone. Candles had been lit and Jarak must have come, because a tray of cheeses and warm bread awaited her.

Had she dreamed it? She reached down between her own thighs and winced at the soreness, but that meant little. For all she knew, she could have masturbated herself to the thought of him.

Sighing, she rolled to her back. The furs that surrounded her smelled like him, but again that meant nothing. They always had. There was no indication that Salin had actually come to her last night and suckled her into oblivion.

But she knew his earlier, anal fucking had happened. She'd yet to come to terms with that. She couldn't deny -- to herself, at least -- that he'd made something that just *shouldn't* feel good, feel wonderful. And while she was making personal admissions, she could admit that he made *everything* feel wonderful.

Disgusted with herself, she rolled from the bed, wincing at her soreness. The timepiece told her most of the day was gone and that it would soon be dusk. Her body had already acclimated to the *raedjour* timetable of sleep during the day and activity at night. Her mouth watered at the smell of the strange, spicy bread they served her. And, as she looked in the mirrored disk on the wall, she could tell that her hair was noticeably lighter.

She was changing.

Avoiding that thought, she used the privy, washed with fresh, cool water, then ate some of the bread and cheese. While munching, she approached the door to her chamber. Tried the knob.

It turned.

Astonished, she opened the door to see the central room of the suite. The only light came from a fire in the carved fireplace on the opposite wall. She knew the doorway to the left was the exit of Salin's suite. Stepping into the room, she glanced to the right and stopped.

Jarak sat amongst large pillows on the floor, busily polishing or cleaning a bit of leatherwork he held on his lap. He stood as she turned, nodding calmly before he met her gaze. "May I get something for you, lady?"

She crossed her arms, not even aware any longer that she was naked. "I should have known he'd leave a guard."

Jarak smiled. "I'm here to attend my master's lady."

She scowled. "I am *not* his lady."

"You are for four more days, at least, lady."

She sniffed, gaze drifting back to the outer door. "What would you do if I went and opened the door?"

"Would you care for a tour of the city, lady?"

Shocked, she blinked, then returned her gaze to his smiling face. "Excuse me?"

"Commander Salin has given me permission to escort you through some of the city, if that's your desire."

"*Some* of the city?" she asked.

"There are parts of the city that aren't safe for those who haven't lived here." He stepped toward her, brushing dust off his trousers. "Just let me fetch some clothes for you and..." He caught her staring at him, which gave him pause. She smiled when he ducked his head, sure again that if his black skin would show it, she'd see he was blushing.

"You shouldn't duck your head away from an enemy, Jarak," she told him conversationally.

That snapped his head up, his blue-black eyes wide. "You sounded just like the commander." He shook his head. "You're not my enemy, lady."

"Just because I can't hurt you, doesn't mean I won't try."

A hint of youthful male crept behind his carefully subservient gaze. "You may *try*, lady."

She couldn't help it. She grinned. She should give him a run for it, just because.

But she felt entirely too lazy to do that. She glanced at the door again, then shrugged. She stepped into the room and dropped down into one of the chairs. "I don't feel like walking," she said.

He cocked his head to the side. "Would you like me to carry you?"

Her eyes went wide, flew to his face. Then she laughed, seeing his impish grin. "All right. Consider me paid back." She flipped her hand at him, motioning him toward the pillows he'd vacated. "Don't let me interrupt your work. I'm sure the tyrant will be put out if you don't finish whatever it is."

"This?" he asked, picking up the leather studded with metal. "This isn't for the commander, lady. Well, not directly."

"Oh?"

He paused, thoughtful. Then he held it up. It took her a moment before she realized it was a collar. When worn, it would stretch from shoulder to chin and lace up the front.

Her gaze narrowed. "Is that for me?"

He didn't answer. When she held out her hand, he gave it to her.

She couldn't deny that the workmanship was marvelous. The gray leather was taut without being stiff, and it was lovingly worked to a buttery softness. The hammered design was cunningly filled with metal brads.

To his utter shock, she raised the collar to her neck and wrapped it on. She tied the laces loosely. As she suspected, it fit perfectly. She stood to see herself in a mirrored disk over the fireplace. "Your work?" she asked calmly.

"Yes, lady."

She nodded, stroking the soft nap with her fingers. "Very nice. You're an excellent leatherworker. What type of skin is this?"

He cleared his throat. "We call it a *yarin*, lady. It's a large deerlike animal with rounded antlers. They're plentiful in the higher reaches of the mountains."

She nodded again, then turned to face him. "How do I look?"

"You're absolutely gorgeous, lady," he said sincerely.

"Thank you. Now, take a good look. Do you see?"

He frowned, but nodded.

"Good." She undid the laces, then ripped the collar from her throat, her brows sinking to a scowl. "Then tell your master what you saw, because he's *not* going to see it on me himself!"

She hurled the collar at him, then stalked to her room. At the last second, she darted toward the outer door. Jarak yelped, but she had to give him credit for reacting quickly.

He needn't have bothered. She bolted out the door and into the muscular arms of a guard.

"What are you doing here, Garn?" Jarak demanded.

Garn held her struggling form easily, infuriating her. "Commander said he didn't want you to have trouble with the lady."

She slumped. She knew it.

Garn shook her slightly. "It's fine to keep struggling, Diana," he grumbled. Leaning closer, he breathed in her ear. "I like it."

She recognized the taunting voice and screamed. He'd been one of her previous lovers. He laughed aloud as he avoided her outstretched claws.

"Stop tormenting her, Garn," Jarak ordered.

"I'll just put her back, then," Garn stated, entering the suite and walking to her room. He deposited her none-too-gently inside.

She stumbled, then whirled to face him. His glittering black eyes watched her, his wide mouth grinning. "You going to try it again?" he asked hopefully.

"No."

He showed his disappointment. "Oh, well." He left the suite.

Jarak appeared in her doorway, looking abashed. "I didn't know he was there, lady."

"I gathered."

"The commander really *did* tell me that I could escort you through the city."

"He just didn't tell you we'd have company, is that it?"

"Well, yes," he said. By his tone, she knew he didn't expect she'd believe him.

Unfortunately, she did. Her anger died a cold death.

"Don't fret it, Jarak," she said, waving him away. "I'm going back to sleep."

* * *

Diana woke abruptly when two pairs of strong hands grabbed her. Before she was fully aware, leather restraints encircled her wrists and ankles, chains chiming.

"What...?" she cried, feebly struggling to consciousness.

No answer. She was hauled into the air, carried swiftly across the room, and placed upon one of the contraptions Salin had yet to bind her to. This one put a padded bar underneath her arched back. Her legs were spread and bent beneath her, the short chains attached to another padded bar beneath her head. Her arms were pulled back and secured to the bottom of the bar under her back. The final effect left her doubled over backwards, breasts pointed to the ceiling, knees forced wide.

"You slimy son of a skunk! Let me go!"

Salin stood from securing her arms, looking to Jarak. "Thank you," he said to the younger man, patting his shoulder. Jarak stared down at Diana. She could only see him upside down, which gave her a wonderful view of the erection tenting his trousers. "Go ahead and take the night off. I won't need you further."

Jarak snapped from his mesmerized gaze to face his master's amused smile. He matched it with one of his own. "Thank you, Commander."

"Did you just send him to go get laid?" Diana asked before Jarak had even left.

"Yes," Salin replied matter-of-factly. "I did. The poor lad's been watching you parade naked before him for nights now. He needs some relief."

"*I'm* not the one keeping me naked!" she screeched.

"Ah, yes. That's true. That's why *I'm* giving him the night off, as *I've* kept you naked and wanting, so *you've* tormented the poor lad."

She glared sideways at him. "You're demented."

He grinned. "Quite possibly."

She tested her bonds as he moved about the room. Returning to her, he slid an arm underneath her back to lift her from the bar. She gasped at the ease with which he held her weight. Effortlessly. Smoothly. He slid something underneath her back before gently returning her to her place, then busied himself with lacing what turned out to be a leather bodice.

"What's this?" she demanded, barely able to see the garment.

"Another of Jarak's pieces," Salin explained, smoothing the corset over her belly. It ended just above her hips. "And these are another. Not practical, I'll admit, but very sexy."

She frowned, trying to decide what he was doing around her hips and buttocks. Finally, she realized he'd tied what might be a pair of panties about her hips and legs, with a leather thong slid through the cheeks of her ass. Only the panties were completely open over her mound and crotch.

"And this," he proclaimed, leaning over her body to spear his hands through her hair, lifting her head. She glared when she recognized the leather collar she'd hurled at Jarak earlier. Salin's wicked grin told her Jarak had relayed the earlier conversation. He took great pleasure in fastening the piece around her neck and gazing at it lovingly.

"Bastard."

He met her gaze. "Thought I wouldn't see you in this, sweet?" he asked mildly.

"Fuck you."

The smile returned. "In due course."

"You keep saying that," she told him as he gently released her head and stepped away. "And you still haven't."

"Remember, my sweet, I await your sweet invitation."

"You didn't need my *invitation* last night," she spat, glaring at the ceiling.

"Well, I'll admit I've been a little inside your body. But there's a difference." He stood above her now, his knees close enough to kiss. Helpless, she gazed up the powerful thighs to the massive erection he cradled in his hand. Where had his trousers gone? "But *this* has not been inside of you."

She licked her lips, unable to tear her gaze away from

the fingers caressing the smooth head of his cock. "So what are you saying? That you *won't* put it inside me?"

"Not until you ask."

She snorted. "I'm not going to ask."

"Don't make promises you won't keep, sweet."

"Go to the hells! I don't want you!"

Grinning, he swung one thick leg easily across her body until he straddled her torso. With effort, she lifted her head to see him bend his knees enough to put his cock on level with her cleavage. She fought a groan as he slid the head against the crest of one breast, then angled further down to smudge a drop of seed into her skin. "How long will you lie to yourself, sweet?" he asked calmly.

"At least four more days," she sneered.

That stopped him. He frowned, suddenly serious. "If you deny me, you'll just go to another man."

"Who won't be you."

"Exactly."

She shuddered. Sweet Mother of us all, he was right. She knew he was right. The thought of another nine days with yet another man sickened her. Somehow, Salin had done the same things to her as many of the others had, but something about him made them special. Add to it that he actually *talked* to her and, damn him, she liked his wicked sense of humor, even though it infuriated her.

She let her head drop back. She couldn't give in. If she gave in, he won. *They* won. And they shouldn't. This wasn't right!

He sighed and left her, to roam the room again. She heard activity but couldn't see beyond her breasts to make out what he was doing.

She jumped when his hot tongue lapped at the skin exposed at the bottom of the corset.

"Did you enjoy last night, sweet?"

She froze. Instantly, she could again feel his mouth on her, forcing her to climax again and again as she scrabbled in the dark.

Stubbornly, she pushed the images from her head. "You mean you in my ass? No. I don't know what kind of spell you cast over me to make me come, but I didn't enjoy it."

"There was no spell, sweet. And you know it. You enjoyed my fingers in your ass." He made her jump again by sliding his fingers over said ass and teasing the thong that covered her opening. "But I realize that particular act might catch you off guard." Another kiss, just at the top of her mons. "But I made up for it later, didn't I?"

"I -- I don't know what you're talking about."

He sighed, nipping at her thigh. "Don't try to explain it away as a dream, sweet. I was there. I made quite a feast of you last day, and you were more than willing."

Damn him! She didn't want confirmation of that. She wanted to believe it was a dream.

"That meant nothing."

"So you said. And I let you believe that. I left you before you awoke. But don't fool yourself. You wanted me last day."

"And you didn't take me."

"No. I want you fully conscious and aware when you ask for me."

"It won't...ah! Happen."

His lips had found her clit. He didn't bother with much foreplay this time, but he didn't need to. The mere reminder of the previous day had her wet. Loudly popping her clit in and out of his mouth, he slid three long fingers deep into her channel. Writhing, she moaned. Fighting the natural buck of her hips in rhythm with his pumping fingers.

"Come for me, Diana," he murmured, slamming his fingers deep just before he nipped her clit.

She was horrified with herself for obeying. She soared through a colorful haze, crying out the pleasure she didn't want to feel.

But he wasn't done with her. He did it again, wiggling the three fingers in her cunt as he attacked her clit. A finger from his other hand snaked underneath the thong and into her ass. "Salin!" she screeched, just before shooting into another orgasm.

"God of war!" she screamed on the fourth, her body trembling. "Fuck me and get it over with already."

At her words, he eased a bit, allowing her to breathe, although three fingers remained deeply embedded. "Sweet, it is far from my wish to get it over with."

"I said it," she panted. "You wanted me to say it. Get it over with."

Abruptly, all fingers left her body. She tried to breathe, barely conscious of his movements until she felt his wet fingers slide into her hair to lift her head.

Burning red eyes locked with hers, a fury she didn't understand evident in their depths. "What do you want?" he demanded.

"Just fuck me and get it over with."

He shook her head once like a mother cat might shake its young. "What do you *want?*"

She snarled, understanding. He wanted her to admit it. "You want me. Take me."

His snarl made a mockery of hers. Cursing in what she could only assume was the *raedjour* language, he bent to release her from the chains that bound her to the bench. Once done, he stalked away from her.

"Where are you *going?*" she demanded.

He whirled as she slid to sit on one side of the bench, easing the ache in her back.

"Do you want me to fuck you?"

"Yes." That she could say.

"Then say it."

She fisted her hands in aggravation, her pent-up arousal feeding her anger. "I said it. Fuck me, damn you!"

His cock twitched, obviously more than willing. But he remained halfway across the room. "No," he barked. "Not like you're relieving an itch. Admit that you want me!"

She rolled her eyes. "What's the difference?"

Growling, he crossed to one of the four clothes chests. After a moment of rummaging, he came up with a long cylinder that was tapered at one end. Scowling, he brandished it, making sure she saw it clearly, before he tossed it onto the bed furs.

"Use that to relieve your itch, Diana." He crossed to the door. "Tell me when you realize you need more from me."

She screamed her frustration, beating her hands against the bench. Defiantly, she went to the bed and retrieved the object. Yes. It wasn't as large as his cock, but it would do. It was made of a strange, warm material that felt like wax but didn't chip away. *Fine!* She dropped onto the bed on her back, letting her legs flop open. Without any preparation -- from her own ministrations, at least -- she plunged it into her core. Her back bowed in pleasure, her body skyrocketing into an immediate climax. But she knew, as she recovered herself, that Salin was right. She needed more. This felt good, but she knew it would feel much better to have his hips behind those thrusts instead of her own shaky fingers.

She subsided with a whimper, letting the tool slip from her grasp. Staring at the ceiling, she nearly cried in frustration.

Chapter Thirteen

Salin could feel something was different before he opened the door the next day. When he saw her sitting on the edge of the bed platform, facing the door, his eyes widened. The leather restraints were strapped to her wrists and ankles. She'd put them on herself?

Lifting her chin, she stared at him squarely. Some decision had been made behind that glittering green-gold gaze, but he hadn't a clue what it was. Calmly, she lifted her arms to pull her long hair into a tail. The movement lifted her full breasts, gaining his attention.

He shut the door carefully and leaned his back against it. Waiting.

She finished with her hair and stood. "What's your plan for tonight, Commander?" she purred.

He crossed his arms, pleased that the movement caused her gaze to drop to his bulging arms. At least she enjoyed the look of him. "I had thoughts, but I'm open to suggestions."

Her long, beautiful lashes dropped halfway over her eyes, a sexy, sultry look that made his cock jerk to attention. Her lush lips curled when she noticed. Eyes locked on his crotch, she approached him. Once there, she took hold of his wrists and guided him to uncross his arms and lay them at his sides. He obeyed, entranced. Was this the same woman he'd left before?

Unconcerned with his skeptical frown, she leaned forward and laid her lips above his right nipple. Against his will, he shuddered. She smiled, opening her mouth so that her warm breath caressed the very edges of his tattoo. Her tongue darted out to flick his nipple. He jumped.

"Edgy, aren't we?" she mused, kissing her way across the broad expanse of his chest to the other nipple.

"A smart warrior is always on edge when an opponent tries something new."

"Wise," she agreed, chuckling. Her hands bracketed his waist, thumbs idly tracing the edges of his abdominal muscles. Cautiously, he reached forward to lay hands on her soft shoulders.

"Does this mean nothing, too, sweet?" he purred.

She lifted her chin to meet his gaze. "Absolutely nothing," she confirmed with a smile.

"Mmm," he mused as she commenced her soft torture of his skin. Although it was tough as leather, *raedjour* skin was attuned to a lover's touch. He slid his hands down her arms to her wrists, removing her hands from his waist. She didn't protest when he started to walk her backwards.

She expected the furs. She *wanted* the furs. Today he'd fuck her. Today she'd have him. She'd spent a long, frustrated time before finally making the decision. She'd seduce him. She'd give him what he wanted, so he'd give her what she'd come to *need*. If he pushed it, she'd even *ask*, damn it! She didn't believe her "truemate" existed among the *raedjour*, so what did it matter if she took a little -- or maybe a *lot* -- of the pleasure he offered? He was the finest lover she'd had to date -- even without having taken her completely -- and she'd be damned if she missed out on having him fully!

She'd donned the restraints as a sign. He was smart. He'd catch on. He was hot enough for her that he'd take it as an excuse without the ridiculous notion of forcing her to ask for him.

She hoped.

She kissed and nipped his breast as he led her backward into the room. He tasted so good! She'd not allowed herself the pleasure of tasting his skin before this. He tasted of midnight mystery and heady secrets, clean and dark and delicious. That light sheen of oil that coated his skin tasted of dark spices. Cinnamon musk and prime male.

She didn't expect it when he abruptly turned her, raising her arms. The clink of chains alerted her that he'd bound her to another one of his infernal contraptions, this one a free-standing post with a set of rings at the top for restraints.

"Salin," she protested, jangling the chains at her wrist.

"Sweet," he responded, kissing the back of her neck.

She shuddered, melting. Fine. If he wanted it this way, they'd do it this way. *This* time.

He nibbled her shoulder as he loosened his trousers and let them fall to the floor. To keep his attention, she wiggled her ass in his direction, spreading her legs slightly. He groaned as he kicked aside boots and trousers. Finally, his hands slid down her sides to her hips. Those he pulled back, forcing her onto her toes as he ground her bottom to his groin. His cock poked her lower back before he drew back, letting it slide down the crack of her ass.

"Yes!" she moaned, willing to voice her approval as long as he continued. If it were true that his pleasure was magnified by hers, he must be insatiable right now. *Take me now*, she demanded silently.

He purred, pulling all the way back in order to re-angle his cock so that his forward slide took it down and through the wet folds of her sex. They both moaned when the tip grazed her clit, sending a rush of fire throughout her body. She bit her lip, tilting her hips to try and push that sensitive spot harder against him. Salin leaned forward, reaching around her body to cradle the tip of his cock in his palm. Using his hand, he pushed the shaft lengthwise up against her folds, hips pumping to create delicious friction. Gasping, she shoved back, not even caring that he chuckled. At least the chuckle had an edge to it. He was struggling to maintain control. But she wanted him *out* of control. She wanted him rampant and lusty and slamming inside of her like the magnificent stallion he was!

She synchronized her rocking hips to his as he began to thrust, trying to force an angle that would guide him inside. She was so close! His hand remained at her groin, guiding his cock against her clit with each forward thrust. She didn't protest when his strong hands slid to either side of her hips and guided her thighs together. Yes! Getting the idea, she willingly pressed her thighs together, making a warm, wet channel for him to...

Too late, she realized what he was about. Too late, she

felt him erupt. "No!" she shrieked, staring helplessly at the spurting white cream that now covered his hand and part of the post in front of her.

He laughed, backing away as she trembled with rage.

"You bastard!" she growled, yanking at the bonds holding her hands.

He came into her line of sight, an infuriatingly smug look on his gorgeous features. "Anger, sweet?" he taunted, leaning against the pole to which she was chained as he idly wiped cream from his fingers onto his belly, making the muscles gleam even more. "Why are you angry?"

His eyes danced with mirth as he watched her struggle with her own emotions. "Care to ask me something, sweet?" he taunted.

She met his gaze. The words were easier to say than she'd thought. "Please fuck me, Salin."

He paused, quite obviously taken aback. "Say it again."

Hope surged in her breast. Relief was coming! "I want you, Salin. Fuck me. Now. Please!"

He leaned in, studying her face. "What are you asking for, sweet?"

"You. So deep inside me that I forget your cock isn't part of my body," she parroted his words right back at him.

That got him. He practically reeled, clutching the post for support. Eagerly, she met his lips when they swooped in to take hers. She wholeheartedly mated his tongue, sucking him into her mouth like she wanted to suck his cock into her body.

"Now, Salin," she demanded, jerking at the chains that bound her wrists. She nipped at his lip.

"Why do you want me?"

"What?"

"*Why* do you want me?"

She moaned, again yanking at the chains. "Not now, Salin. Not now. Can't this wait?"

He shook his head. "Is it so hard to admit what you want? I *know* you want me." His look turned suddenly serious. Reaching forward, he cradled her face in his big, warm hands and tilted her head up. His fingers smelled of their combined juices, made her thoughts spiral. "I'll make it easier for you, sweet Diana," he murmured, capturing her gaze. "I'll say it first." He paused -- gathering his courage? "I love you, Diana," he murmured, shocking her. "I don't know how I know, but I know you're my truemate. I know we belong together." He planted a soft kiss on her surprised lips. "Ask me. Tell me you want me. Let me make love to you, Diana," he begged softly, breath a warm caress to her lips. "Let's seal the bond between us."

She stared at him, mind whirling. She barely registered when he reached up and released her wrists from the pole. She backed away when he reached for her.

"You don't know that," she protested.

"That I love you?"

"Why would you say that? I've been nothing but horrible to you."

"Perhaps that's exactly what I need."

She shook her head. "How could you want such a thing?"

"What? A fiery mate who keeps me on my guard? In focus? A woman with stubborn strength of will? A woman whose body's pleasures make my blood sing?"

She walked away, toward the privy chamber. "Stop saying those things. You can't mean them."

He froze, watching her retreat with predatory interest. "What are you frightened of, Diana?"

She whirled. "What?"

"Why does the mention of love send you running?"

"You don't know what you're saying."

"No. But something makes you deny everything that your body feels. I mention 'love,' and suddenly all the lust you felt runs cold. Something is making you deny me." He caught her arm, hauling her up against him. "Tell me what's wrong!"

"I'm denying you because you're a killer and a rapist!" she spat, tearing at his grip to escape him. "How could I love something like that?!"

He went stone-still except for the fingers that suddenly released her. Her blood ran cold, her own words, said in fright, sinking in. She backed away helplessly, unable to think of a way to take them back. Confused by the fact that she *wanted* very badly to take them back. He watched her retreat, his sensual mouth smashed in a furious line.

Abruptly he turned, snatching his trousers from the floor. "Deny me for another three nights and you'll have your freedom," he said, bending to tug them on.

"What?"

"I'll tell Nalfien what I suspect. He knows my instincts, and he knows they're usually true. He can confirm it. If I'm right and you are my truemate, you're of no use to another man other than as a fuck toy." He tossed a disdainful glance her way. "I assume you don't relish a life in the brothel?"

She shook her head, still confused. "What are you talking about?"

"The brothel. It's where we keep the women who haven't found a truemate. They still have needs, you see. Needs that only a long line of lovers can try to appease. Only your needs would be worse, because only your truemate could fully satisfy you."

She gaped, horrified.

He nodded coldly. "Just so. I didn't think that would appeal to you. And with your reputation..." He shook his head. "Once Nalfien confirms I'm right, I'll let him know that I don't want you. It will take some convincing, but he'll cast a spell to erase your memories."

She staggered back against the wall, unable to digest all that he was saying. "*What?*"

He ignored her. "He'll have to put some alternate memories into your head. After all, you'll need an explanation why Gala is no longer with you. You'll think she's dead."

"Salin, wait."

"Why?" he demanded, rounding on her. The fury in his eyes flattened her instinctively against the wall, even though he was across the room. "Isn't this what you wanted? You haven't turned fully yet, so it's still not too late. We don't tend to tell women that it's possible to leave, but before a certain time, it is. The problem, of course, is that you'll never quite be right in the head again. A symptom of having manufactured and missing memories." He spread his arms. "But you'll have your wish. You'll be away from here, away from us. Away from *me*." He glared. "Of course, you'll never be fertile. But that shouldn't bother a lone warrior like you."

She scowled. "Now wait just a moment…"

"No, Diana. This is it. Think very carefully. I offer myself to you, wholeheartedly. Myself and my life. A very *long* life compared to the one you'd have as a human. Or I offer a way out." His upraised hand silenced her. "Choose one."

With that, he stomped out.

Chapter Fourteen

"You told her *what?*" Nalfien demanded.

Salin, sprawled on a bench to the side of Nalfien's workroom, waved a negligent hand. "What will it matter? You've done it before."

"That is not common knowledge. Radin should not have told you."

Salin shrugged.

"And what, pray tell, happens if she decides to stay? That knowledge is dangerous if she imparts it to other women."

Salin grimaced. "She won't stay."

Nalfien studied the top of the younger man's head. He'd never seen Salin like this. The commander was always in top form, his quick mind often reaching conclusions long before others had an inkling of an issue. Part of it was those damnable instincts that invariably proved correct, but much of it was pure genius. A genius currently without his spark.

"How do you know that?"

Salin shook his head, dragging long fingers through his short hair. "She's too stubborn. There's a wall in her mind that she's trapped by. I don't seem to have the key."

"Would you like me to change her mind for her?" Nalfien offered carefully.

"No," Salin snapped. "If she doesn't come to the conclusion herself, it's not worth it."

"Salin, think carefully on what you say. You still have a few days with her. Perhaps if you…"

"I know what I say, Nalfien." Salin lifted furious eyes to meet the sorcerer's. "My truemate denies me. Do you think I haven't thought on this? Do you think I want to watch her go to the brothel pit to be used by any man who believes he can handle her? No. I'd rather she was out of sight."

"But you…"

"What about me? I'll be childless. Is that such a horror?"

"Salin!"

"Or perhaps I'm wrong," Salin continued, wilting back onto the bench. Wearily, he closed his eyes. "Maybe she's not my truemate. You should test her to find out."

Nalfien wished fervently that Radin were not away on one of his extended treks through the mountains. Radin was one of the few who could talk sense to the commander.

"Salin, if you haven't taken her, I can't…"

"Spare me, Nalfien. Radin's told me that you can tell."

"What secrets has Radin *not* told you?" Nalfien muttered angrily. But the anger died quickly in the face of Salin's obvious pain. "I'll test her. But, Salin --" The younger man had stood, resigned, and started out the door. He paused at Nalfien's words. "-- do not give up just yet. As you said, she has a wall in her mind to hurdle. You've likely shocked her with words of love. Allow her *some* time to think on that."

Salin nodded, and left.

* * *

Salin didn't come to her the next day. Or the next. She waited. She was aware when Jarak came to the room, kept her fed, but she feigned sleep. She *knew* before Jarak entered that he wasn't Salin, and Salin was the only one she wanted to see.

He loved her? How could he know that?

Images of her mother haunted her. The woman had left when Diana was still a young child, but Diana recalled enough. Recalled her spiteful words. Recalled her disdainful tone when she spoke to Diana's father. She never loved him. Never loved them. Four children together, Diana the last, before Diana's father finally gave up. He wished her well, helped her pack, and saw her on her way. The woman had never looked back.

Diana saw reflections of this in herself. She wasn't worthy of love. Her measly few friendships had taken precious, agonizing time to forge and lasted only through the resolve of the other, not Diana. Gala was the only one who'd taken the time and energy, taken the blows and cuts, to be her true friend. Diana knew this.

Gala had been the only one until now. Until Salin. He'd played her game masterfully. He'd shown her the error of her ways without making her lose face. He'd bared his soul and allowed her to rake it apart.

She was just like her mother.

She didn't bother to touch the food Jarak brought. She watched the flame in the hands of the little goddess statue turn midnight blue then sunny yellow then blue again, and still no Salin. Not that she blamed him.

Her body ached, lust coursing through her veins. But she couldn't bear the thought of bringing herself to climax. The toy he'd given her lay unused on a table. It wouldn't help. It couldn't help. She needed him.

Did she love him?

The goddess's flame had turned a greenish blue, indicating the nearing of sunrise on the second night without Salin, when the door again opened. She automatically scowled at the sight of Nalfien.

"What are you doing here?"

"Salin asked me to come test you."

Her heart cracked, recalling his words. "I don't want you tasting me," she warned, although she didn't bother to rise from the bed furs.

"That isn't necessary for this," he said, crossing halfway into the room. He hesitated. "Should I bind you?"

She grimaced. "I won't attack you."

He seemed to take her at her word, for he closed the distance and sat on the edge of the bed platform.

"What do you do this time?" she asked, listless. "Scour my brain with your magic? Shove your fingers inside me?"

"No," he replied softly. "For this, I need to gauge your heart."

She blinked rapidly as he placed a warm hand over the center of her chest. She was *not* crying! She felt nothing but the warmth of his hand. Glancing toward him, she saw him watching her face. No glowing eyes. No sign of magic. Nothing but kindness showed there, a bland warmth that showed a caring for another living creature. She closed her eyes.

Presently, he removed his hand.

"Well?" she prompted when he said nothing and didn't leave. "Is he my truemate?"

"What do you think?"

"You're the sorcerer."

"You're the woman."

She paused. "Is it true you can erase my memories and send me away from here?"

"Yes."

"Will you?"

"If necessary."

Another pause. "Why would he want me?"

"Love rarely follows any path we perceive."

"How could he love me?"

"I've known Salin his entire life. He's never taken the easy road."

She barked a laugh, little amusement in it. "Then I'm perfect for him," she sneered.

He stood. "Yes," he said softly, turning to leave. "You are."

She scrambled to sit, watching his retreating back. "What's *that* supposed to mean?"

He was at the door. "If you continue to resist Salin until the end of his nine days, I will cast the spell he described to you." Red eyes bore into her from across the room. "It won't be painless, but you'll not recall any of your time here."

She swallowed.

"Be certain that's what you wish, Diana," he murmured as he opened the door. "Be certain you know what it is you're giving up."

Chapter Fifteen

The ninth day. Panic overwhelmed her.

"Where is he?"

Jarak, having just entered, hesitated in the doorway, tray in hand.

"Jarak," she warned, sitting up on the bed platform, "where is he?"

"The commander is practicing with his men."

"Go get him."

Jarak blinked at her.

Impatient, she stood and stomped across the room to take the tray from him. "Go yourself or get Garn to do it, but I have to talk to him." Then, when he still hesitated: "Please!"

"Yes, lady."

Krael backpedaled from Salin's furious advance. Their sparring match had taken a decidedly dark turn some minutes back, and Krael was still deciding how to extricate himself from it. That distraction cost him.

He fell with a grunt, Salin instantly atop him, almost pinning him. Almost. Through instinct and practice, Krael had a dagger out and pointed upward at Salin's belly. A good enough thrust and he could gut the other man. Kill him.

Burning red eyes met violet blue. Salin eased up the dulled blade he held at Krael's throat. "Do it," he ordered.

Krael blinked. His mind raced. No one else could have heard the command. No one else could see the pain in the commander's eyes.

"Damn you, I gave you an order!" Salin hissed.

"Salin…"

"Commander!" cried another voice. Krael stared into Salin's furious gaze as Jarak ran up to them. "Commander, the lady is asking for you."

Krael saw it. The sudden hope quashed by burning anguish. He saw it, but no one else. Of that he was glad.

Suddenly, Salin pushed back to his knees, his angry gaze pointed up at his squire. "What does she want?"

Jarak shook his head, his concern for his master obvious in his gaze. "She begged me to come and find you."

"Begged?"

"Yes, Commander."

Salin took a deep breath, scrubbing a hand roughly through his shorn hair. "Fine. I come."

She *felt* him enter the outer room. She knew he was taking his own sweet time, making her wait. She accepted that. He entered the room to find her waiting, and hesitated.

She knew what he saw. Her. Naked. Kneeling not on the

bed platform but on the bondage bench. Leather restraints on her wrists and ankles. The leather collar Jarak had made laced around her neck. A length of chain connected her wrists and lay in a loose *S* on the bench before her.

She looked up, locking with his skeptical gaze. She let him see the longing, willed him to see the traces of her tears. Taking a deep breath, she lifted her bound arms toward him in a pleading gesture. "Please."

He scowled, not moving from the doorway. "What game are you playing, Diana?"

"No games," she said softly. Although she'd determined to say them, the words came hard.

He crossed the room to stand by the bench. He made no move to take the chain or her hands, although she kept them outstretched toward him.

"Please," she repeated.

"Please what?"

No "sweet." She cringed, lowering her arms. "Do you still want me?"

Did he still want her?! Was the woman daft? He could barely contain himself. Her body vibrated with uncertainty, and he knew she fought every base instinct she had to remain kneeling before him. But he had to push her that extra step. She had to do this, or else she'd accuse him of forcing her into it for the rest of their long lives.

"That's not the way this will work, Diana," he warned.

She risked a glance at his face. Another at his crotch. Evidence of his arousal was prominent, but she'd likely attribute that to his race's high sexual appetite. After all, what *raedjour* male had she encountered who *didn't* have an erection for her?

She swallowed. "Please, Salin," she begged.

"Please what, sweet?"

The endearment worked wonders. He felt the rush of hope that coursed through her veins, perhaps giving her the courage to continue.

Taking another deep breath, she looked up into his eyes. "I want you."

His heart soared, but he struggled not to show it. "Why?"

Why?!

She fought the instant rage. That anger had been her ready answer to everything, and the introduction to disaster for nearly every situation she brought it to. She swallowed. She was intelligent enough to know why he asked. But was she brave enough to give him what he wanted?

"Because I...because..." Frustrated, she tried to breathe over the pounding of her heart.

His gaze softened, those bulging arms lowering from across his chest. Slowly, he lowered himself to sit on the bench.

She lowered her gaze to the chain before her, unable to look at him and admit her feelings at the same time. "Because I think...I...love you," she said softly. "I want to stay with you."

His hand crept out to take hold of the chain. She watched his long, elegant fingers wind about the links. Were they trembling just a bit? He twisted his wrist to wrap the chain around his hand -- once, twice, again and again, until her wrists were snug against his hand and each other. He shifted, and his knees came into her lowered view. His free hand appeared, cupped her chin, made her look up at him.

"Be sure, Diana," he warned gently once their gazes locked. "Once we're mated, it's over. You're mine." There was a moment's hesitation, and a softening of his lips to the barest of smiles. "And I'm yours."

She stared at his face, really seeing him for the first time. Without her blinding sheet of rage between them. He was truly stunning. His face was all sharp angles except for the smooth curves of his lips and the curl of his lashes. The tattoos on his chin and forehead made him look even more exotic. The fall of his curly hair over his eyes made him mysterious, secretive.

"Will I be more attractive to you once I've turned?"

He smiled fully, and it lit her heart. "I can't imagine a sexier woman, with any color skin."

"Will I be able to see in the dark?"

"Yes."

"Will my eyes turn?"

"No. Your eyes will remain their perfect golden green."

She smiled. "But my hair will turn white."

"Beautiful, snowy white," he agreed, sinking his free fingers into said hair.

"Will my skin be as tough as yours?"

"Smooth as silk but tougher than leather," he promised.

"Will I be as fast as you with the sword?"

"Maybe not as fast, but we'll work to make you the best

you can be."

"I do love you, Salin," she said before she could think about it.

His mouth closed on hers, her instant reward for bravery. She willingly parted her lips, welcoming the assault of his tongue.

She pulled eager hands toward his face, frustrated to find them still bound. Laughing, he parted their lips only long enough to unwind the chain from his hand and toss it over his head. The cold metal slithered over his back as she let her greedy hands take their fill of his hair, yanking him back to her kiss. She climbed forward into his lap, steadied by his strong grip on her waist. Straddling his hips, she ground her groin against his, drenching the front of his trousers with her juices.

"Salin," she muttered against his lips, loath to part them for very long, "if you don't fuck me now, I'm going to have to hurt you."

He laughed and she gasped as he lurched suddenly backward. To her amazement, he gained his feet in one fluid move, without losing his grip on her or parting their lips any further. "Mmm, you're strong," she purred, confident now. "Is that why I have to change? So you won't pound me into pulp?"

He chuckled, lowering them both into the soft furs of the bed. "Partly," he admitted, tumbling her onto her back so he could get out of his trousers.

She scrambled to her knees before him, eager to help. "Only partly? What's the other part?"

She almost didn't notice his hesitation at her question,

too busy unlacing the ties and freeing his cock. She'd never handled it before and was fascinated. Hot and long, soft and hard. She squeezed experimentally, gratified to produce a raw moan from deep within his chest. She bent her head, wanting to taste him.

She couldn't understand why he put his hands on her shoulders, stopping her.

"Sweet, I've got to tell you something."

She froze, her blood running cold. She hated the tone in his voice. "What?"

"A *raedjour* pregnancy lasts two cycles."

She blinked, still looking at and holding his cock. The organ that would plant a seed inside her that she would carry for *two* cycles.

"That's the other reason for the change. Humans can't survive a *raedjour* pregnancy."

She licked her lips, still staring at his cock. Slowly, she moved her fingers down the shaft, watching the loose layer of skin slide back with her hand. "Well," she said as she slowly pulled her hand back up the shaft, watching the skin bunch and nearly cover the head. "I'll just have to make you suffer every moment of the way, won't I?"

Salin groaned, releasing her shoulders to allow her to dip her head and finally take the head of his cock into her mouth. He nearly came out of his skin. No mouth had ever felt so good! Even the scrape of her teeth as she struggled to gulp as much of it as she could felt good!

He let her nibble and suckle for precious moments, growled when she slid a free hand to cup and handle his balls.

"Ah, sweet!" he cried, pulling her away just as she'd discovered the sensitive underside of the head with her agile little tongue. She protested, but he shoved her back into the furs, coming down atop her, "We can explore that later," he promised, reaching down to grab his cock, "but I need to be inside you."

"Oh, yes," she purred, spreading her legs and canting her hips to a better angle.

He met her gaze. "You want me inside you?"

"Yes," she said, without blinking. "I want you inside me. Fuck me, Salin. Now!"

Gladly, he obeyed. With one, smooth thrust, he was inside her to the hilt. Despite his size, he'd known theirs would be a perfect fit.

Diana gasped. They both froze, locked together. His mouth was pressed to the curve where her neck met her shoulder, his massive shoulders hunched over her smaller body. Her cheek pressed against his temple. Her arms wound as tightly as possible about his neck, his arms twined beneath her back and around her waist. Neither wanted to end this perfect moment, their first as one. Both squeezed their eyes shut, memorizing the feeling.

But she had to move. She had to feel him. Rotating her hips, she gasped again as that huge cock ground against the walls of her channel. Once felt, she couldn't get enough, couldn't stay still. Neither, it seemed, could he. His breath came in gasps as he pumped his hips against hers, slowly, carefully. She wondered if he was being easy on her, or if he was struggling to maintain control. It didn't matter. She wanted him *out* of control.

"Fuck me, Salin," she breathed in his ear.

His whole body shuddered, his cock swelling larger. She groaned, catching his ear again, which made it repeat. She'd found a sweet spot! Experimentally, she reached out with her tongue to trace the delicate tip of his pointed ear. He growled, fingers clutching painfully at her buttocks. But she didn't care about the last, because it was accompanied by firmer, longer thrusts from his cock.

"Yes," she hissed, sure her breath caressed his ear. He moved to pull his head away, but she clutched handfuls of his hair to keep him there. She *liked* this reaction and wasn't about to release him from it.

"Diana," he groaned, using his hands at her hips now to slam her more firmly against his pumping groin.

She muttered into his ear, unconscious of the words, uncaring. She suckled the lobe, delved into the recesses, but -- although he clearly liked it all -- it seemed to be the very pointed tip that was most sensitive.

He broke free, rearing up over her, ear out of reach. She grunted a protest, struggling to pull him back. They fought for supremacy, and he won, trapping her hands with his over her head. Not once during their battle did he stop the rhythm of his hips.

Deprived of the distraction of his ear, Diana lost herself in the feel of his cock. He was so deep! Surely he'd punctured her belly, her chest! She was sure he'd emerge in her throat soon. Oh, but it felt good! Sweet pumping rhythm. Sweet delicious cock. Sweet...

"Salin!" she cried.

He groaned, halting movement, allowing her to shudder into climax around him, pinning her hips with his, her hands with his, until she stopped writhing.

She blinked up at him, sweat plastering her hair to her face. He grinned.

"Bastard," she spat, grinding against him, ready for the next round. "You have to come, too."

"I will," he promised, pulling out and pushing back in slowly.

"I thought my pleasure was your pleasure," she accused.

"It is. Which is why I'm selfishly prolonging it."

"Bastard," she repeated, this time on a shaky laugh.

"Diana," he purred, releasing her hands and lowering himself to press chest-to-chest. His lips found hers, soft, sweet playing of lips and tongue. And his hips kept pumping.

She let him lead, content to take what he gave her. And he gave so much! She came again. Then, on the third climax, he roared, slamming into her quivering pussy as he came.

Warmth flooded her, body and soul. Followed by an amazing, sated feeling she'd never before encountered.

She cuddled Salin's weight atop her, smoothing his back as his breathing calmed. Presently, he chuckled. She gasped when he twitched his hips and she realized that not only was he still inside her, but he was still hard! After such a hard climax, any of her other lovers -- human and *raedjour* -- had needed *some* time to recuperate!

Still smiling, he propped himself on his elbows so he could look down at her. "Did I mention that you're in heat? And that increases my sexual appetite?"

She grimaced, knowing her true delight showed in her eyes. "No. You failed to mention that."

"Hmm." He kissed her lips. "You'll have to punish me for that."

~ * ~

DARK ELVES 2: MASTERED

Dedication

This book is dedicated to those who gave me those last pushes to actually submit my story somewhere. Nythande and Suzana for helping me finish. And Angela Knight for shoving me in the right direction.

Chapter One

Sunlight had faded from the cracks within the thick blanket of leaves and branches overhead. Soon it would be night. When the wagons reached a small stream that ran alongside the road, the caravan master called a halt. Quietly, quickly, the dozen guards dismounted and set about their nightly tasks. The horses were watered, fires were built, and the caravan master himself lit the cooking fire and set out the nightly stew. The master's main assistant, a small man in a homespun tunic and wearing a slave's collar, filled the water bags and set to watering the slaves within the wagons.

Suzana waited her turn, quite used to the routine after several nights of the same. As the smallest of the five women within the wagon, she was the last to get water, simply because she did not fight to grab the waterskin first. As she waited, she continued to glance out into the surrounding trees. With the onset of night, the gnarled giants took on a more sinister look, branches reaching up and over to intertwine above the wide road and babbling stream.

At first she had wondered why camp was always made on the road. Then one of the women had explained that this was the Dark Forest. At Suzana's blank look, the woman and some of their companions had embarked on tale after tale of people entering the trees, never to be seen again. Of haughty men, who thought the world of themselves, stepping off the road, only to have their bones found days later and miles away *still within their armor*. When bodies were found, it was clear that the damage could not have been from an animal attack. Bodies were always those of men, never women or children. Something intelligent guarded the forest, something that would often -- but not always -- allow isolated trade caravans to cross beaten tracks within the periphery of the forest, but rarely allowed individual travelers to be seen again. Suzana was not sure she believed the stories, but if even a quarter were true, it was worth the caution.

She took the waterskin from the last woman and drank her fill. The filling stew was next. Not tasty, but not horrible. At least the wooden bowls were always rinsed in the streams by which they stopped every evening.

This night was eerily quiet. On previous nights, animal sounds abounded in rustling grass, distant snorts, and far-off cries. The animals had learned, it seemed, that the humans were restricted to the road. But tonight, all sounds were muted. Or absent.

The guards huddled about the fires that marked the corners of the camp, all facing the darkness beyond the light. They would sleep in shifts. Those who remained awake would not take their eyes off the sinister trees. The caravan master came to stand by the door of the wagon that held his female slaves. As his assistant took them one by one to the creek's bank to relieve and rinse themselves, he stood sentry himself. Although he had hired them, the master did not trust his guards with the females. They were precious cargo and *would* reach his destination unmolested.

Especially Suzana. When it came her turn, he personally escorted her to the creek's shallow waters. She fought the nightly embarrassment of taking care of private business with an audience. The caravan master knew she was a virgin, because he had seen her among her family before the shipwreck that had killed them all. And he took great pains to keep her pure. She waited, eyes averted, as he unlocked and removed the chastity belt fastened about her waist. He did not so much watch as hover over her, alert for any of his men who might take a chance to gain his prize. She ignored him as best she could, finished her business, then waited for him to secure her again.

"You will fetch *such* a price!" He smoothed a hand over the crown of her head, petting her long black hair. She avoided his gaze, hating the look she knew was there. He lusted after her. Not for her body, but for the gold her sale would bring him. It was disgusting!

She preceded him past the nearest guards, headed for the wagon, her eyes directed at the ground before her and not at the curious faces that would dart glances her way. She had made the mistake of looking up during one of the first nights, and she could still feel the palpable lust aimed her way from the guards.

The assistant stood beside the wagon's open door, a blank look on his face. She frowned up at him, but he didn't see her. The sound of a heavy fall had her spinning around just in time to see the caravan master slump to a heap on the ground. She stood, shocked, unable to believe what she clearly saw. Not only was the caravan master laid out asleep, but all of his guards seemed to be in a likewise state!

"What's happened?" asked the frightened voice of one of the female slaves.

Suzana shook her head.

"Mother of the gods!" cried one of the men from the other wagon. Suzana glanced over to see him pointing at the trees.

She looked. And gasped.

Men like none other peeled away from the shadows. At first she saw only floating white, which soon materialized as the hair on a number of heads. The bodies beneath the hair were astounding, skin darker than night, gleaming in the patchy moonlight. Male bodies, muscles chiseled under the dark flesh. Only a few wore anything but trousers and boots, and those few wore open vests that still revealed acres of skin.

Suzana spun to see more of them emerge from the opposite side of the road. They were all around! The slaves, the only ones not passed out in deep slumber, cried and muttered piteously as the black-skinned men approached. Suzana could only stare, dumbfounded. Terrifying, yes. But they were all incredibly beautiful!

They spoke to each other in low, rumbling voices. It wasn't commonspeak. Even Suzana, who was fluent in two languages and could recognize at least a dozen others, didn't recognize it. Some stopped just outside the men's wagon, studying the cowering human contents. The majority of them, though, approached the women's wagon.

A pair of them in particular caught her eye. From the way one pointed and called out and the others obeyed, it was clear he was the leader. He stood half again as tall as Suzana, his lean torso minimally covered by a dark purple vest. His milky white hair was smoothed back and fell in loose waves to just below his shoulders. He turned his head, and the number of rings that pierced his right ear sparkled. His *pointed* ear.

Elves? But Suzana had met elves before at court. Never in her life had she seen any with skin so dark or eyes so vividly red as those of the leader, who came to stand an arm's length before her. His companion, equally dark and exotically beautiful, crossed behind the stunned -- *spelled?* -- assistant, who still stood at the door of the wagon. The elf's bleached-honey hair fell forward, obscuring his face, as he leaned over the man and muttered. The assistant's eyes rolled back in his head, and he slumped to the ground.

A woman in the wagon screamed, the sound piercing the quiet night. Suzana tried to step back, only to find her back pressed against the side of the wagon.

"Don't be afraid," said the leader in clear commonspeak.

"Who are you?" Suzana heard herself say.

His eyes, red as fresh blood and faintly *glowing*, fixed on her. Obsidian lips pulled back into a half-smile; one snowy brow arched. "We've come to save you, lovely lady."

Her heart skipped.

"Save us?" demanded Kyla, one of the other slaves.

"Quite." The leader's eyes never left Suzana. She clutched her arms about her torso, trying to hold closed the loose tunic that was all she wore. Unfortunately, it was so short that as he glanced down, he could see the glint of the chastity belt. "We've come to rescue you."

"What do you plan to do with us?" Suzana asked.

His smile spread across his face. His companion chuckled. "Why, we'll take you home, of course."

"Home?" squeaked one of the women. "You're taking us home?"

The man turned to her. "But, of course. *Our* home."

Radin closed the small distance between himself and the tiny woman. "What astounding eyes," he said to Savous, switching to *djinar.*

She shied but didn't bolt. Carefully, he tipped up her chin with his forefinger so he could see her better. Her face was perfectly round, every line within also softly rounded, from plump lips to soft brow. Her heavily lashed eyes looked almost too large for her face, and he had to wonder if she had pixie or fae blood, as the extraordinary violet of those eyes was not any color he had ever witnessed in a human. Entranced, he lifted his free hand to brush aside a heavy lock of pitch-black hair. Even dirty and tangled, it fell in thick waves almost to her knees.

"What's that about her hips?" Savous asked.

"A belt humans use on women to keep them from having sex."

His apprentice was shocked. "Why?"

Radin inhaled deeply. "Unless I miss my guess, that delicious scent means this one's a virgin. I've heard they strap them so to keep them 'pure' sometimes." He rolled his eyes. "One of the stupidities of human males."

Interest piqued, Savous eyed her carefully. "Are you sure she's of age?"

She knew they were talking about her. Those expressive eyes darted toward Savous and back to him, dying to know what they said.

Radin laughed. "She's of age. No child could smell so ripe."

"I still don't understand the belt."

"She's worth more when she's sold, if she's a virgin."

"Ah!"

His nostrils flared. *Ah!* The scent of aroused woman. With six *raedjour* standing about the caged wagon, the female cargo was beginning to react in that blessedly familiar way. Glancing up, he could see the fascinated stares the women laid on his men. One leaned against the open door, preening as Savous reached up to stroke her cheek.

Radin smiled, turning back to the little one. She would bear watching, but he had other responsibilities at the moment. In *djinar* he asked, "Savous, how long will your spell hold?"

Savous kissed his fawning companion gently, then led her down the steps to stand before him. "Not much longer. There were more of them than I thought."

"Hmm. Trying to stick your cock into too many holes?"

Savous glared, handing off the woman to one of the raedjour, then reaching up to take the hand of the next woman. "You could help."

Radin grinned. "And why would I do that? This is your test."

"And a farce," said another voice from the vicinity of the men's wagon. The male slaves were off-loaded, as well. "We should just kill them and have done with it."

"Now, Krael," Radin chided. "It was Savous's choice."

"And he chooses to spare them. And show off."

Savous growled. "You meat-brained lout! We can't just keep killing every human that comes across the mountains!"

"Why not?"

Savous rolled his eyes, leaving the women's wagon to confront his adversary. "If you *knew* anything, you'd know that the human population is expanding at an astounding rate. We can't keep them at bay forever. And if we keep *killing* them, they'll gather together and attack us!"

Krael yawned in Savous's face. Although he was nearly a head shorter than Savous and not a mage, Krael did not back down. He never would. He was one of the *raedjour's* prime warriors, second only to Commander Salin. "I've lived longer than you, pup, and seen more. Humans are good for taking women, and that only. Human males are servants, fuck toys, or walking corpses that need to be put down."

"You know nothing."

"I know your virgin is escaping."

Savous spun, gaping at the space where the violet-eyed woman had stood. Radin was aware of her escape, but chose to do nothing.

"Radin, you let her go?!"

"I did no such thing." Radin looked to Krael. "I thought Krael might need to chase off some frustration."

Krael chuckled, tossing the long fall of his loose, silver-white hair behind his shoulder. "I would."

Radin raised a cautionary finger. "Remember, she's a virgin. You can't have her."

Krael snorted. "Yet. If she's worthy."

"She's getting away," Savous pointed out.

Krael glanced disdainfully at him, then returned his gaze calmly to Radin. "Where should I meet you?"

"The old tree entrance."

With a nod, Krael took off, sprinting after the woman.

Radin cast his gaze about to see that his men had all but disappeared into the trees with their human cargo. The wagons were bare, the caravan master and his men sprawled in heaps on the ground. Some were even snoring. This would make quite a good story to perpetuate the legend of the Dark Forest.

He returned his gaze to Savous, who glared at him. "Yes?"

"What was *that* about?" The younger man gestured into the trees where Krael had departed.

Radin shrugged, kneeling beside the caravan master. "If she was aware enough to run, then she needed to run, virgin or not."

"What if he fucks her?"

Radin snorted, digging in the caravan master's pockets. "You don't think I'm going to trust him that far, do you? Aha!" He produced a tiny key from a chain within the man's waist pocket. "Besides, Krael's not likely to get at her sex without this to unlock that blasted belt." He stood, dusting off his knees. "Take the others and return home. I'll fetch

Krael and she of the violet eyes and meet you there."

Savous's face was skeptical, but he questioned no further. With a last, wicked grin, Radin took off after Krael.

Chapter Two

Suzana ran. Shadowy branches reached out to grab her, and rocks burst forth from the ground to trip her. She fell often, but picked herself up and continued.

Stupid! She railed at herself, even as she continued. She had only the scant clothes on her back, no food, and no survival skills. She did not have the key to the belt around her waist. Nor was her body fit for such exercise. She fully expected a huge, wild animal to come crashing down on her at any moment and end her life.

In fact, she welcomed the idea. Her entire family was gone. Everyone she had loved. Gone in a shipwreck she had somehow managed to survive. By rights, she should be dead, as well, deep in the depths of Lir's watery embrace.

She stumbled again, fell to her face and tasted dirt. Stunned, she lay for a moment, catching her breath. Her fingers dug into the scrubby grass as she tried desperately to think what to do.

Weight descended on her. She screamed, instantly struggling, but went nowhere. Shadows encased her wrists, pinning them to the ground, and a solid mass straddled her hips, imprisoning her without smothering her.

Her screams stopped abruptly when a sheet of white came hissing down from the shadow above her. Shocked, she watched it catch the scant moonlight, glowing faintly blue as it curtained her and the shadow above her.

A dark chuckle sounded over her head. "Caught you, little one," said a voice that resonated in her very spine.

Slowly, she twisted her neck to see his face, which loomed just above her left ear. Even in the meager light, she could see his strong features and could just make out the lightning tattoo that crisscrossed his features. He smiled, flashing white teeth from between ebony lips.

Suzana felt her existence halt. Her entire self lost itself in those eyes, eyes she was suddenly obsessed with seeing in the light so she could know their color. Her body heated, and reality faded away. Her nostrils filled with the strangely exciting scent of him, unlike any other male she had ever encountered.

His grin faded, burned away by the heat of his gaze. In one swift, sudden move, he backed up and flipped her over. Before she knew what had happened, the length of her front was pressed against the hard mass of his body. Only her clothes separated them, as he was gloriously bare from the waist up. Instinct rolled her hips to rub her aching center against his flat belly, the short tunic riding up her hips. But the horrid metal of the chastity belt covered her pleasure and denied her the touch she sought.

"What's your name?" he demanded, the fingers of his big hands spearing the hair at either side of her head to force her to face him. Not that she wanted to look away.

"Suzana," she breathed, fascinated by one short stray lock of white that drifted down from the crown of his head to caress her cheek.

"Suzana," he rumbled, bending his head to seal their lips.

Suzana had never been kissed. Not like this. Not by a man. Even her suggested suitors back home had only kissed her cheek or hand. No man had ever before crushed his mouth to hers, stolen her breath by inhaling it himself.

He pulled back slightly. "Open your mouth."

She did, more out of surprise than anything else. Instantly, his tongue plunged in, shocking a groan from deep in her chest. She pulsed upon hearing an echoing purr from him. He took from her, and she could only lie there and accept. And enjoy. Oh, he tasted good!

Her hands sailed up the slick skin of his arms to find the wealth of hair that hung from his head. Gods of water, he smelled *good!* His calloused hands slid from her face, down her sides, to command her hips. His fingers slid in under the metal panel between her thighs, stroking her dripping core. Her gasp was lost in his groan.

"Krael!"

She heard the voice only distantly. Her hands had filled themselves with silky white hair, clutching it near his head as his fingers struggled to enter her body.

"Krael!"

Abruptly, he tore from her. Eyes open, she shuddered at the fierce growl that vibrated in his chest, matched by the snarl on his upraised face.

He was beautiful!

"Krael, you can't take her like this."

Again the snarl as he glared at someone over her head. Someone she irrationally hated for interrupting their tryst.

"Leave off, Radin."

"I can't do that."

Krael growled, his lips peeling back from his teeth just like a caged black jaguar she had once seen. Unable to help herself, she whimpered.

Distracted by the sound, Krael's attention returned to her. He instantly forgot the other man's presence, again bending his head toward Suzana.

Eagerly, she parted her lips, anticipating his kiss. Unfortunately, she fell unconscious before he could touch her.

Krael knew she was gone when his lips touched hers. They were slack and unresponsive, worlds apart from the heated return kiss he had enjoyed just moments before.

"Radin!"

"Don't snarl at me." Radin's purple boots appeared beside Krael. "You know Rhae's edict just as well as I do."

Krael muttered every obscenity that came to mind. Added a few more. This choice little bit in his arms was far too tasty to release. He ached to tear away that damned belt and rough-spun tunic to bare all her creamy skin to his gaze. To his hands. His cock threatened to burst through his trousers to reach the moist, heated entrance he could smell but barely touch. He wanted to devour her, to live in her for days.

Which is what gave him pause and allowed him to catch

his breath. What was he doing? Never had a woman affected him like this. Not so suddenly and not so harshly. Did all virgins affect *raedjour* like this? Not ever having known one -- at least, a *female* one -- he wouldn't know.

Still muttering, he eased away from her. Suzana. He took a long moment to gaze at her lush body, so tiny, but beautifully curved and full. He picked her up, delighted to find that she was heavier than expected, not a weak little flower that would break if breathed on.

He rose easily to his feet with her in his arms. A groan tore from his chest. He'd never make it back to the city.

"Here," he told Radin, unceremoniously dumping his precious bundle into the startled man's arms. "You take her back."

"Where are you going?"

Krael's hand lingered in her tangled hair. He yanked it away. "To hunt." To run. To kill something. To do something, *anything*, to put down the fire in his blood.

Chapter Three

She woke in a small bedchamber, nestled in a pile of blankets. A cheery fire kept the room warm as well as lit. A basket lay on a small table beside the bed, a loaf of bread and several cheeses poking out from the linen in which they were wrapped.

Suzana sat up and gasped. Her tunic and the chastity belt were gone! What remained was a pretty, if small, embroidered vest and a tiny pair of panties. Her hair had been brushed. What had they done to her?!

The door clicked, and she clutched the blanket to her near-nakedness.

The red-eyed leader of the men who had taken her entered. *Lir! He looks even better in full light!* He was mostly dressed, at least from the waist down. Pale gold trousers hugged his muscular thighs and tucked into knee-high boots of soft violet leather. His sculpted chest and arms were bare. A thick silver choker hugged the base of his throat. The rings in his right ear twinkled in the light.

"Greetings, little one," he purred, shutting the door

softly behind him. "Did you sleep well?"

She nodded, watching him warily as he approached.

"Do you have a name?" he asked conversationally. "Or should we continue to call you 'little one'?"

"Suzana." She supplied only her common name.

"Ah. How beautiful! It is a pleasure to meet you, Suzana." He sat on the bed at her feet. "I am Radin."

"My clothes are gone." She said the first thing that occurred to her.

"Not so, Suzana. I left you with some clothing."

She hugged the blanket closer. "You undressed me?"

He nodded. "And got rid of that horrible belt. You're welcome."

"Thank you," she said automatically. Then she lowered her gaze, staring at the hand he had casually rested on a muscular thigh. "Did you...?"

"No, Suzana. Your virginity is intact. For now."

"For now?"

He chuckled, edging closer. "For now. You see, I must fill you in on some details of your new situation."

New situation. As a slave. Still as a slave! She blinked back tears. This was not happening!

Radin's hand appeared at her cheek to gently brush away the tears. "Now, little love. Don't cry. I promise you this new life could be heaven."

"It's *not* my life."

Suzana widened her eyes in a vain attempt to keep further tears at bay. Her family was dead. Her beloved homeland lost to her. Yet she survived. Perhaps this capture was punishment. Perhaps she deserved this.

The fear and anxiety of the days since her capture crashed onto her. She crumpled, sobbing, burying her face in the blankets.

"Oh, little one," Radin crooned, immediately leaning forward to scoop her, blankets and all, into his lap. "It's all right, Suzana," he soothed, seemingly sincere. "You won't be hurt. You'll be treasured."

She barely heard him through her body-wracking sobs. Distraught, she clung to him as a warm comfort. Despite his being a stranger, he was the first source of comfort she'd encountered in what seemed like a lifetime.

Radin held her throughout, tenderly stroking her hair. At length, her sobs subsided. He prompted her to use the blanket as a handkerchief, assuring her that other blankets would be forthcoming. She huddled in his lap, accepting this strange man's comfort.

"Are you hungry?"

She glanced at the basket of bread and cheese. Nodded.

Securing her with one arm, he leaned over to snag the basket. Bringing it back, he opened it and laid it in her lap.

She ate silently for a moment, staring fixedly at the contents of the basket while entirely too aware of the muscular body that held her. The blankets had fallen down during her crying fit, which meant that her right arm was snugged up against the smooth, hot skin of his chest. Completely hairless. Out of the corner of her eye, she saw the strange white tattoo that flowed down his belly, like parallel waves, each inward point aimed down so that the entire tattoo drew the eye toward his groin. She slowly became aware of the smell of him, as well, a warm, musky scent that spun her thoughts far from depression and into melting interest.

"As I was saying before," he began, either oblivious of her interest or ignoring it, "you will be treasured among us. You see, we're a race entirely of men."

She frowned. "How can that be?"

"All children born to us are male."

She frowned harder. "But who gives birth to them?"

"The women we take from the world above."

She froze, a bite of bread momentarily forgotten in her mouth.

He took advantage of her silence to continue. "We're a long-lived race. We think we're related to the elves we've heard about but never seen, but we can't be sure. We do know that we were created as a race by our goddess, Rhae. To be blunt, She created us as sexual consorts and bodyguards. When the gods left our world, She tried to do what She could for us. She told us to take human women and change them."

"Change them?"

"To *raedjour*. We have a spell that will change you into one of us."

She looked pointedly at the glossy skin of his chest. "Do you mean black skin?"

"I do mean black skin. Which, by the way, is almost as hard to cut as cured leather but --" He smoothed a hand over the outside of her thigh. "-- is much more pleasant to the touch." She squirmed at his touch and heard him laugh softly. "I also mean you will develop night vision and a long lifespan. Changed women tend to add at least three to four hundred years to their lifespan, possibly more."

"Three to four hundred?"

"Yes."

"You mentioned living underground."

"I did. But, as you can see, we don't exactly live in bat-infested caves."

She had to smile.

At his urging, she stood, and he stood with her. He led her to a window and parted the curtain. She gasped. Beyond lay a wondrous world she could never have fathomed. Her window was at least four stories up and looked out over single-story buildings. The layout was roughly like that of a castle, complete with a wall marching across the terrain in the distance. And there *was* distance. Stalactites hung from the ceiling, some touching the floor to cause columns, but the open space extended for miles. She glimpsed other structures, a few as massive as a castle, others the size of a house. Beyond the walls was what looked like a city, complete with meandering streets and a cleared town square. Scattered figures walked the roads. In the distance…was that a lake? The shining, shimmery surface had to be water.

"It's beautiful!"

"It is."

"Are we under the forest?"

"No. We're much farther under the mountains. We are in the heart of the city here. Most *raedjour* live within the main foundation, but many choose to live in the outskirts.

We also have small gatherings, somewhat like villages, throughout the cavern system."

"I could never have guessed such a place could exist."

"It will be your home now."

She stepped back, but kept her eyes on the distant shimmer of the lake. "What happens now?"

He tugged at her hand to turn her, then released it to cup her face with both his hands. "I start the process to make you one of us, little one." He leaned forward even as she began to protest. "Welcome home."

She wanted to protest. She suspected that part of making her one of them included taking her virginity, and, as it was all she had left, she did not just want *anyone*, even this beautiful man, to take it from her. But his kiss overwhelmed her. More than a kiss, more than a meeting of lips. She tried to push away, needing to argue, sensing that his next actions would seal her fate. But her body already pulsed with a need she didn't understand. Her hands slid along the slick surface of his skin. Finally, she gave in to her desires.

Radin delved deep into Suzana's mind. As she was ungifted in magical defenses, her natural shielding was child's play to penetrate once he had distracted her with the kiss and a little push to the natural attraction humans felt for *raedjour*. With a sigh, she sank against him, and he had to release her face to surround her body with his arms to hold her upright. Her firm, high breasts pressed against his flesh, tempting him to take more than he should.

If only she weren't a virgin. He sighed, putting his thoughts back on track as he sifted through her mind. If she weren't a virgin, he could volunteer to be her first and enjoy the lush body he felt against him. However, there were very definite rules regarding virgins, and he would be defying his goddess if he broke them.

Although he couldn't read Suzana's precise thoughts or memories, he could get feelings and inklings. He read enough to know that she had to be well-born, and he read her guilt over the death of her family. He felt for her, but he could only hope that these pains from the past would ease in time.

His first task was to judge her capability. Could she handle the change? Could she live amongst them? He saw nothing within her to convince him she needed to be freed, and he saw ample that convinced him that her compassion and demeanor would be welcome among the *raedjour*.

Task complete, Radin broke the kiss. Suzana fell easily into his arms as he scooped her up and carried her to the bed. He laid her down, then stretched out beside her. Her eyes were closed, her plump, moist lips parted slightly. He smiled ruefully. Unfortunately, the planting of the spell would make this experience with him hazy in her mind. She would only remember fragments.

Taking his time, Radin smoothed his hand down her body, flipping aside the flaps of her vest to expose her breasts. His mouth salivated, but he didn't taste. They weren't his to explore just yet. If ever. But he could look!

His fingers trailed down her softly rounded belly to the

silky panties that guarded her sex. He pulled aside the flimsy fabric and fluffed his fingers through the curly hair there. Delving deeper, he found her moist heat. A moan escaped her lips as he caressed, finding and coaxing her little nubbin of pleasure to waken. It did, pushing at his finger.

He concentrated on her face as she began to writhe in pleasure. Her hips rocked into his hand, but he was careful to keep his fingers from her channel. He couldn't take her innocence. The rules were very explicit. He was to plant the spell, leaving her virginity intact. It was an interesting task for Radin, who had never planted the spell without also planting his cock deep inside a woman. He'd known the theory that it could be done, but had never seen the reason to deny himself before.

He fondled her, allowing the natural oil from his fingers to mix with her already copious lubrication. He often wondered how other males existed without the oil that covered a *raedjour*'s body. The scent delved deep into a human's sexual center, starting the simmer of pleasure that a *raedjour* man learned to cultivate with skill.

Suzana writhed, and more oil from the skin of his chest rubbed off onto her arm. Even in her semi-conscious state, the smell and warm burn would push her just enough...

When she burst, he was ready. As her body convulsed in orgasm, he sealed his lips to hers and planted the spell within her. The orgasm weakened her defenses further and made her receptive. Her pulsing body and racing blood tangled with the spell, helping to lace it through her being, to tie it to her soul. Before she subsided with a contented sigh, it was done. The seeds were sown to convert Suzana into *raedjour*.

Sighing, Radin pulled back his fingers and restored her panties. He licked his fingers clean of her cream, then shifted away from her and stood. Carefully, he arranged the blankets and pillows around her sleeping body. Then he left.

Chapter Four

Leaving a suitable guard outside Suzana's door, Radin emerged into the hallway, took a sharp turn, then climbed. It took precious minutes before he was in range. As soon as he was, he probed mentally in the direction he was going.

Are you there?

A sleepy thought met his, not coherent. Smiling, Radin probed a bit harder. Finally, Salin woke.

Ah! Finally he answers me!

When did you get back?

Nearly seven days ago.

Really? Salin gave a soft laugh. *I must have been distracted.*

I noticed. Is she that good?

Salin didn't have to answer. Radin could feel the overriding warmth in his brother's thoughts. Having shared a mind-to-mind contact with Salin his entire life, he knew the difference and was intrigued by its strength. As far as the brothers knew, they were a unique pair among the *raedjour.* No others shared a mind-bond, at least not to Radin's knowledge. Selfishly, they'd not told anyone of their secret, not even Radin's master, Nalfien, enjoying it through their youth and finding the secret useful in adulthood.

We could never have guessed at this, Salin assured him.

Mind if I join you?

Yes. I believe she's ready. Salin chuckled sleepily. *I thought you'd never get back.*

I tried to reach you when I got back. Then I had to take Savous on a caravan hunt. We found a virgin.

Mild interest. *Really?*

Complete with chastity belt. I'll present her tonight.

Excellent! Diana is ready to leave our rooms. The feast is a perfect excuse.

Radin emerged from a stairwell to the floor on which Salin's suite was located. *Is she awake?*

Salin's mind warmed with another chuckle. *Yes. And coveting Jarak's ass as we speak. I know we promised that the first of us to truemate would include the other in the first threesome, but you'd better hurry.*

Diana's eyes were riveted to the slight dip in Jarak's lower back, just above where the waistband of his trousers covered the intriguing gleam of his skin. Young and ripe and firm. She bit her lip hard as she struggled not to think of what else was ripe and hard on Salin's squire.

Whore! she called herself, fiercely shutting her eyes. Jarak was unaware she watched him. He knelt before one of Salin's chests, putting away freshly laundered clothes. She lay on the bed, peeking at him through the furs tucked around her head. Of course, the worst part was that she was also spooned into the naked curve of Salin's sleeping body.

For weeks now, she had been with him and only him. After she'd given up and admitted her love for him, they'd been enclosed in this room, fucking almost constantly. When they occasionally came up for air or weren't sleeping, Salin assured her that this was normal. Even though she was already pregnant, her craving for his body, his seed, his very presence was necessary. She thought it was waning. She was pretty sure she could now think of a few things besides Salin's cock buried somewhere deep in her body. But now she was looking at *Jarak!*

Jarak rose from his crouch, and she shut her eyes, feigning sleep. The squire had been their only contact to the outside world in the past few weeks. He brought their food, fetched water for baths, and replaced any soiled linens or broken furniture. So why did she want him *now?*

Scowling to herself, she decided she needed Salin. Determined, she rocked her hips, grinding her butt into the erection that had never quite fully gone away in the last few weeks. A sleepy moan reached her ears.

"Awake?" she asked innocently.

He growled. The hand which had been resting on her thigh slid up and forward to glide over her belly and between her legs. "Awake," he muttered, the sleepy rasp in his already deep voice causing ripples of delight down her spine. Or was it the long finger that probed her drenched folds?

She sighed. "Good."

Squirming, she twisted her body until she lay on her back, the thigh near him draped over his hip. The position opened her further to his exploration while allowing her to reach for a handful of his silver curls and bring his lips to hers.

She heard the door opening. She assumed Jarak had forgotten something. She certainly didn't stop. The squire had witnessed far more lately than Salin fingering her pussy.

Salin's kiss was not near deep enough. He held back. Growling, she moved to force the issue, but he pulled back completely.

"What are you...?" Then she saw him. A tattooed *raedjour* stood at the foot of the bed platform. Glowing red eyes marked him a sorcerer, and she was pretty sure the designs on his chest and face similarly marked him. She was immediately intrigued by the belly tattoo that spilled over a perfectly shaped abdomen and pointed toward the promising bulge at his crotch.

"Who are you?" she demanded. There was something familiar about that face.

"Diana," Salin began, voice laced with amusement. "Meet my brother, Radin."

So *this* was the famous Radin! Salin, she knew, was quite close with his brother. Radin the brilliant. Radin the rogue. Radin the wanderer. Radin the powerful.

Radin the fucking beautiful!

He tilted his head in greeting, his gaze freely roaming her naked body. Diana realized that she probably should close her legs, but she was amazingly turned on by allowing him to see. Besides, she didn't really want to stop Salin's marvelous fingers from their task.

"You're a lucky man, Salin." His voice was every bit as beautiful as Salin's, deep and rich as honey. Perhaps a touch more...*refined?*

"I am, aren't I?" Salin mused, nuzzling Diana's ear.

Diana made note that he didn't seem at all bothered either by his brother's presence or by his brother's perusal of her wet and welcoming body. Interesting.

"Nice jewelry."

Salin raised his head to frown at Radin. Diana smirked. On each wrist, her truemate wore leather restraints. They matched the ones on her wrists, except that hers were black and his were white. "My truemate's idea," Salin explained. "To show I'm as much hers as she is mine."

"Your men will love it."

"I couldn't care less."

Radin nodded. Smiling, he cocked his head to the side. Sleek white hair fell in waves to his shoulder. She was beginning to wonder anew why he was there, when he said, "Mind if I join you?"

Her interest perked. Radin's eyes were on her face now. She quirked a brow, then turned to Salin. Her bastard truemate was smirking at her. "I take it you don't mind?"

"Not at all."

She narrowed her gaze. "Why do I think that even if I said 'no,' you'd try to *persuade* me?"

He pursed his lips, unsuccessfully hiding a smile. "Are you saying 'no'?"

She returned her gaze to Radin, who waited patiently. The smirk matched Salin's. Obviously, the family resemblance was not just in appearance.

She sat up, her thigh still draped over Salin's. Casually, she wrapped her arms around the upraised knee and raked a gaze up and down Radin's body. "Can I at least *see* what's being offered?"

They knew, of course, that they had her. They could smell her arousal, and Salin, no doubt, could feel it. She failed to care. Salin had thoroughly altered her way of thinking, at least sexually. If he was game, she was game.

"I believe I can oblige." Radin stepped back.

He bent and showed wonderful balance as he removed his violet boots without having to sit. Diana couldn't remember ever having seen a man in leather of that particular shade.

"Nice boots."

Salin laughed. "Radin is, shall we say, fond of color."

"I am." Boots dropped to the floor.

The gold trousers came next. She had yet to encounter a *raedjour* who wore undergarments, and Radin was no exception. *Oh, my!* Unless she missed her guess, he was actually longer than Salin, who was *quite* enough, thank you very much!

He stood back, arms spread. "Do I meet with your approval?"

Oh, quite! But she didn't want to give in *too* easily.

"Hmm." She heard Salin's chuckle as she pulled away, but he seemed content to let her pretend to consider the situation.

She sat on the edge of the bed and motioned for Radin to move closer. He did, and his erection bobbed a little fuller.

Just a tad lower than her mouth. Perfect. But she ignored it for the moment, instead sliding her hands up the hot skin of his thighs, over the sharp bones of his hips. She considered the tattoo. "Someday, I want to know where these come from," she announced to the room, delicately tracing the patterns. His skin twitched beneath her touch.

Finally, her fingers found his erection. She teased him, using only her fingertips to smooth over the tracery of veins. She tilted his length up and gently pulled the loose skin of the shaft back so she could rub one thumb along that sensitive spot just under and below the head.

His entire body shuddered. "Ah, Salin, you've shown her a trick or two."

Salin snorted. "I showed her a few tricks, but she comes up with quite a bit on her own."

"Mmm, you sweet talker, you," she murmured, leaning forward to flick her tongue out and catch the drop of moisture that seeped from the head of Radin's cock.

A soft moan escaped him. "I take it I meet with your approval?"

"Not so fast," she said, making sure her breath caressed him. "I'm still judging."

She pursed her lips and leaned forward to slide the head and much of the shaft into her mouth.

Goddess! Radin cursed.

Feel good? Salin asked lightly, clearly amused.

Radin shut his eyes, the better to enjoy the slow, gentle raking of Diana's teeth as she pulled away from him. She kept the tip trapped by her lips and used a wicked tongue to lash over what remained in her mouth.

"Hmm." He shook again as her hum vibrated his cock. Opening his eyes, he watched her moist lips swallow him whole, her hazel eyes half shut.

I'm so glad we made our pact, Radin decided.

Yes. I'd imagine you would be. At least she seems to be enjoying you.

A corner of Radin's mind wondered what it was like for Salin to be truemated. Radin could feel the echo of her pleasure, as could any *raedjour*, but he knew Salin's enjoyment of Diana's pleasure would be magnified. Not only was he her truemate, but they were also still in the throes of the initial heat. It was the first heat, the first furious melding, that cemented the truebond for the rest of their lives.

Salin shifted, moving up behind Diana. Radin kept his eyes open to watch his brother's long black tongue drag up Diana's spine. It was her turn to shiver, and she again moaned around Radin's cock.

"Ah, Salin! Do that again," he moaned.

"Wait," Salin muttered. "This is better."

Radin watched as his brother's mouth hovered over Diana's right shoulder, a hand fisting in her hair to move it aside. She tilted her head to expose more of her neck, clearly anticipating even as she continued to lave Radin with her tongue. At first, Salin only breathed on her skin, his lips almost but not quite touching. She moaned. Then he reached the bend of her neck, just at the apex of her shoulder. His tongue darted out, and her body jerked, surprising Radin. Salin laughed, and her ripple of arousal grew. Lovingly, he lapped at her nape. Salin's head blocked Radin's view of his exact movements, but he soon didn't care. Diana's reaction to Salin's attentions was to clamp her fingers and mouth around Radin's cock and pump it.

I'm going to come, Radin informed Salin.

Do it. Take the edge off. You'll need it.

But still. "Diana," Radin warned, placing his hands gently on her head.

She growled. Pulled back enough to pop him out of her mouth and glare up at him. "Come, or I don't do this," she threatened.

Pleasantly surprised, he gave in as she swallowed him whole. Salin shook with laughter as he continued his assault on Diana's neck. His hands reached around to pluck at her breasts. She moaned. Radin let the urgency burn, released his control, and came. The lovely woman swallowed most of it.

He leaned back from her, still half hard. Salin sat back, pulling Diana with him. Radin enjoyed the sight of Diana sprawled and open, back against his brother, one of Salin's hands plucking at an engorged nipple, the other sunk deeply into her plump, wet sex. Her eyes were shut tight, her fingers digging into Salin's thighs. It didn't take long. She was already primed. Suddenly she arched, nearly pulling free from Salin. He had to clutch her to keep her. It looked painful. Perhaps it was. She didn't seem to mind.

He held her as she subsided, muttering nonsensical words up her neck to the curve of her ear. Her skin was beautifully flushed.

Finally, she took a deep breath and opened her eyes to look at her truemate. A sudden worry crossed her lovely features. "Salin?"

"Sweet?"

"Are you sure?"

Radin recognized the fear, but he let Salin explain.

"Yes, sweet, I'm sure. Radin is the closest person to me other than you. I'm delighted to share you with him. If it would please you."

She smiled. Some private lover's joke? "But..."

"No, Diana. Don't worry that I'll be jealous. *Raedjour* are lucky in that we don't have a human's need to make sure his mate is his by keeping her from all others. We *know*."

Without looking, Salin reached out a hand to Radin. Seeing his cue, Radin placed his hand in his brother's. Salin tugged him forward and down until he was kneeling on the floor, draped over the side of the bed.

"Let Radin taste you, sweet."

Her sharp eyes were on Radin, hazed by lust. Salin released Radin and used the same hand to part her sex for him.

Not one to pass up such an offer, Radin leaned in.

The fierce echo of Diana's desire punched through Salin when Radin's tongue touched her folds. Another benefit of sharing his woman was that, as her truemate, he could enjoy her desire and feed off it without the necessary distraction of performing.

Carefully, he slid out from underneath Diana's twisting body and moved to stretch out beside her. He plumped one firm breast as she arched under a particularly pleasant assault from Radin. She subsided, and her head fell to the side, those beautiful hazel eyes opening to capture his gaze. She stared a moment, then reached out to grasp a handful of Salin's hair and haul his face to hers.

"Mine," she muttered before sealing their lips.

Who's tamed whom? Radin asked wryly, sensing the surge of fierce pleasure that heated Salin's blood at Diana's declaration.

Jealous?

Both brothers subsided as Diana's body tensed then exploded, her hands pulling painfully at Salin's hair while her thighs clutched Radin's head.

She let her thighs flop open, wonderfully spent. For the moment. Radin laid a fond kiss to her nether lips and stood. She released Salin to watch as Radin fondled his cock, pumping it slowly to draw her attention to it. She blessed Rhae for giving her consorts such wonderful recuperative abilities!

Granted, it was a pretty sight, but she wanted it in her! She looked up and realized he was waiting. She glared. "Fuck me already."

"As the lady commands."

Oh, didn't he just drip sexy? He knelt between her thighs, bending forward to brace himself above her. He hovered, lips a breath away from hers. The heavy weight of his cock rested on her belly. *Not* where she wanted it. He bent his head to take her lips, plunging into the inviting cavern of her mouth with his tongue. She sank one hand into the thick, silky hair at the nape of his neck and wrapped the other around his cock. His moan matched hers, his hips pushing his cock through her fingers.

She cried out, her pussy bereft. "This is not fucking."

He laughed, letting her guide his cock lower, waiting for her to aim, then pushing home with one slow thrust. Her back bowed.

"Feel good, sweet?" Salin murmured. His lips caressed the side of her jaw as Radin dipped his head to nuzzle her neck on the other side.

"Gods!" Intense! She groped and found Salin's cock, taking possession of it as Radin began his exit slide.

"I can feel it, sweet," Salin rasped as he traced her ear with his tongue. "You're loving this."

"Oh, yes," she moaned. Then screamed when Radin abruptly slammed forward.

Salin's head fell forward to press against Diana's shoulder. *Rhae's tits, that feels good!*

Radin didn't reply, busily working his cock into and out of Diana's tight passage. Salin trembled with her, almost feeling the friction of Radin's cock inside her. If this was what it was like to share a truemate, Salin was all in favor! He forgot himself, forgot his own bodily pleasures as waves of Diana's crashed over him. She pumped back into Radin, wantonly sucking him deeper into her body.

It took Salin a moment to realize she was tugging at him, trying to get his attention. He raised his head to meet her gaze, struck by the blazing heat within. "I want to suck your cock," she told him. "Now."

Not one to disobey that particular command, Salin dragged himself to his knees. He laughed at himself, at his seeming weakness. But it wasn't weakness, exactly. He was not at all used to the bombardment of sensation from not only his body but hers.

Radin readjusted, sitting back on his heels. He pulled Diana's hips up until her buttocks rested on his thighs, her legs spread to either side. Salin crawled up to kneel beside her, but she slapped his thighs to maneuver him until he was above her head, nearly straddling her face. Satisfied that he was where she wanted him, she grasped his cock and gulped him halfway down her throat. He cried out, shocked by both the move and the sensation. She moaned, adding a vibration that was nearly his undoing. He fell forward, trying to brace himself, trying to hold back.

Too much? asked Radin's amused voice.

I...ah! He cried out as Radin pumped his hips forcefully, causing Diana to clamp about his cock in her pleasure and to pass that pleasure along in a chain reaction to Salin.

He ignored Radin's mental chuckle, too unnerved for a quick rejoinder. Finding his brother's shoulder near enough, he used it to brace his head. His hands found Radin's thighs, doubled up under Diana's splayed legs, and clutched them for support.

Radin's amusement was laced with unadulterated envy. He cradled Salin's head to his shoulder, supporting his brother as Salin obviously dealt with incredible sensations. In the past, they had shared women. They had shared men. But this was far more intense. The addition of Diana added another level to Salin's pleasure that neither of them had clearly anticipated. Oh, they'd known that a man could feel pleasures through his truemate. But knowing and feeling were clearly two different things.

Radin worked his cock within Diana, a sensation wholly enjoyable in itself. She was tight and wet, with a strong grip. And she was a demanding little bitch! Each time she thought he wasn't going fast or hard enough, she threw herself at him or rotated her hips in clear instructions.

He tried not to be distracted by Salin, but how could he avoid it? It was amazing to watch his strong, always-in-control brother fall apart at the seams. The mental bond they shared allowed him to hear the mental stutters, the incoherent groans, and Radin briefly wished their connection were more like a truebond so he could feel the sensations himself.

Sensing Salin was on the edge, Radin picked up the pace, his goal to drive Diana to an orgasm that would set them all off. Salin groaned, his thoughts incoherent as he tried to hold on, tried to let the pleasure go on.

He snapped first. His release into her mouth triggered Diana. Radin let her clutching channel fire his own release.

Salin sagged against Radin, breathing hard. Radin held him gladly, enjoying his own after-warmth.

Radin moved first, lowering Salin down to lie beside Diana, whose eyes were closed as she tried to catch her breath. Slowly, Radin pulled out, dragging a small moan from her. He left them on the bed and went to retrieve a bottle of Salin's favorite wine, chilling on a side table. *Bless Jarak.* Pouring a cup of the rare light, fruity wine, he drank it himself before taking another full glass to the bed. The truebonded pair hadn't moved.

"Drink?"

Salin cracked an eye. Apparently thinking it a good idea, he pushed up to sit and took the cup from Radin.

"How do you feel, sweet?" Radin asked, unthinkingly adopting his brother's endearment.

Diana groaned, lifting a hand to run through her hair. "Is this normal?"

"Which?"

"Just tell me that I'll get a break from sex *sometime*. No, scratch that. That I'll *want* a break from sex."

The brothers laughed, prompting an angry glare from her.

"It's already waned, sweet." Salin lazily caressed her thigh. "Days ago, we were hardly conscious of other people."

"So, what now?"

"You'll always want Salin," Radin assured her, taking the empty cup to refill it. "But the initial heat is done. You'll feel more like interacting with others, and you won't feel the need to fuck him *every* moment of the day."

He returned with the cup, handing it to her. She struggled and, with their help, sat up. She drank, then eyed him. "You explain nicely. I like you *so* much better than Nalfien."

He smiled. Salin laughed. "Thank you."

"Where were you when I was taken?"

"Likely on the far side of the mountains. Radin wanders," Salin answered for him. "He's often gone for moons at a time."

"Where do you go?"

Radin sat beside her and tucked her hair behind her ear. "Anywhere I can. I'm limited to the forest and mountains, and I need places where I can find shelter for the day, but I've explored most of our limits."

"Alone?"

He smiled. "Usually."

She nodded, accepting that. Yawning, she slumped to her side, cradling against Salin. "So. When do I get to leave these rooms?"

"Tonight."

Surprised, she twisted to see Salin's face. "Really?"

He nodded. "There will be a celebration tonight."

"What for?"

Salin hesitated.

What's wrong?

She's not going to like this.

Why not?

Her gaze narrowed at the verbal pause. "What?"

Salin sighed. "Radin found a virgin."

"I assume you mean a woman. So?"

"Virgins are a cause for celebration."

"What the hell for?"

Hmm.

Yes. Salin sighed. But another part of him perked. Diana's anger aroused him. *The hellcat emerges.* "We don't often get virgins, sweet," Salin said reasonably.

"So?"

"When we find one, there is a celebration. Unmated males are invited to compete to see who will win the honor of being her first."

Scowling, Diana pushed up to sit, the better to fully see her truemate. "What?"

"It's a coveted honor to be a woman's first."

"Why?"

"It can only happen once," said Radin, trying to help. He grinned, warming to the topic. "Also, Rhae's given us a spell that amplifies a virgin's lust so that everyone can share it. I'm told it's a heady feeling."

"Because it only happens once."

"Yes."

"Just women?"

"Virginity isn't the same for men."

"Yeah. It doesn't hurt." She scowled. "And it does hurt, you know. I'd think it'd hurt more to be breached by a man hung like a fucking stallion." She made her point by reaching down to flick a finger at Salin's semi-hard cock. "You make an honor out of torturing the poor girl?"

Salin brushed his fingers lightly down Diana's cheek, the look in his eyes infinitely sad. "I'm sorry your first time was traumatic, sweet." She flinched away from him.

Her scowl still firmly in place, Diana shoved out of the bed. Both Salin and Radin had to duck to avoid getting kicked. "Just when I thought it's gotten as bad as it's going to get," they heard her grumble, "you pull another surprise on me."

"Where are you going?" Salin asked mildly.

"Away," she proclaimed, finding one of Salin's tunics and sliding it over her head.

"Alone?"

"Yes."

"No."

She growled at his tone. "Fuck you."

Ominously, Salin rose to a crouch, eyes fixed on her as she tore open a clothes chest. "Diana, you're not going anywhere without me."

"That's too damn bad, because *you're* the one I want to get away from."

"Or Radin."

"As if *he's* any different."

"Diana."

She leveled a finger at him. "Don't you dare. Don't you fucking dare!"

The nerve! She fumed, watching the too-quiet predators that eyed her from the bed. Somewhere in this hellish cavern was a poor, terrified woman who was about to be a *prize* in a fucking competition. As the prize, she would get ripped apart from the inside when some over-eager *raedjour* shoved his cock into her. At least when Diana was taken, she had known sex. Not *good* sex. Nothing like what she had with Salin. But at least his mammoth cock was not the first she'd fit inside her body.

She spun, racing. She reached the door and actually got

it open. Farther than she really expected. She knew that look on Salin's face. Knew the narrowed slant to his dark crimson eyes, the tiny hint of a grin to those black lips. There was no way she would make it out of the suite.

But she would damned well *try*.

One set of hands caught her shoulders and hauled her back. Another set ripped the door from her grasp and slammed it. Salin's arms wrapped about her shoulders, one hand spanning her neck. Squeezed just enough to make breathing difficult. She snarled, furious that this fired her blood. Her foot shot out at Radin, but he caught it and tossed her foot aside. He stepped into her widened stance so that she ended up sandwiched tightly between them.

"Get off me!" She clawed Salin's arm, swinging the other arm in what would have been a good jaw punch if Radin hadn't caught her hand.

Together they walked her back. Salin caught both of her arms and dragged them behind her as he sat, forcing her to kneel, spread wide over his thighs. Although she kept telling them to let go, she never said stop. Could not bring herself to do so.

Radin knelt, sliding his fingers through her weeping pussy. Bending forward, he sucked her clit into his mouth as his fingers slid down to rim her back entrance.

"No, wait!"

"Yes," Salin hissed, his teeth at her neck. "We're going to fuck you now, sweet. Both of us. Together."

She squirmed, fear momentarily overriding pleasure as Radin's finger penetrated. "No, Salin. You won't fit."

"We'll fit."

"Salin..."

"Trust me, sweet."

She groaned, all thoughts flying from her head save those of two beautiful obsidian rods impaling her.

Radin slicked her with her own juices, then positioned Salin's cock himself. "Push down, sweet," he murmured. Behind her, Salin breathed heavily into her shoulder.

She did. She had had him there a few times, knew the sensation by now. But not in this particular position.

"So fucking tight," he muttered, lapping and nipping at her sensitive neck.

She made him moan with a twist to her hips. Gasped when Radin reminded her of his presence by again catching her clit between his lips. Crying, she fell aback against Salin. He released her arms to take control of her hips, bracing her so she wouldn't hurt herself too much.

She came in Radin's mouth, her ass clutching Salin. Her truemate panted, biting her shoulder to maintain control. He fell back on the bed, taking her with him. She opened her eyes in time to see Radin crawl onto the bed, over them. Smiling down at her, he positioned his own massive cock at her pussy and penetrated.

"Fuck!" she screamed, the heat spiking when he hit her just *there*.

Inexorably, he kept coming, smoothing through her slick walls. Beneath her, Salin pulled out, making more room for Radin to slide home. Then Salin pushed in while Radin pulled out. Diana clutched the furs beneath them, pinned between them in midnight ecstasy. If she closed her eyes, they were one massive male body, invading her from both sides. As one, they worked together, finding a rhythm of push and pull that left her mindless and squirming, screaming and crying into orgasm. Another. Or maybe the same. Finally, as one, they growled. As one, they came, triggering another shuddering release within her body.

Chapter Five

Suzana awoke with a start when a hand softly shook her shoulder. She opened her eyes to behold a woman smiling down at her from the bedside. Her skin was dark, pearly gray, not nearly as dark as any of the *raedjour* men Suzana had seen. Her eyes were a startling ice-green that seemed wrong for her skin color. But she had a kind, pretty face, and her smile was filled with warmth.

"Hello, Suzana. I'm Gala." She stepped back, politely giving Suzana space as she sat up.

Modestly, Suzana gathered blankets around her nudity. Then it dawned on her that this woman was practically naked herself. Her slim, muscular body was covered only by a silky green wrap about her hips and soft leather boots dyed a matching color. Her pale blonde hair spilled in smooth waves from the crown of her head past her shoulders, some of it curling delicately just above the smooth mounds of her breasts.

Gala smiled, extending a bundle of fabric she held in her arms. "I brought you something to wear." She looked down at her own "clothing" and snickered. "It's not much more than I'm wearing, I'm afraid. But I managed to get a vest to cover up top, if you like."

Suzana glanced down, embarrassed. "Will I ever get to wear proper clothing again?"

Gala laughed. "Therein lies the problem. To the *raedjour*, this *is* proper clothing." She held out the bundle again. "Come, get dressed. I promise you've nothing I haven't seen before." Feeling silly, Suzana slipped from under the covers, but her eyes went immediately to the closed door. "No, don't worry. They'll wait outside for a while yet."

Suzana took the bundle. "They?"

"Radin. My truemate, Hyle, and a few others. We're here to escort you to the festivities."

"Your truemate?"

Gala sighed, turning toward a small table to retrieve a brush. "Didn't Radin tell you anything?"

Suzana shook out a tiny lavender vest, a color she knew would bring out the color of her eyes. Delicate silver embroidery made the vest sparkle. She slipped it on, only to find that it wouldn't quite close across her ample bosom.

"Here." Gala dropped the brush on the bed, took the ties in front of the vest, and helped to lace Suzana in. "What *did* Radin tell you?"

Suzana thought about it. Truthfully, her memory of her time talking to Radin was a bit of a blur. She remembered seeing the city and talking about a few things, but after that, nothing. "That I would be treasured. That he was going to change me into one of them. That this was now my home."

"That's it?"

"For the most part."

Gala sighed. "Typical. I'm glad they allowed me to talk to you, then. What little he said *is* true. You will be treasured. The *raedjour* as a whole treat us very well."

"Us?"

"Women. But for a race that follows a goddess, they're remarkably domineering of women." Gala shrugged. "But in that, they're very like most men. Also, Radin did cast the spell to begin your change into one of us. It will take a while, from what I'm told."

"Then you…"

Gala nodded, smoothing the now-laced vest over Suzana's breasts. The edges barely covered her nipples, and the taut laces pushed her breasts in and up, creating a deep and bountiful cleavage.

"The change was started for me a few moons ago." She held out her arm, displaying the gray skin that gleamed in the light. "It's remarkable to watch your skin turn color. Not that I notice, most of the time." She ran a hand over her forearm. "And it *feels* different. Tougher but softer." She shook her head, as if unable to explain it. She fingered a lock of her pale hair. "And my hair was dark blonde." She shrugged. "As I said, it's gradual and gets more pronounced as time wears on. I think the pregnancy helps it along. Or causes it. I haven't quite pinned that one down."

"You're pregnant?" Suzana couldn't help her smile. She *loved* babies!

Gala matched it, smoothing a hand over her very flat belly. "I am."

"Congratulations."

"Thank you." Picking up the brush, Gala climbed onto the bed behind Suzana and took hold of her wealth of hair. Someone had brushed it since her run through the forest, but her hair could always use brushing. "You have beautiful hair!"

"Thank you."

"You must never have cut it for it to be this long."

"No. Only trims to keep it healthy. My people only cut their hair as a sign of grief or shame." She felt the pang of loss at speaking about her lost home. She *should* cut her hair, a sign of grief for her lost relatives.

Gala must have sensed that, for she went on. "Life among the *raedjour* for me has been a wonderful experience. It's so beautiful down here. I would never have guessed that an underground kingdom could be so varied. You must visit the main bathing cavern some time. It's a huge cavern with dozens of pools. Some are big and you can go swimming. Others are small and naturally heated." She babbled on a bit, her talk and manner putting Suzana at ease. "And since I found my truemate, Hyle, I couldn't be happier. He's wonderful! So sweet and loving. You see, one of the other drawbacks for the *raedjour* is that they're only fertile with one woman. Ever."

Gala spoke in a stream of words that Suzana was pleased to find she had no trouble following. Gala was a lot like a few of her friends back home. "Only one?"

"Only one. That's another reason that they're very careful with us. They'll make note of what you like and who you like so they can find your true match. So you'll be taken from man to man until your truemate is found."

Suzana started. "From man to man?"

"Yes." Gala's friendly manner all of a sudden seemed hesitant.

"Do you mean...?"

Gala sighed. "There's no good way to say this, so I'll just be blunt and say it. You'll be given to one man before today is through, and you'll stay with him for nine days. He will have sex with you." Gala's voice was warmly amused. "A lot." Suzana's face flamed, and she was glad Gala was behind her so couldn't see it. "At the end of the nine days, you'll be tested to see if you're pregnant. And yes, they can tell after such a short period of time. The sorcerers, anyway. I'd imagine Radin will test you. Anyway, if you're not pregnant, you'll be given a night or two of rest. After that, you'll be given to another man for another nine days. That will be your life until you truebond or until they decide that you're not likely to truebond."

Suzana froze, hearing Gala's words. This was truly happening?

"But you're special. Because you're a virgin. Rhae thinks virgins are special. So, you get a contest to see who gets to be your first," Gala continued blithely, still stroking Suzana's hair. "They're going to hold a contest for you, tonight. *Ilk vet metmre*, Radin called it. It means 'brawn and domination.' He's spread the word, and any unmated male who thinks he's worthy and is of a mind is going to come fight for you."

Mind racing, Suzana shook her head. "No."

"Suzana, really, it's not that bad. Their goddess, Rhae, created them for sex. She gave them a special sense. They can actually feel your pleasure or pain. So it actually *benefits* them to see that you enjoy sex." She chuckled. "They've made the act of making love an art form. Because, to them, it's the way they worship their goddess."

"But... No! They can't! My virginity is all that I have left!"

Gala sat back on her heels. "Suzana, calm down. Really, it's not..."

"No! They can't!" She stood, ripping her hair from Gala's grasp. Frantically, she eyed the room, settling on the open window.

"Suzana, please. Calm down. There's nothing you can do --"

Again, Suzana shook her head. "I can't."

"Radin!" Gala screamed as Suzana darted to the window.

Behind her, the door crashed open. But she was at the sill. She... Froze. Not of her own volition. The air itself coalesced around her body, confining her in the spot where she stood. Magic.

"Trying to take flight without wings, little bird?"

She felt Radin coming up behind her but could not move a muscle to turn toward him. He materialized at her side, head cocked in question. He seemed calm, but she thought that might be anger or annoyance burning in those red eyes.

Her mouth, she found, was not confined. "You can't take my virginity."

"I didn't, Suzana."

She shook with the effort to move, her gaze cast out the window and down at the welcoming cobblestones below. "You're going to give me to some man to take my virginity tonight. You can't."

"Why?"

"It's all I have left."

He leaned casually against the edge of the window, crossing his arms over her chest. "Small comfort in a thin barrier buried deep inside your cunt, Suzana."

She flinched at his vulgarity.

"Besides, did you think we *weren't* going to take you? You were headed for a slave auction when I first saw you, Suzana. What do you think your new master would have done?"

"Radin, don't be cruel," Gala admonished.

He waved a hand in her direction but kept his eyes glued to Suzana. "Talk to me, Suzana. Don't you think we've been rather kind so far?"

Tears welled in Suzana's eyes.

Radin sighed. "Don't cry, little bird. It's not as bad as all that. You're not headed for a vulgar rape. After all, *you're* going to choose the winner of the contest."

She blinked, trying to contain her tears. "I am?"

"In a manner of speaking."

"What does that mean?"

"Part of the virgin contest involves a spell that's tuned to your arousal. I'm actually quite excited to see how it works, as I've never cast it before."

"You haven't?" This from Gala, somewhere behind Suzana.

Radin's eyes remained on Suzana. "No. Suzana's the first virgin we've found since I reached my majority." He smiled.

"And I reached my majority nearly two hundred cycles ago." He waited for Suzana to digest that tidbit of information before continuing. "The spell takes your arousal and allows everyone at the contest tonight to experience it on a low level. The men fighting for your favor, however, will feel it more strongly." He lanced her gaze with his, making sure she heard his next words. "Your focus will give your favorites a needed edge in winning you. So, in a way, you will be choosing the winner. If you can't decide, then those who are among your favorites will fight it out until one remains the victor."

She swallowed the last of her tears. He was right. She was being given far more choice than she would have received as a slave. They were being *nice* to her. She was warm. She was clean. She instinctively trusted Gala. And Radin. Despite his mischievous grin and exotic nature, she did feel that she could trust him. Her instincts were rarely wrong.

"Will Krael be there?"

Radin laughed. "You remember his name, then? I noticed your instant attraction for him. Your reaction to him in the forest is the reason I chose *Ilk vet metmre* for you." He eyed her, red eyes shining. "Yes. He, and those like him, will be among the combatants."

"Can't I just choose him?"

Radin's eyes widened. "A moment ago you were protesting that anyone take your innocence, and now you're asking for Krael? Are you so sure, little bird?"

She nodded, so intent she didn't realize that she could now move freely. "Yes."

"How do you know? You've only met a handful of us. I assure you that Krael is not the only arrogant, long-haired warrior among us." He snorted. "We have those in abundance."

She shook her head. "No. I want Krael. I know it."

His humor slipped. "You *know?* How?"

She lowered her head. "I just do."

"Yes. I sensed some magic in you," he mused. "But it was faint, so it must be mostly instinctual."

He reached out and gently grasped Suzana's shoulder. "I'll make a bargain with you, little bird. Come with us to the contest. See the combatants. If it's Krael you truly want, your attention alone can ensure that you have him."

He guided her firmly away from the open window, turning her to face the room. Gala stood at the bed, an encouraging smile on her kind face. Another *raedjour* man, shorter and younger than Radin, stood behind her. Suzana assumed it was Gala's truemate, Hyle.

"Do I have a choice?"

"Truly? No," Radin answered, voice stern but not unkind. "Regardless of anything you or I say or do, you will be taken by a *raedjour* tonight. Potentially fertile women do not go untried among us. But take my bargain and at least you'll have some say in the matter."

"Do as he says, Suzana," Gala urged. "It was more choice than I was given at first."

Suzana considered. Radin was right. The offering was far more than she would have received from whoever would have bought her from the caravan master. After a short silence, she nodded.

"Good." Radin turned her and tipped Suzana's chin up with one finger. "Don't be afraid, little bird. We'll take very good care of you."

Chapter Six

Suzana was overwhelmed. She sat amongst a wealth of silken, embroidered pillows on a dais raised perhaps four feet above the dirt floor of a small arena. The perimeter of the cleared central area was lined with similar pillow-strewn platforms, only one set higher than hers. That one stood against the wall to the right of Suzana, empty.

Radin lounged beside her, half seated among the pillows. A low table -- more of a tray -- lay between them, supporting a trencher of rich stew as well as assorted small loaves of different kinds of bread. Gala and her truemate, Hyle, lay loosely entwined next to Suzana, sharing their own tray. To Radin's other side sat another woman, introduced to Suzana as Diana. Diana, unlike the other women, wore a burgundy leather tunic, which cut off just below her breasts, and snug matching leather trousers. Oddly, about her wrists and neck she wore restraints, but these she treated more like jewelry than bondage.

The other platforms were rapidly filling with a multitude of people. The far majority were *raedjour*, men and women, their shining onyx skin mostly bare. Men wore trousers and boots. Women wore skirts or wraps and sandals or boots. Most of the women were topless. There were a few human-looking women within the crowd, each paired with a man. There were a few human men, as well, but they seemed to be servants of some kind as each wore at least a collar around his neck.

Krael was nowhere in sight. When Suzana asked Radin about him, he would only say that the warriors would "soon make their appearance."

At present, a man sat in the center of the arena, entertaining the crowd with song as he played his lute. Born to a people who held music in the highest regard, Suzana paid him the attention he deserved. When he rolled into his next song, she was delighted to discover her name in the phrasing. While he sang, he focused smiling blue eyes on her. When he completed his ballad, Suzana was not the only one to applaud enthusiastically. He seemed to be a crowd favorite.

"Donnal, haven't I heard that ballad before?" Radin asked, amusement lacing his low voice.

The musician darted an anxious glance at him. "Uh, no, Radin."

"Really? I could have sworn I'd heard it. Although, the name was 'Tiana,' not 'Suzana.'"

Suzana covered her mouth with her hand to hide her giggle.

"You're correct, Radin," shouted a female voice from across the room. A woman stood on one of the platforms. Her white hair was piled atop her head in luxurious curls, held in place by violet ribbons, and a matching violet sheath hugged the curves of her black-skinned body. "Donnal, I'm wounded." Her smile and amused voice ruined her act.

The musician cast an agonized gaze at Suzana. Raised among musicians, Suzana took pity on him. "It's a lovely song, sir bard." He puffed up at her choice of title. "Thank you."

"Come here, *sir bard*," said the woman as Donnal left the area. "*I'll* give you something to sing about!"

The crowd laughed, Suzana with them. Happily, she accepted a plate of sweets from a young boy and turned to share them with Radin.

"All right, Radin. When does this show start?" Diana grumbled once the laughter had died.

Radin looked at Suzana instead. "Please forgive Diana. She's a bit put out, being separated for the first time from Salin since they truemated."

Diana snorted. "I'd be less 'put out' if I didn't have to witness this farce."

"Diana," Radin warned.

"What? It's barbaric."

"No," Radin disagreed lightly. "'Barbaric' would be if we laid her out on a table and then stood in line to take a turn at her." Suzana gasped, but he smiled at her to make light of his words. "Which we won't do." He looked back at Diana. "Despite what you want to think, we do want her pleasure."

"Of course." This from Gala. "Remember, the *raedjour* feel your pleasure."

"And tonight, everyone here will feel your pleasure." He waved at the crowded arena. "Which is why there are so many of us here tonight. As Suzana's arousal grows, so everyone will feel it."

Suzana's face flamed at the reminder.

"Well, isn't Rhae just full of surprises," Diana muttered.

Of a sudden, the din of the crowd hushed. Confused, Suzana looked up to see most attention directed toward the largest entrance directly across from her. The crowd parted. And *they* entered.

The first man to enter was a marvel to behold. Tall, slim, and completely naked, the *raedjour* was nearly covered head to knee, elbow to elbow with gleaming white designs. These seemed more vivid than the tattoos on Radin, nearly as bright as the shimmering white hair that fell in heavy waves to his knees. From across the room, Suzana could plainly make out the burning orange of his eyes. To each side, he was flanked by another man. The one to his right was slightly taller, with short gray-white hair. He wore loose trousers and tall boots, and swords were tucked in either side of the embroidered red sash that bound his slim waist. Weblike tattoos decorated his chest. The man on the left was shorter and rounder, his white hair bound and braided close to his head. He wore a vivid red robe that swathed his body from shoulder to ankle but was left open in front to reveal nudity beneath.

Behind the trio were at least a dozen other men, warriors all, to judge by the weapons at their waists or held expertly in their hands. And Krael was at the head of this group! He strode just behind and to the right of the short-haired swordsman in front. Gleaming obsidian muscles rolled, a sinuous predator in motion. His shining white hair followed as an unbound cloud behind him. Krael's eyes locked on Suzana, and an evil grin possessed his lips.

The procession advanced until all the warriors were within the open area. The warriors stopped while the man in front and his two companions continued to the empty raised dais. Radin tapped Suzana's shoulder, leaning close. "That is Valanth, our *rhaeja*. Consider him our king."

Suzana only nodded, her eyes still glued to Krael, who now stood at the head of the procession of warriors. He fingered a long black whip that was curled up and attached at his hip. Mesmerized, she watched him slide the tail of the supple leather weapon through his fingers, the gleaming black the exact same shade as Krael's skin. She wanted to feel those fingers on her skin, have them caress her as they caressed the leather. Her mouth went dry at the thought.

"Radin," came a strong voice from the larger the dais, startling her. "Bring forth the virgin so I may see her."

With a small sigh, Radin rose and extended a hand to help her to her feet. A glance at the *rhaeja* showed his attention on her, and fear pulsed in her throat. Luckily, the training drilled into her since birth as a noble lady also kicked in. Head bowed, she allowed Radin to hand her down the shallow steps at the back of the platform, then lead her to meet the *raedjour* ruler.

The *rhaeja* lounged back among a wealth of pillows atop the dais. A woman had been brought to him and now served as his backrest. She was as naked as the *rhaeja*, her lovely onyx skin smooth and unadorned except for a white leather collar strapped around her neck. A chain dangled down her chest to the pillow below her, the handle conveniently located for the *rhaeja*'s hand. Her white hair fell in thick waves past her shoulders. She sat placidly, but not as a lover would. She stared blankly to the side, her face and green eyes entirely devoid of emotion or feeling. She focused on a space inches before her nose and seemed to see nothing. *What could cause someone to look like that?*

"*Rhaeja*, may I present Suzana," Radin pronounced, halting her at the foot of the steps leading to Valanth.

Valanth no more noticed the woman against whom he lay than he noticed the silken pillows beneath them. "Come closer."

Hesitantly, Suzana mounted to the final step, keeping her head bowed.

"Look at me."

She did and found that meeting his gaze was nearly impossible. Every fiber of her being wanted to stumble back down the steps and hide from this man. His eyes burned fiery orange, hotter than the glowing red of Radin's eyes, and the wicked slant to the lips below them did not convince her that he was entirely sane. His skin was not wrinkled, but he did look older than Radin somehow. Perhaps his skin gleamed just a little less, or perhaps his muscles were a tad less defined.

His voice was smooth as silk. "Aren't you tiny? Where are you from, child?"

"Dinnah Mar, my lord. Just off the north coast."

He nodded. "I have heard of such a place. An island nation, yes? Under the god Lir?"

"Yes, my lord. *Rhaeja.*" She ducked her head, but the view was no easier lower on his body. The white designs on his flesh were disturbing, much brighter than those on Radin's chest, face, and abdomen. If she stared at any of them too long, the design looked like it moved, or began to hover over his skin. His stenciled cock lay long and semi-hard against his flat belly.

"We have never seen the sea, of course, but we have heard of such a wonder. You are a long way from home."

She settled her darting gaze on his shoulder, knowing he would take offense if she simply looked away. "Yes, *rhaeja*."

"And exquisitely well behaved. You are familiar with courtly manners."

"Yes, *rhaeja*."

"Nobly born, then?"

"Yes, *rhaeja*."

"Ah. Would that I could teach the *raedjour* to respect courtly behavior. I fear we are quite lax in the proper modes of respect."

By his words, she knew his kind. A man who thought much of his position and thrilled at others' recognition. The trouble with such men was they rarely *earned* the recognition they sought.

"Perhaps I may rely on you to…" His words trailed off. Suddenly, he rolled forward to his knees, leaning toward her. On instinct, Suzana stepped back, but he grabbed a handful of hair just behind her ear to still her. Frowning, he stared at her face. "This one's a mage!" He glared over her shoulder. "Radin, all mages are to come to me *first*."

An abrupt hush settled over the arena.

Radin spoke calmly. "Beg pardon, *rhaeja*, but she's not a mage."

Valanth sneered over her shoulder. "Do you doubt my

abilities to tell such things, *sorcerer?*"

"No, *rhaeja*. She does, indeed, have magic, but she is not a mage."

Valanth turned back to her. "What say you, virgin? Are you a mage?"

"N-no, *rhaeja*." Terrified, she trembled under his glare. "M-my family, my lord, is born with some magic, but it is very specific."

"Such as?"

"Music. I'm a bard."

"You cast spells with your voice?"

"N-not exactly s-spells, my lord. I can enhance and sometimes cause strong emotions."

The death grip on her hair eased a touch. "I see. A useful trait."

"Yes, *rhaeja*."

"But she's not a mage, my lord."

She swallowed a cry as Valanth thrust her aside, bringing her to her knees beside him while keeping hold of her hair. "You're new to your position, *sorcerer* --" The word was said with a sneer. "-- to be judging magic for me."

"My apologies, *rhaeja*."

Suzana knelt, frozen, as Valanth turned back to her. The fingers in her hair pulled cruelly, but she bit her lip over the pain. Like a frightened bird before a cat, she stared up at his considering gaze.

"Perhaps in this, you're right." Suzana held her breath when he tilted his head, the long fall of his silvery white hair tumbling across his shoulder. "She would have to have more power to be the answer to my needs. Besides, I don't have the patience to train a virgin." He released her, pushing back slightly to force her to struggle to keep her balance. A smile took his lips as he settled back against the empty-eyed woman. "So tell me, are you prepared for a thick black cock to take your virginity?"

She gasped. He chuckled, grasping his own organ with a long-fingered hand. Suzana watched, unable to tear her gaze away, as it grew in his grip. The odd stenciled designs reformed as it grew. "*Ilk vet metmre*," Valanth murmured. "You are certain of this, Radin? She doesn't strike me as the type."

"Quite certain, *rhaeja*."

Valanth nodded, still stroking his cock. Suzana struggled not to squirm where she stood, aroused despite her fear of the august presence before her. "Stare like that, virgin, and I may reconsider my decision not to train you."

Blushing, Suzana dropped her gaze to the planks at her feet.

Valanth laughed. "Very well. Let's get on with this."

Krael clutched the whip, his relief slow to diffuse through the boiling rage in his blood. He was as loyal as any to the king, but he wanted that tasty virgin morsel for himself.

Radin led Suzana back to their original seats, accompanied by Salin. Salin relinquished his usual spot beside the *rhaeja* in favor of wrapping himself around his truemate. Krael watched the hellcat snarl at him, putting up a token struggle before Salin finally settled her in his arms. Krael shook his head. Salin was quite obviously pleased with his truemate, but Krael didn't understand it. The woman had put him through hell, had repeatedly denied him. She'd forced the commander to practically beg for her. Krael well remembered that one horrible moment when his closet friend had ordered him to sink a dagger into his heart and end his misery.

Krael dragged his gaze away from the happy couple as Diana finally relented to a kiss. That wasn't for him. Krael knew the joys of a woman's flesh, knew how to pleasure a woman, but he wouldn't be tied to one. There was far too much angst involved.

He barely listened as Radin stood and proceeded through the formalities of describing the contest for the crowd. The litany was for young *raedjour* and the virgin herself. Any seasoned man knew what was about to happen, even if they, like Krael, had never actually participated before. Contests of *metmre* were common among the *raedjour*. A way of easing tensions and expelling the need for violence that went with their highly sexual nature. The only difference in this contest was the prize.

She sat like a jeweled statue on her pillows, eyes wide as she gazed at the crowd, her wealth of thick black hair strewn about her like a blanket. The tiny vest she wore guided attention to the fullness of her breasts. Krael idly wondered about the color of her nipples.

Radin didn't call him for the first battle. Not that it mattered. Some of the others were fierce, but they were not him. They were not marked as a warrior by Rhae Herself. He barely recalled the time in the dark, when he had given himself to Her will, but he had emerged victorious, with lightning strikes etched across his face. It made him a primary captain, answerable only to Commander Salin and the *rhaeja* himself. Few other warriors could boast such a feat or would even try the test to see if they were worthy of Her favor.

He sat back to wait his turn

Suzana winced as the first contest ended with one combatant out cold on the floor. The winner stepped toward her, saluting with the long staff he had used to pummel his opponent.

"Would you reward this warrior with a kiss?" Radin asked mildly.

Suzana blinked, still trying to come to terms with the heated arousal that tingled on her skin and deep in her belly. She had never felt anything like this before.

She turned her eyes, trained them on the man's handsome face. "I --"

"It's not required," Radin continued lightly, plucking a sweetmeat from the tray between them. "But you may. If you wish."

She felt the weight of Krael's stare. Despite her fixation on him, the first battle had captured her attention. Horrified and fascinated, she had watched every moment. The warrior before her was tall and wonderfully built. His obsidian skin shone with what should be sweat, but didn't quite look right. His black eyes flashed with his warm grin.

"I…" It seemed only fair to reward him somehow, did it

not? Besides, what would his lips feel like? "I wish."

The warrior's grin grew as he stepped forward. Radin's hand steadied Suzana among the pillows, helping her to her knees. With her kneeling on the platform and the warrior on the ground, he was still a bit taller than she.

"I'm Rigiel," he informed her, leaning forward. His hands he kept to his sides.

"Rigiel," she repeated, resting her hand lightly on his shoulder to steady herself as she touched her lips to his.

He leaned into her, a slight moan catching in his chest. Radin cleared his throat, however, and Rigiel abruptly pulled back. He smiled at her. "Thank you, little one."

"You're welcome," she breathed.

Radin helped her sit as he called two more names.

Krael barely contained himself, watching that whelp Rigiel kiss the girl. Then Callip after he trounced Garn. Then Dreidon when he beat Waldaz. After each battle, with each kiss, Krael -- and all those around him -- could feel her arousal grow. Suzana's sweet, heady lust permeated the room, caressing the skin of every *raedjour* in the arena. Krael's cock pressed against his trousers, hard and ready. All around him on the pillow-strewn platforms, couples and threesomes were well into kissing and caressing, tasting and exploring as they enjoyed the pulse of the virgin's innocent appetite.

Krael suffered through yet another two matches and another two kisses before it was finally his turn. He only barely calmed as he stepped forward to face Vanzanter, his opponent in the final match of the first round.

He uncoiled his whip, watching Vanzanter eye it warily. Fool. Vanzanter was better than that. After his nine days with Suzana were over, Krael would take the man to task for showing a weakness so obviously.

Vanzanter fought with two cudgels, expertly flipping them in his hands. A distraction technique that didn't work on Krael, who knew the cudgel as well as the whip. Krael simply waited for the less-experienced man to attack.

Sssssthack!

Suzana nearly jumped from her skin when the whip hissed through the air and caught the man on the back as he tried to duck away. Such a sound! She felt as though invisible fingers pinched a sensitive spot between her legs.

Krael pulled the whip back, all the while dancing aside and away from an attack. The other man tried to engage the whip, tangle it, but Krael used it as a six-foot-long, snaking extension of his arm. The other arm, he used to bat away any advances Vanzanter might make.

Suzana fidgeted, aroused beyond measure at the sight of the wild male who had chased her down in the forest. His long, lush hair billowed about him like wings. How he avoided tangling it with the whip, or how he managed to keep Vanzanter from grabbing it, she had no idea. Like the whip, it simply seemed an extension of his body that he controlled effortlessly.

Krael wrested one of the cudgels from Vanzanter, using the butt end of the whip to knock the man aside. Now he fought with both weapons, corralling Vanzanter with the whip, then rapping any available appendage when the other man came too close. And he was often close. How could he use a six-foot whip effectively at close range?

With a particularly loud *crack*, the match was over. Vanzanter fell to his knees, then to his side, clutching his head. Dismissing him, Krael tossed the cudgel to the side and boldly strode to the edge of Suzana's platform.

She heard Radin chuckle. "Again, Suzana, you may choose not to bestow reward."

"No, I --" She stared longingly at the smooth expanse of Krael's chest, the wicked smile he pointed at her. "-- I want to."

She knelt on her own and edged forward. Krael's hands lifted to reach for her.

"Krael," Radin warned.

Krael snarled at the sorcerer, and Suzana very nearly swooned on the spot. His lip lifted, revealing gleaming white teeth, and the lightning bolts that crossed his face sizzled to life. Her skin burned to feel the touch of those hands. She failed to swallow the moan that vibrated in her throat.

Obviously pleased, Krael switched his attention to her, even as he braced his hands on the edge of the platform. She stopped when she knelt before him. She was shocked to find that he was not as tall as the other *raedjour* she had met. Still far taller than she, but not a towering mountain like some of the others. Kneeling on the platform, she was about on eye-level with him. It was comforting, made him seem more tailored to her. At least in her own fanciful thinking. She reached out a tentative hand. A thick hank of silky white hair rested on his chest, and she laid her palm on it. Instantly, her fingers moved, weaving into it.

His smile turned feral, and again Suzana thought she might melt. A sensible woman would be frightened. She *was* frightened. But, oh, her body responded to this man!

She leaned forward, and he tilted his head to more fully catch her lips. She started back when she felt his tongue swipe the seam of her lips.

"Krael," he told her, naming himself as the other men had. Even if it wasn't necessary.

She nodded, knowing she couldn't possibly forget.

The final match. Krael's cock was hard enough that he could have used it as a weapon itself against Callip. Suzana's lust was thickly palpable, driving him insane. It was like but unlike the feeling a *raedjour* experienced with a lover. It was that tingling sense, that phantom echo of pulsing pleasure, that drove a *raedjour* to please his lover. But this virgin lust was slightly different, a lighter taste but no less potent.

Around him, few of the onlookers watched the contest. The sounds of sex, slapping skin and frantic moans, had accompanied that of the clashing weapons during the last battle, which had seen Dreidon unconscious under Callip's mace. Some of the audience had left for private quarters, but most simply stayed and enjoyed the impromptu orgy while they siphoned off Suzana's arousal.

Krael tuned out the activity about him. He concentrated solely on the man before him and the surge of extra confidence he received from Suzana. Her attention was on him and him alone! He felt it as clearly as if her tender flesh was pressed against his.

Impatient to experience her flesh in the physical sense, Krael faced Callip. It was over almost before it began. His aim had never been finer as his whip wrapped about Callip's neck, his arm never stronger as he pulled the startled man off his feet and kicked the side of his head. Callip, victor of three fights this night, was out.

Chapter Seven

Triumphant, Krael spun to face his prize. Her huge violet eyes rounded impossibly larger as he approached, but she didn't take flight. Frozen, she awaited her capture. He saw Radin's smile and his faint nod. Beside Radin, Salin had rejoined Diana. They were locked in an embrace, as were Gala and Hyle to Suzana's side.

"Well done, Captain," boomed the *rhaeja.*

Krael stopped in mid-step and forced himself to turn and face his ruler. Valanth was alone with Tishna on the platform, the empty-eyed woman spread across his chest like a blanket. Valanth's stenciled cock was buried deep in her pussy, but his eyes speared Krael's.

"Treat her well, Captain," the *rhaeja* told him, turning an admiring gaze toward Suzana.

"Yes, my lord." Krael turned his own gaze to her, smiling as he felt her trembling need hammer at him. "I intend to."

Crossing the distance between them, Krael scooped Suzana from the platform, tossing her high before him like one might a toddler. Again he tested that delectable weight he had discovered when he held her in the forest. She looked delicate, but there was solid woman in that body. Solid woman to wrap around his cock. Unable to meet those eyes directly any longer lest he throw her down and take her right then, he threw her over his shoulder, keeping a tight grip on her plump little ass.

He followed a boy to the room the winner of the virgin was assigned. It would be bigger and better equipped than his rooms, and at least one squire would be assigned to attend them during the nine days. For that, Krael was thankful; he never took on squires of his own.

They reached the room, and he took his trembling bundle inside. He knew she was frightened, but he also knew she was aroused. If he couldn't already feel it, he could certainly smell it wafting from between her silky thighs. He tossed her carefully onto the pillows and blankets heaped atop an overlarge bed. Primly, she pressed her legs together, turning her hips so that she was closed to him. His gaze narrowed. He didn't realize he'd growled until he saw her cringe.

He thought to reassure her, but words were beyond him. After the fight, his heart rate was skipping furiously, and it was all he could do not to tear into her. Also, her fear added a tangy spice to her scent.

Slowly, he knelt before her. Never taking his gaze from hers, he took hold of her ankles and placed them to either side of his hips, spreading her nicely. The silk wrapped about her hips annoyed him.

Snarling, he twisted a finger in the knot holding the wrap and yanked. Suzana gasped as the shimmery fabric tore.

He flipped the cloth aside and fastened his gaze on her exposed sex.

Suzana didn't know if she wanted to scream or groan. All reassurances from Radin and Gala flew from her thoughts as she was confronted with the wild man before her. His movements were carefully contained, barely leashed violence evident in everything about him. But even the knowledge that he was probably going to hurt her didn't detract from the deep, pulsing arousal that suffused her body. She knew arousal. She knew attraction. Both were paltry feelings from her innocent past compared to the heated blaze that burned in her belly and pooled in her groin as she lay spread before this man.

Heavy eyelids and thick white lashes didn't hide the dark, vivid blue of his eyes. As he leaned forward, a heavy hank of his long, straight hair fell from the top of his head, over his shoulder, to curl deliciously on her thigh. She moaned. The sound brought his gaze to hers. She could only stare in fascination at his harsh features, the gleaming obsidian skin bisected with a crisscrossing lightning design. He continued forward, closing the distance between them, his brawny arms keeping his body from touching hers. More of his hair hissed forward to curtain them on either side. She squirmed, wanting to run but wanting to grab handfuls of that hair to rub all over her body.

"Suzana," he breathed, lips hovering over hers for just that moment before he sealed their lips.

The kiss was hard. Not hurtful, just demanding. He pulled back long enough to demand, "Open." Just like in the forest. Now, like then, she parted her lips to his plunging tongue, squirming deliciously beneath his assault. This was all-encompassing, explorative and possessive. He touched every surface of her mouth that he could reach, branding it his own.

Suzana clutched the blankets beneath her, wanting to reach up and touch him but scared to do so. She could only follow his lead because this was a new experience. She was deathly afraid she'd get it wrong, that she'd displease him, that he'd stop this glorious exploration. She couldn't think on her own. She was his to direct.

He pulled away, leaving her bereft. Muttering darkly to himself, he took hold of both sides of her vest and tugged. The two laces that held the sides closed snapped. His nostrils flared as the vest fell apart, exposing her breasts. One huge hand closed around one of those mounds of delicate flesh, plumping, pinching. He wasn't exactly gentle. She cried out when he dropped his head, sucking her nipple into his mouth. Dark, fiery warmth spread through her chest, melted through her belly, and oozed from between her thighs. He worried her nipple with tongue and teeth, a rumble in his throat setting off a vibration in her breast. Her hands flew up of their own accord to grasp the hair near his head. Eagerly, she tangled her fingers in the cool silk of it, pulling to press his face closer to her breast.

He switched to the other breast, each hand now cupping one mound. He brought the other nipple to painful awareness, then opened his mouth wide to suck as much of her breast into his mouth as he could. She held her breath, unsure whether to enjoy the sensation or brace herself for intense pain if he bit her.

Krael reared back, dislodging her hands from his hair as he sat back on his knees. "Suzana," he groaned again, sliding his hands down her ribs to smooth over the curve of her belly. Sweet, creamy skin, flushed a lovely pink by her arousal. The curve of her belly entranced him. His entire hand could splay the width of her waist! His hands trailed lower, smoothing out to the sway of her hips, then down over the plumpness of her thighs. With both hands, he gripped those thighs and tugged her forward so that her bottom rested on his knees. All the while, his gaze remained riveted on the dark triangle of curls between her legs, curls that parted due to his action to reveal juicy, wet lips and an intriguing, seeping hole. He glanced up to see her eyes locked on the fall of his hair, and he smiled. She'd fallen under the spell of his hair, a common occurrence for most of his lovers. While she gazed at him, he trailed his fingers through her pussy lips, his cock stiffening when he realized just how *big* his fingers looked. If his fingers looked big, his cock would truly find a snug fit!

She moaned, her eyes finally falling shut as he smeared her cream over her sex. He found the nub of her clit easily and had to grasp her thigh with his free hand to keep her still as he rubbed it. Her cute little mouth pursed to frame the "Oh!" that escaped her lips.

Oh, he wanted to fuck her! He wanted to wear her ankles as a necklace as he pounded into her. *Later,* he promised himself. He had nine days with her. Despite the boil of his blood, he had to be careful.

Her hips started to pump. He wasn't surprised she was close. The entire night had been one long foreplay session for her. He kept rubbing her clit, bringing one finger of his other hand down to her entrance to probe just inside to find the right spot...

There! She shattered, her hips pumping furiously at his fingers, instinct seeking to drive him deeper. He shut his eyes, letting her orgasm roll over him like a warm tide, allowing it to ease some of the urgency in his blood.

Leaving her limp among the blankets, he slid out from under her and stood beside the bed. Breathing heavily, she rolled her head to watch as he bent to remove his boots.

"Don't move." She froze in the midst of sitting up. Uncertain, she remained on her elbows. "Keep your legs spread. I like the sight of you."

That helped her embarrassment. Her thighs relaxed, bowed open as instructed.

One boot then the other found the floor. He straightened to unlace his trousers. Even now, her manners tried to rule as she wondered whether to watch or not. *How cute.* She finally decided on his eyes, and he let his gaze heat as he finally pushed his trousers down over his slim hips. She practically panted in the effort not to look, and, since he stood calmly, it finally overwhelmed her. Her gaze dropped, and those huge violet eyes got even bigger at the sight of him. Her thoughts were plain. How was she going to fit *that* inside her? He was hard and thick, and he wasn't entirely sure he'd fit it all, either. But he'd fit as much of it as he could!

He dropped to his knees beside the bed, disregarding her panic as he scooped his hands between her thighs and under her lush buttocks. With a practiced move, he let his hair fall forward and flipped it slightly. Hair fell to obscure his face as locks of it pooled over her belly and waist. Distracted by the hair, she didn't realize what he was about until his pointed tongue just touched her engorged clit.

A ragged groan rattled through her, her hips instantly rocking forward to slide her clit neatly between his sucking lips. His own groan settled into her pussy as he lapped at her juices. Rhae's mercy, she tasted divine! Warm, salty, almost flowery, her nectar coated his lips and tongue. Reveling, he rubbed his chin over her fleshy lips. He dipped his tongue down to her channel, plunging inside before licking back up to torment her clit.

She groaned, writhing, and he left her sensitive little organ long enough to remind her, "Be still." She froze again, and he grinned at the agony on her face as he again put his mouth to her sex. He knew very well it was impossible to stay still. But the struggle would make it all the hotter for her.

Screaming, she came around his tongue, her thighs thrashing against his cheeks. He held her firmly, opening his mouth over her sex so that his teeth pressed her clit, sending her right over the edge into another climax.

Suzana was blind. Her sight had gone the way of her voice. She could only moan as her body writhed incessantly beneath Krael's assault. She had never felt so alive yet so helpless. Never so out of control.

She sighed in relief when he finally lowered her bottom to the blankets and released her cunt. But then he crawled up her body, carefully lowering himself so that his hips were fitted to hers.

Her eyes flew open, sight suddenly returning as she realized what was happening. This was it.

That blue gaze seared hers, barely contained behind heavy eyelids. "It will hurt, Suzana," he promised, bending to kiss her forehead. Her own juices smeared her skin. "But it will also be worth it."

"Please," she squirmed, panic rising.

"Be still." She instantly complied. What was it about this man that her body obeyed him before her mind realized the fact? "It's been nothing but pleasure so far."

She had to concede that fact. But still, as he shifted his weight and she felt a nudging at her entrance, she squirmed.

A hard smack on the side of her thigh froze her. And exhilarated her. To her own surprise, she felt another gush from herself moisten the head of his cock. He chuckled. "Relax, or it will hurt more." His voice was dark, rich cream that oozed over her chest and sank into her heart.

Smoothly, he breached her opening. Now, that felt good! He forged forward an inch or so, then pulled mostly out. The heat of his cock felt wonderfully odd within her body.

"Scratch and scream all you need." He pushed deeper. Retreated. She clutched at his shoulders, feeling the unfamiliar stretch of inner muscles. She hissed, trying to decide where this was supposed to hurt. Because it didn't. It filled a void she'd only just realized was there.

"Now!" he grunted, yanking her hips to thrust even more deeply into her body.

There was the pain! She howled, nails digging into the tough skin of his shoulders. She kicked out feebly with her legs, her struggles ineffectual. He remained absolutely still until the first of the pain subsided; then he pulled out slowly. She whimpered, tears in her eyes. His lips caressed her forehead, nipping at the hair atop her head. The fingers of one hand slid from her hip to the side of her breast, toying lightly with it. She wondered at his actions, until he pushed back in. She tensed, ready for more pain, but was shocked when there was only a faded echo from before.

He took hold of her hands, pulled them out to the sides, and braced them to the bed with his own hands. He hovered above her, connected only by his cock within her, watching until she looked up at him.

Grinning, he pulled out and thrust back. She groaned. The pleasure she'd felt before was back, and deeper. He did it again, and she was sure he butted at the entrance of her womb. No, she changed her mind. He was nudging her heart!

Her eyes drifted closed as he found a rhythm. Her body followed suit with his, arching, twisting, clutching. Oh, yes, clutching! She concentrated on that. It still hurt some -- he was big, after all! -- but the pain wasn't enough to detract from the pleasure. In fact, it might have been making it better!

He growled, and she opened her eyes to a glorious sight. Framed by that wonderful, shining hair, his face was contorted in sheer pleasure. His belly contracted as his hips worked. Looking down, she could even glimpse that onyx rod, wet with her cream, as it dipped in and out of her channel.

Too much!

"Ah!" she cried, riding the orgasm. She was beginning to

recognize the sensation. That implosion deep inside that caused her entire body to tense and writhe.

Suzana lay limp in the pillows, trying desperately to catch her breath. Krael was poised above her, breathing deeply but not quite heavily. She peered up at him through a sweaty haze. While her long black locks were plastered to her damp skin, his ever-flowing white hair still drifted about them like a curtain. Rather than sweat, he was covered in a fine, glossy oil.

He smiled, a dark, possessive expression that curled her toes. She drew in a startled breath when he slowly pulled back his hips, withdrawing the cock that was still huge and hard within her. Her heart skipped a beat. Wasn't there something missing? She knew the rudiments of sex, though her poor nurse's explanations fell *far* short of what she'd just experienced. He was supposed to empty himself. In her nurse's words, his "tool will spill its seed in you and get soft. Then you know he's finished, and you've done your duty."

What did it mean that he was still hard?

He stepped off the bed and padded across the room to a small door she had not noticed before. A short moment later, he returned with a bowl cradled in one hand, two thick, soft cloths in the other.

"Be still," he told her when she would have moved aside as he sat.

He told her that a lot. Why did she like it? She'd never particularly enjoyed it when coming from her father and brothers. Why was it exciting when this man demanded it of her?

Calmly, ignoring the erection between his legs, Krael dipped a cloth into the water in the bowl and then very tenderly used the cloth to wipe moisture and blood from between her legs. She bit her lip, her heart expanding at the sweet gesture.

"You're sore," he declared, a statement rather than a question. "That's normal." He dropped the cloth he'd been using to the floor. Dipping the second into the water, he used it to wipe perspiration from her brow, her neck, her torso. She welcomed the coolness, as the room was toasty warm from the fire and their exertions.

She glanced at his cock, opened her mouth to ask, but stayed her words.

He noticed and smiled. "Yes?"

She looked up at him, instantly lost in the crystal-blue world of his gaze.

"Ask." He discarded the second cloth and bent to place both cloth and bowl on the floor beside the bed.

"Did you...finish?" she asked, unsure she'd used the correct words.

But he understood. Was amused. Leaning back, braced on one muscular arm, he idly traced his fingers over the shaft of his cock. "You mean did I come? No."

Her eyes were riveted on the long organ, fascinated by the bunch and pull of loose skin, the domed head when it was revealed. "Did I do something wrong?"

"No. It was your first time. I did all I could not to make it too painful for you. My concentration didn't allow me release."

"It was wonderful!" Sitting up on her knees, she winced only slightly at the soreness between her legs.

She felt her face mirroring the warmth in his smile. "I'm glad you were pleased."

She glanced back at his cock. His big hand surrounded the gleaming shaft. She licked her lips. He chuckled. "Do you have more questions? Or..." He leaned into her, breathing softly at her temple as she continued to stare at his cock. "...would you like to do it again?"

"I --" Her mind, just now awash with questions, cleared completely when a pearly drop of liquid seeped from the tiny hole at the end of his shaft. She could not have said why the sight arrested her, but it did.

He released his cock and reached over his body to grasp her hand. She watched in wonder as he folded her fingers around his hot organ, amazed that something she couldn't even encompass with her fingers had actually fit within an opening of her body. And said opening, while admittedly sore, pulsed with a need to be filled once again.

"You're mine to teach over our days together," he purred, freeing his braced arm so he could use it to cuddle her closer to his side. She laid her cheek on the broad muscle of his shoulder, her eyes still fixed on their hands as his led hers up and down the length of his cock. "We'll find out all the things you enjoy. All the things that will make you come."

"Come?"

"That explosion of feeling you felt." He dipped his head to nuzzle her ear. "Four or five times, if I counted correctly."

She giggled, smoothing her thumb over the head of his cock to smear the liquid. His purr made her squirm. "Is it always that way?"

"No. I'm told some women have difficulty coming. Rarely with one of us, though."

"'Us'?"

"A *raedjour.*"

"Oh. Is it because of your goddess?"

"Yes."

Impulsively, she squeezed, gratified to cause a shudder to race through his body. He groaned. His hand left hers, and she paused. "Keep doing that, Suzana," he demanded softly, his hands now burrowing in her hair to turn her lips to his.

Assaulted by his kiss, she could barely remember her name, let alone how to move her hand. But he pulled back and again demanded, "Don't stop." Obedient, she squeezed, and he groaned. The sign that she pleased him encouraged her. She caressed his shaft as he again plundered her mouth, his long tongue twining with hers, coaxing her tongue to foray into his mouth, as well.

At length, with a growl, he pulled from her. He grasped her hips and bodily swung her up and around until he dropped her across his lap, her legs to either side of his. He was so big that her knees didn't even touch the blankets on which he sat. Scowling in need, he placed one big hand across her buttocks and slid her forward until her hips were locked to his, her open sex caressing the shaft she'd been forced to release. She moaned, instinctively rocking her hips to bring his hardness in contact with that little nub of nerves he'd found with his mouth earlier.

"That's it." He took possession of her mouth again, fisting a hand in the hair at her nape while sliding the other down her back to grip her buttocks.

They came up for air, barely. The only distance he'd allow between their mouths was hardly enough for air to escape their panting lungs. The hand left her hair to grip her hips. Again he lifted her bodily "Suzana, reach down and guide me inside you."

Shuddering, she braced one hand on his shoulder, then obeyed. His cock was wet with both her juices and his own. As he lifted her, she placed him. He let her slip down just enough to lodge him snugly inside her.

"Grip me with your thighs and take as much as you're able."

Biting her lip, she nodded, concentrating on the sweet ache as he filled her. She reached her limit at last, sure she could feel him bumping at her heart.

"Lean back and brace your hands on my legs."

She did. Bent back, the position gave him better ability to control how far down she went. She let him have her weight, sighing as he lifted and lowered her on another forever slide.

"Ah!" She gripped him with her thighs, which tightened her channel around him. Both of them cried out at the added friction.

"Ride me, Suzana."

Shyly, she rocked her hips. Oh, that felt so good! She shut her eyes, throwing her head back, and did her best to move. Awkward at first, she finally got the rhythm. Rolling her hips with his help, she found places to aim his cock that felt positively exquisite!

Holding her to make sure she didn't hurt herself, Krael nonetheless let her weight bring her down farther than before. How did such a little woman take so much?!

All of her curves were sleek with sweat, her body completely open to him as she leaned back. Her luscious breasts bobbed to her rhythm; her long hair caressed his thighs and calves. The ass in his hands flexed, helping those muscles inside her squeeze the life out of his cock. And the trust! That was the most amazing part. Her instant obedience and open trust were not lost on Krael.

He felt her impending orgasm and knew he had to let himself go this time. She likely wouldn't make it through another. He pumped up her rhythm, adding a roll from his own hips. She stiffened. Screamed. Nails dug into his thighs. Pulsing lust washed over him. He followed her over the abyss and lost himself in her sweet, warm depths.

Chapter Eight

"...no sooner had Dreidon said 'Well, naturally *I'm* in charge,' than Salin walks in. Only Dreidon doesn't see him, so he goes on about how, now that both Salin and you are laid up, he'll be taking charge and running the place." Radin and Krael shared a belly laugh. "Calm as you please, Salin taps him on the shoulder -- when he's done, of course --"

"Of course."

"-- and asks him if he 'may proceed.'" Radin shook his head. "I'm told Dreidon collapsed from exhaustion by the time Salin was through with him."

Krael grinned at Radin's story, glad the commander was back at his duties. The men *could* function without either he or Salin watching over them, but they really *shouldn't*.

He drummed his fingers on Nalfien's worktable. It was late in the day, judging by the time statue, and Krael had only recently awakened. Regretfully, he'd eased away from Suzana's warmth to come to this meeting. It was expected. The sorcerers kept an especially close eye on a woman's first few lovers, using the initial experiences to hone their future choices for her. It helped to find a truemate. Krael had served the function many times in the past.

Why did it bother him this time?

"Are you all right?"

Krael scowled. "I'm fine."

"You don't look fine. Was it hard on her?"

"What?"

"Suzana. Did last night not go well?"

"Oh. No. It was fine." Great. Stupendous. Exquisite! Why?!

"Then what aren't you telling me?"

Nalfien's arrival spared Krael from answering. The elder sorcerer swept into the workroom with Hyle in his wake. The younger sorcerer carried the requisite journal and quills. In that journal, he would record what Krael told him about Suzana. He would make note of the fact that she responded well to dominance. That she had a fondness for long hair. That even in her first times, she took an amazing length of cock into her tight little body.

Why did it bother him that they would know this?

He felt Radin's gaze on him but ignored it as the other sorcerers sat at the table.

He answered the same questions he had answered on previous occasions, and he answered them calmly. He ignored the hard pit in his gut at the thought that he was preparing Suzana for another man. *Sharing* her was an attractive idea -- giving her over to another was not.

Nalfien proclaimed himself pleased that Krael had made her first experience a memorable one. Nalfien had presided over the last virgin found by the *raedjour*, but Krael, Radin, and Hyle had not even been adolescents, much too young to participate back then.

The interview had just about completed when the door opened to admit Betaf. In his flashy, shiny red robes and with his silver hair bound with numerous braids, the man was one of the king's pet sorcerers, rather than Nalfien's, and was therefore not precisely welcome in Nalfien's quarters. Krael sat back, content to stay outside their animosities.

"Excellent, you're here." Krael was surprised to see Betaf's attention on him. The lanky man's red gaze pinned him from beneath heavy eyelids. Then he scanned the others, nodding slightly.

Radin toyed with his wine goblet. "What do you want, Betaf?"

"The *rhaeja* has decided that he'll have the virgin after Krael's time. He's sent me here to arrange it."

Krael froze. Valanth wanted Suzana?

"Why?" Nalfien voiced Krael's question.

Betaf sniffed. "It is not your place to question the *rhaeja*."

"Humor me."

The younger sorcerer considered Nalfien, but was just intelligent enough to know he was no match for his crafty elder. Fear of Nalfien was one of the reasons he remained plastered to Valanth's side. "If the *rhaeja* wished you to know his reasons, he would tell you. But he will have her. So be it."

With that and a flourish of his robes, he was gone.

"Why?" Krael turned to Nalfien.

The elder sorcerer's eyes trained on the shut door,

squinting, as if the answers were written there in miniscule script. "I can only guess."

"You can't let him have her."

Nalfien turned at Krael's insistent hiss. They shared a weighty gaze.

It was known, but never talked about. The *rhaeja* was...not right. Sanity had not been his for nearly a hundred cycles. Not since the death of his truemate. The *suspicious* death of his truemate. The pair had gone into chambers one day, and the next she was dead. He mourned her, of course, and the *raedjour* watched him carefully for several moons afterward. It was uncommon for truemates to outlive each other by more than that, *if* that. Once the connection was formed, breaking it through death almost always broke the will to live in the survivor. But Valanth had not only lived, he'd thrived. After a hideously short mourning, he had emerged and claimed one of the women in the brothel. He claimed that Rhae Herself had deemed he should not remain without a partner. She had even given him a prophecy: "A mage's love to save the *rhaeja*."

The woman he'd claimed had survived, physically, but she was forever after mute. And withdrawn. There was no discernable reason. She was also quite timid and avoided contact with others until and unless her sexual urges became too much. She died within a few cycles of being with Valanth. After a short remorse, Valanth took another. That one stayed with him for many cycles, but she also lost herself somewhere along the way. No one knew what happened -- or if they did, they didn't speak of it. The woman simply became a walking, breathing body without a mind to speak of. After she died quietly, Valanth took another.

"What will we do?" asked Hyle.

The *raedjour* endured Valanth's odd, cruel behavior only because there was no heir. Rhae very clearly marked those she deemed worthy, and Her *rhaeja* she marked profoundly. Nalfien, for all his power, had not emerged from Rhae's test with the marks of *rhaeja*. Nor had Radin or Salin. Nalfien had even undergone testing a second time, only to emerge without any additional markings. No other likely candidates were of age to yet be tested.

Nalfien glanced at Radin, who barely contained his own anger.

"We do nothing." Nalfien raised a hand to forestall arguments from three mouths. "Allow me to rephrase. Radin, Hyle, and I will do what we can to discover why the *rhaeja* wants Suzana. If possible, perhaps we can persuade him differently. You," he said to Krael, "will return to Suzana. You have eight days left with her. I suggest you make them memorable for her."

Krael heard the ominous undertone loud and clear. Make them memorable, because they might be the last pleasant memories she has for quite some time.

Chapter Nine

A knock woke Suzana from a deep sleep. She roused, disappointed to find herself alone. Krael had been such a marvelous warmth curled about her when she fell asleep, she had hoped to awaken with him still there.

The door opened, and a young *raedjour* stepped halfway through the opening. "Lady," he greeted, smile wide, "I'm Rhon. I'm to see to your needs during your time with Krael."

She smiled. He was very cute. His face was rounder than any of the full-grown males she'd seen, his hair a tumbled mass of short curls that barely touched his shoulders. She wasn't sure how she knew he was young. He just seemed to have an unfinished look to him. He glanced down. If his face weren't pitch black, she was sure she'd see him blushing. Not that she could fault him. She was, after all, quite naked, even if she was covered by the blanket she held to her chest.

"Would you, uh, that is, should I bring food or a bath?"

She perked. "A bath?"

He looked up and beamed at her excitement. "Yes, lady. I could order a tub and bring all that you need."

"Oh yes, please do. And, Rhon..." She stopped him as he turned. "A meal would be wonderful, as well. And, um, clothes?"

His smile took a decidedly wicked turn. "I'll bring the meal, my lady, but not the clothes. You won't need them."

It was her turn to blush. No, she supposed she wouldn't.

She studied the room around her. She hadn't gotten much of a chance to see it the previous night, as she'd been distracted by Krael. She sighed, the very memory of what they had done causing things low in her belly to melt.

The room was quite cozy and surprisingly roomy. The stone of the walls was gray, with shots of yellow and green that made the room seem lighter. A fire in a large fireplace warmed the room nicely. The floor was polished stone covered in colorful, scattered rugs, both fur and woven. Aside from the bed, the only other furniture was two sturdy chairs set at an equally sturdy table, and three smaller tables set against the walls. The smaller tables held bottles of various kinds, along with a brush-and-comb set on one. Three beautiful woven tapestries hung on the walls, each depicting a peaceful forest scene.

She wondered if these were Krael's personal rooms, then decided not. There were no personal effects. And somehow, the room just didn't have the *feel* of him.

She shivered. Where *was* he? She didn't want to waste a moment!

Rhon returned with a tray of food. Famished, Suzana wrapped a blanket around her torso and joined him at the side table. The youth was nearly a head taller than she, a fact that seemed to surprise him but didn't faze Suzana at all. The bread was sweet and nutty. Responding to her questions,

Rhon told her that the deep-golden spread was butter but that the milk was from a *yarak* rather than a cow. She asked about the *yarak* as he emptied the tray of a plate of sweetmeats, another of plain bread, and a last of cold meats.

Before he was done, the door opened and two more youths carried in a small copper tub. They set it before the fire, then took buckets from within the tub and disappeared through a door she knew led to the washroom.

Curious, she followed them to the door to watch. The facility was small but fascinating. Part of one wall was a trickling waterfall that shimmied down the stone into a polished stone basin set at hip-level to the young men. They took turns filling the buckets from this and going back to the main room to fill the tub. Peeking in, Suzana found the room also contained a covered hole on the far wall that could only be the privy. Cleverly, a bit of the waterfall had been diverted to run through it, as well.

Once the boys were done, she discreetly excused herself and closed the door to use the facilities in private. When she emerged, an older youth had joined them. This one was more of a man, taller, with muscles far more defined and developed. His hair, white with faint honey highlights, fell in soft, loose curls that decorated the back she initially saw. When he turned, her eyes widened. She recognized the second man who had been in charge of the party of *raedjour* that had captured her. The younger one who had escorted the female slaves from the wagon.

He smiled. "Greetings, lady." He held out his hand, and she automatically placed hers within. She watched, wide-eyed, as he bent nearly double to place a warm, dry kiss on her wrist. He straightened, and his eyes lingered over her, causing her blood to heat. "You are beautiful, lady," he murmured.

"Thank you," she breathed.

"I'm Savous."

"You were in the forest the night I was taken."

He smiled. "I'm pleased you remember me."

She blushed. "I'm Suzana."

"Excellent," chimed in an annoyed voice. Suzana jumped away from Savous, spinning to face Krael, who lounged against the doorway. Her lover, however, only had eyes for the youth. Angry eyes. "Now that official introductions have been made, you can heat the water and go."

Savous only grinned. "Are you sure you don't need...help?"

Krael growled low in his throat. Suzana shuddered, sure there wasn't a sexier sound. Savous glanced at her, a brow raised, then heaved a melodramatic sigh. "Whatever you say, Krael."

Krael snorted and continued to glare as the younger man approached the tub. Humming to himself, Savous extended a hand over the water. Back to Krael, he cast a sly, sidelong glance at Suzana. She gasped when she saw steam begin to rise from the water.

"The red eyes," she said before she realized. "That means you're a sorcerer?"

His grin hiked up a notch. "It does."

"He's an *apprentice*," Krael corrected.

Savous rolled his eyes.

"Oh!" Recalling herself, she glanced at Krael. He was very carefully not looking at her. She smiled at Savous, manners drilled into her from her cradle coming naturally. "Um. Thank you, my lord."

Savous chuckled, walking to stand before her again. "I'm no one's lord, Suzana. We only have one, and that's the *rhaeja*. I --" He recaptured her hand. "-- am simply Savous."

"And he's leaving," Krael snarled.

At that, the younger man laughed outright. "And I am leaving." A kiss to her palm this time. "Farewell, lovely lady."

Krael hated Savous at that moment. It was simple. Radin's apprentice was simply too cocky! Obnoxious. Smart. Powerful. The youngest son of the *rhaeja*, he had mage blood from both his father as well as the *rhaeja*'s deceased truemate.

But that itself didn't piss off Krael. The fact that he had impressed Suzana did.

Krael glared at Savous as the younger man passed, receiving only a cheeky grin in return. Suzana, however, was more interested in the steaming water than in the retreating sorcerer. She stood by the tub, bending to put one finger tentatively into the water. The look of sheer delight that glowed on her rounded features punched at his heart. She was so tiny. The blanket she held closed just above her breasts trailed nearly two yards behind her and dipped enticingly low on her back. Her tousled black hair fell to her knees and glowed from the firelight behind her. Those cute, plump little lips were drawn into a delighted "O" and her eyes... He could drown in those eyes.

She looked up as he closed the door, shutting out anyone but the two of them. Those eyes speared him, first with attention, then slowly with interest. Ha! She enjoyed the sight of him more than Savous!

"Drop the blanket," he said.

Immediately, she let go. His cock kicked the inside of his trousers at the alacrity with which she followed his instructions. She kept her gaze on his face, devouring him whole as he stepped up to her, stopping two paces away.

"You *are* beautiful," he murmured, palms itching to cradle the luscious round breasts that almost seemed too big for her frame.

"Thank you, my lord," she responded, clearly pleased by his words.

"I'm not a lord," he felt compelled to explain. "As the whelp told you, we've only one lord, and that's the *rhaeja*. I've a number of men that I command, but I'm their captain, not their lord."

Her gaze dropped a moment, thinking, then returned to capture his eyes. In all sincerity, she responded, "But you're *my* lord."

His heart stopped. Of that he was sure. He stared into those violet pools that served for her eyes, and with that one statement he was willing to do anything for her. *Anything*.

He forced himself to calm. Forced a small smile rather than the foolish grin his mouth wanted to form. Unable to help himself, he reached out to brush a stray lock of hair from her face, his fingers lingering on her ear as he tucked the strands behind it. "Does it please you to call me 'lord'?"

She turned her face into his palm, tilting her head to rub

it like he'd seen jaguar cubs rub their mother. Pure affection. "It pleases me that you're my lord."

If he could, he'd purr. He trailed his fingers down the soft curve of her jaw to her rounded chin. "Then the taking of your virginity was a pleasant experience?"

"The most wonderful of my life, my lord."

Ah, yes, he had died and was in Rhae's bed!

He leaned in, carefully, slowly, and brushed her lips with his. She stayed absolutely still, only her lips pursing in a slight return of his kiss. Her tiny sigh thrilled him.

Torturing himself, he stepped back.

"My lord?" she asked, not moving.

He made no reply. He spun one of the chairs so that the back faced her. He straddled it, folding his arms over the back and leaning his chin on his hands. "Proceed with your bath."

Suzana licked her lips, imagining that she could taste him even though she knew it wasn't true. The kiss hadn't been enough. But she could smell him, all musky male and something else that was *raedjour*. And she felt the soft caress of his lips, of the loose hair that had fallen forward to lightly drape her shoulder as he leaned into her. And now he was across the room. Close, but entirely too far away!

"But, my lord…"

He raised a brow.

She glanced at the tub. It was inviting, but… "I thought we…"

He chuckled, leaning his strong chin on one palm. "Rest

assured, Suzana, I'm going to fuck you. I'm going to fuck you for a very long time." He nodded to the tub. "But first, I want to watch you bathe."

She colored at his language even as it thrilled her. Watch her? No one had ever watched her bathe except her nurse.

"Suzana."

She returned her gaze to him, and her knees nearly gave way at the intensity in his eyes. "I want to watch you bathe."

Slowly, she smiled. She understood. A sensual game. An arousing performance. *Oh, yes!*

He pointed to a side table. "The bottles to your right contain soaps and oils. Use the yellow bottle."

She took the two steps to the side table. An array of perhaps a dozen glass bottles was laid out. "May I ask why, my lord?" she asked, even as she picked up the bottle of shimmery yellow glass and unstoppered it. The strong scent of honeysuckle assailed her nostrils.

"It suits you."

She warmed. It was one of her favorites. She peeked over her shoulder at him, allowing her hair to partially obscure her view. In the past, she had seen other women use such looks, and they seemed to work on men. "Thank you." Judging by the way his eyes shuttered halfway, by the way one corner of his mouth quirked up, it seemed to work.

She picked up the bottle and a similarly scented bar of soap and returned to the tub. "May I ask a question, my lord?"

"You may."

"I was told the *raedjour* are unable to withstand sunlight," she said as she stepped into the tub. The water was deliciously hot, just the way she liked the start of a bath. "Where, then, did you get honeysuckle oil?"

"Caravans."

She grimaced, reminded of the slave wagon. "Are there many slave caravans that cross the mountains?"

"Enough. We get most of our information and goods from them. And they're not all slave caravans. There are others who brave the mountains."

"So some do pass?"

"Yes. Some."

She leaned back in the tub, tilting her head back and ducking quickly under the water to wet her hair. She emerged to find an enraptured expression on his face and wondered if he knew his lips were parted.

She asked a few more questions. Small, meaningless matters. She didn't want to touch on anything serious. She rather enjoyed the light chit-chat. It enabled her to concentrate on her performance.

And perform she did. She sat up straight in the tub because that kept her breasts visible. She made sure that her movements were languid, lathering the soap in her palms, then raising her arms to scrub it into her hair. Perhaps she *pushed* some of the foam off her head so that it trailed down her neck and dribbled over her breast. And, yes, it took a while to scrub her hair, and perhaps she lingered a bit overlong, but who could blame her when Krael so obviously enjoyed the sight? She rinsed her hair by again dipping back. Unfortunately, she couldn't see his reaction to that, but she hoped it was good.

"My turn to ask," he told her as she settled against the curved back of the tub to soap her skin.

She glanced up and smiled. "Ask me anything, my lord."

"Last night you mentioned a magical ability. You can affect others with your voice?"

"Yes, my lord."

"How is it you're not a mage?"

She shrugged. "It's actually a fairly common trait among my people. I've a higher ability than most others. But it's not a matter of spells. It's a matter of feeling."

"Do you have more ability because you're of noble birth?"

"Perhaps. One of my brothers also had the ability."

Do not think of them!

She stood, happy to distract him for a moment as she soaped and washed her hips and thighs. She sighed when she ran her soapy hand between her legs, risking a glance to see his eyes riveted on her hand.

She sat back down before he continued their conversation. "Do you play an instrument?"

"Yes. I had a lovely harp that was handed down from my grandmother. It's...gone."

"I know of someone who would love to fashion one for you. He doesn't get much call for instruments."

"No?"

"There are precious few *raedjour* with any talent for music. Or any desire to make it."

She frowned as she lay back. Her bathing was finished. The water was still nicely warm, and the fire at her back supplied more heat. She was lazily content. "How many *raedjour* are there?"

He shrugged. "Perhaps a thousand of us."

"So few?" Even the three other elven races she knew of had numbers in the thousands.

"You know our problem with procreation."

"Well, yes, but you do have women."

"Yes. And once you're truemated and turned, you'll only be fertile once every five or six cycles."

"Really?"

"Pregnancy itself lasts for two."

Two cycles pregnant?!

Krael stood, distracting her. Suddenly, she was no longer content. She wanted to lick him all over! He stopped at the foot of the tub. Took a moment to rake his gaze over her naked body, mostly hidden by the murky water. He extended his hands and she took them, allowing him to raise her to her feet. He stepped to the side and indicated, by his actions, that she should step from the tub. She did, onto a thick woven rug. He motioned for her to stay and retrieved one of two thick, long cloths Rhon had left. Unfolding it, he lifted it and laid it atop her head, gently rubbing. Oh! He was drying her! She bit her lip.

"Are you all right, Suzana?"

"Please call me Suza, my lord."

"Suza."

She trembled. "Yes. I'm wonderful, my lord."

The cloth drifted to her back, and warm lips pressed to

her forehead. "Yes, you are."

He used the cloth on her from head to toe, kneeling for the latter. He retrieved the bottle of oil. Kneeling before her again, he poured it into his big palm and, starting at her toes, rubbed the oil into her skin. She moaned, unable to help herself. He smiled, but didn't stop the wonderful massage. His hands traveled up one leg, then the other, skirting her drenched sex. Meeting her gaze, he slid his hands around her hips to her buttocks. Deliberately, he squeezed. She gasped, reaching forward to brace her hands on his shoulders. Still smiling, he kneaded her buttocks, a cheek in each of his big hands. Once the globes of her butt were oiled, he dipped his fingers between. Her jaw fell open in surprise as he delved the depths, rubbing oil in thoroughly. Eyes still glued to hers, he used one finger to tease her opening, dipping in marginally. An embarrassing squeak piped from her lips, but she forced herself to relax. His smile of approval and a brief kiss to her belly were her reward.

He pulled back to pour more oil into his palms, then proceeded to rub it into her belly and sides, reaching behind to reach her back. It was easy for him. He could probably wrap his arms around her twice without trying. Remaining on his knees, he took her right arm and oiled it from shoulder to fingertip, then did the same to the other. Pouring more oil, he started at her neck, then slid down to circle her breasts. Her nails dug into his shoulders as he toyed with her, skimming her skin with the lightest touch he could manage while still transferring the oil. He tested the weight of her breasts, supporting them with his hands, squeezing gently. She closed her eyes and moaned, unable to stand it. She was alive with need.

"Suza," he breathed, and she opened her eyes just in time to see him stick out his tongue and use it to lightly trace her nipple.

"Oh!" She arched her back to bring him closer.

He glared at her playfully, hands at her hips to push her back and keep her there. She moaned. "Please."

"Please?" He traced the other nipple.

"Oh, please, suck them."

He grinned. "Happily."

She gasped, arching again, as he took the nipple and half of her breast into his mouth and bit gently. Her feet shifted, her hands sliding over his skin. She was positively unable to keep still as he pulled back until only the hard peak of her nipple was in his mouth. Between his teeth. Mercilessly, he lashed her with his tongue.

He pulled her to him, allowing her to press her hips to his chest as he feasted on her other breast. He wrapped his arms around her waist, one big hand sliding up to grab a handful of her wet hair and yank it back. It arched her into him, kept her off balance, so that she only remained upright because of his support. Gladly, she gave over control to him, entirely willing to be his plaything.

He stood, lifting her easily. She floated in his arms across the room until he laid her gently on the bed. His hands on the inside of her thighs spread her wide, and she cried out when his mouth engulfed her sex. Her back bowed, and she eagerly reached forward to grab two fistfuls of his hair. Giving in to the urge, she drew the silky sheet up and over until it covered her to her neck.

Krael's heart swelled. Her taste was finer than any sweet he'd ever sampled, by far the most delicious cunt he'd ever lapped. Growling, he slid his fingers closer until he could sink both thumbs into her channel, pulling her open to further expose her sweetness to him. His hair covered them, but he paid it no heed, content to let her enjoy it while he plunged inside in further search for treasure. He tongued the sensitive spot just inside and had to hold tight as her hips bucked. Withdrawing his tongue, he twisted one thumb to put it against that spot, rubbing hard.

She came in a glorious gush of cream and a matching scream. Before she'd subsided, he sucked her clit into his mouth, still massaging her from inside with his thumb. She shuddered and writhed, pulling his hair. Not that he minded. He wanted her mindless, and the pain just added an extra edge to what he was feeling.

He took her to edge after edge until her body subsided. He licked at her clit, and she could only shudder and moan, her muscles remaining lax.

Grinning, he pulled back and stood, careful to let his hair linger and caress her as it fell away. Her fascination with it was not lost on him.

With effort, she turned her head and cracked open her eyes. A sheen of sweat had joined the oil on her skin, making her sparkle in the firelight.

Silently, he put his hands to the tie of his trousers and unlaced them. Using the bedpost for support, he bent to remove first one boot, then the other. Then he shucked the trousers. His aching cock sprang up, eager for her. She eyed it appreciatively.

Bending forward, he tucked his hands under her armpits and lifted. She easily slid farther up the bed, and her hips were a welcome cradle to his as he lowered himself atop her.

"Sleepy?" he asked, calmly brushing sweaty locks of hair from her face.

"No," she assured him, sliding her hands up his arms to his shoulders. Her legs wrapped around his waist.

"Are you certain?" he teased, tracing her lips with one finger. A finger that still smelled of her juices. "I wouldn't want to tire you."

She sucked his finger into her mouth and he groaned, watching the black digit penetrate her wet, pink lips. "Please," she said finally, without releasing his finger. "Please wear me out, my lord."

He laughed. Pulling his hand away, he brought it down to grasp his cock and place it at her entrance. He laughed again when she wiggled forcefully to impale herself on that first inch.

"Impatient, Suza?"

"For you, my lord. Yes!"

"Mmmm." Seated, he slid forward a bit, loving the way her breath stuttered and her eyes lost focus. "You want me to fuck you then?"

"Oh, yes."

He slid in some more. "Say it."

Her eyes flew open, her mouth as well. He took the opportunity to suck at that plump lower lip briefly. "Say it," he repeated.

"Fuck me," she said softly.

Another inch. "Mmm." He watched her lips. "Again."

"Fuck me," she said, bolder.

"Ah." He reached her limit, butting up against her womb.

She pushed up against him, her arms snug about his torso as far as she could reach. He hissed in a breath when her wet little mouth closed about his nipple and pulled. He braced himself above her, careful not to pull too far away and lose her mouth, then rolled his hips. She moaned against him and clung, eager to take as much of him as he could fit into her snug channel.

He pounded until she shattered around him, taking him into oblivion with her.

She dropped to the bed with a little sob. He remained braced above her, breathing hard. "Are you all right?"

She nodded, unable to open her eyes. Her small smile reassured him. "I believe you have worn me out, my lord."

Teasing? He chuckled, dropping to her side, then scooping her small body into the curve of his. "Sleep then, vixen."

She giggled tiredly. Within moments, she was asleep. Surprisingly, he was not far behind.

Chapter Ten

"A mage's love to save the *rhaeja*."

Krael looked up at Savous. The younger man shrugged. "That's what he said when he emerged. I wrote it myself."

Krael switched his gaze to Nalfien, who stared thoughtfully into the fireplace. "What does it mean?"

The men again sat in Nalfien's study, but they had yet to discuss Suzana's sexuality. The subject hadn't drifted from Valanth's request to have her.

Nalfien shook his head. "Likely, exactly what it states."

"But he doesn't need saving."

"Doesn't he?"

"No. Save him from what?"

"Himself?"

"Speak sense, old man."

"He is speaking sense." This from Radin, who stood in the corner, toying with his belt knife. "Valanth very likely knows that he's sick. He killed those women."

"Radin," Nalfien warned.

"No, Nalfien, let's be blunt. He killed those women. There is no denying it, no matter how hard we try. The question is, why? And how? Rhae may have let him escape with one accidental death, but they can't *all* have been accidental." His voice was low and the walls were solid stone, but each man in the room tensed just the same. Radin's words could easily get him killed.

"You're saying that Rhae's looking for a mage to put his head right?" Krael asked.

"Maybe."

Both men looked to Nalfien, who now studied Radin. "Perhaps."

"But he's already had a truemate. That's ridiculous!"

Neither sorcerer answered. Savous, when Krael looked to him, only shrugged. Krael sat back, pounding the thick table with his fist. "It's not Suza."

"I agree." Nalfien turned to face the table, calmly folding his hands before him. "But my belief is not what will save her."

"If he takes her, he'll ruin her."

Nalfien watched Krael closely. "Yes."

Krael snarled, shoving from the table. "I will *not* let that happen."

"Tell me, why --"

Nalfien stopped at a knock at the door. He glanced at Savous, who instantly rose to answer it.

All four men stood and froze. Valanth himself strode in blithely and stood at the end of the table. He actually wore robes, the voluminous white silks settling softly about his body. He was accompanied by only two bodyguards.

Thankfully, he had left Tishna, his latest mindless plaything, behind.

"Krael. I have something for you." He held out his hand. The robe's sleeve fell back to reveal what he offered. A whip.

Krael extended his own hand and accepted the slap of the whip's handle into it. "Thank you, *rhaeja*."

Valanth's eyes danced as he smiled into Krael's face. "You're to use it on her."

"*Rhaeja?*"

"Use it on the virgin. She's to be used to it by the time she comes to me."

Krael could only stare at Valanth, unwilling to put words to the thoughts careening through his mind.

"Don't disappoint me, Captain." With that, he turned on his heel and led his bodyguards away.

Krael stared at the whip in his hand. Memories flooded his mind of the many times he had trained women to the whip. The weapon was his specialty, and the use of it in sexual play his forte, as well. It was another oddity that it had not yet occurred to him to introduce Suzana to that particular aspect of sex. Not during her first nine days.

Savous cursed softly. "Krael, you can't..."

Krael lifted his gaze to meet the eyes of the youth who might someday be *rhaeja*. "It's what the *rhaeja* commands."

Savous threw furious glances at both Radin and Nalfien, but neither sorcerer had words.

"Are we done?" Krael asked softly.

"Yes."

Savous caught him by the arm as he went by. "You *can't!*"

Krael shrugged him off and left the room.

He pictured Suzana's lovely, creamy skin striped by marks. *His* marks. Her succulent round buttocks would dance becomingly as he struck her. The thought inflamed him.

But, no. He couldn't. Not yet. First she had to know and appreciate sex without pain before she could truly enjoy whipping. *If* she could ever enjoy it. Krael was well aware that not all women could stand it.

But neither could he directly defy Valanth. The *rhaeja* was owed absolute loyalty as Rhae's chosen. There were rules to *raedjour* society, in place for a reason. To keep the race of all men in line. The two primary rules were that you never jeopardized a truematch and you always obeyed the *rhaeja*.

He compromised, stopping by his personal rooms to pick up a necessary object before returning to the rooms he shared with Suzana.

He entered the outer room of the suite and placed Valanth's whip on a chest. He had seven days more to enjoy her company. He had time to prepare her for Valanth's request. Then he strode to the bedchamber door and opened it.

And froze.

The thick wood had obscured the sound, but now he heard it perfectly. Suzana's beyond-lovely voice traced the air, accompanied by the harp she cradled in her lap as she fingered it. Rhon and two other boys stood transfixed just within.

He was just in time to hear the last of the song. Suzana trailed off, her fingers causing a twining ring of music to disperse in the air. The boys clapped appreciatively. Suzana smiled, then turned her face to him. It was then the boys noticed his presence. Together, they bowed their heads and vacated the room.

Krael stood transfixed, hardly noticing their absence. The music he'd heard coming from this woman astounded him. He could not believe she was real. Nor could he quite believe she smiled so beatifically at him!

Her gaze trailed down his body, and her smile died at seeing the flogger dangling from his hand. Anxious, she returned her gaze to his face. "Have I displeased you, my lord?"

He glanced at the pleasure-weapon. Unlike Valanth's whip, this was meant for sexual play alone. Loose leather straps fell like a tail from the handle he held in his grasp. A few of the strands were knotted at the end. He slapped it smartly against his shin. "No."

Carefully, she set her harp on the floor beside the bed. She stared at the flogger the entire time. He lifted it, slid the loose black straps through his hand. As he approached, he gripped the ends, snapping the flogger taut before him, displaying it for her. She held rock still, her eyes trained on the leather in his hands. He stopped before her, extended the weapon out and over her too-still body. Slowly, he dragged it up her back until he could wind it around her neck. She shivered as he bent, using the flogger to draw her close for a kiss.

Carefully, he monitored her response. Fright. Uncertainty. Desire! Yes! She was afraid he would hurt her, but if he didn't -- or if he did it just right -- she was game.

He touched his mouth to hers, lips slightly parted. She waited, trembling, but he did no more. Finally, she needed the contact. She leaned forward that little bit to seal them in a kiss. He responded languidly, parting his lips, caressing hers. Waiting. After a moment, she whimpered, and he felt her hands grip his arms as she pressed her lips tighter to his. Still he teased, until finally he felt her tongue tentatively foray between his lips. He opened further, luring her in. Flicked her tongue with the tip of his. With an impatient little moan, she thrust her tongue further. Humming softly, he suckled it, toying with her as she grew bolder.

Ever so slowly, he released the loose ends of the flogger, letting them trail down her naked back. She stiffened, but didn't stop their kiss. He pressed forward, forcing her to fall back into the pillows. Kneeling, he straddled her hips. He played the flogger over her body, letting the supple leather caress her naked skin.

"There are people who find pleasure in being whipped." She stiffened again, eyes wide. "And there are people who find pleasure in whipping others."

She licked her lips, stammered once. "I-is that what you enjoy, my lord?"

"Which?"

"Either."

He smiled, nudging the underside of her breast with the end of the handle. "I've enjoyed whipping others."

She swallowed. "I-is that what you --" She hissed when

he rubbed her erect nipple with the handle. "-- wish to do to me, my lord?"

The smile drained. He let her see the heat of his gaze. "Yes."

The surge of her arousal nearly made him groan. Vastly trusting, her body went limp, her eyes trained on his. "I'm yours, my lord. Do with me what you will."

His nostrils flared. "And if it hurts?"

"If it pleases you, my lord, it pleases me."

He heard the growl before he realized it came from deep within his chest. Her trembling response made it worse. He threw back his head, breathing deeply of her intoxicating scent. She *was* turned on.

Slowly, he lowered his head and edged back, straddling her calves, so he could trail the flogger down her body until the straps trailed over her thighs and groin. Her breath caught when he nudged the edge of the handle between her thighs, grazing it through her drenched pussy. His smile returned. "Bend your knees." She did, eyes closed. "Watch, Suza."

She dragged open her eyes. Her heart still pounded in fear. She wanted to believe that he wasn't going to hurt her, but that weapon! She glanced down. In the sparse lighting, the black leather almost seemed an extension of his arm. She groaned when he seated the handle more firmly in her pussy and used it to rub her sensitive skin. Gods, that felt good!

He took her hand and closed it around the handle. "Pleasure yourself."

Another groan, but she did. Just as he had, she used the leather-wrapped wood to press against her aching center.

When he was satisfied that she was obeying, he stepped back off the bed. A toss of his head sent his cascade of hair flying behind him and a clutch of warmth to Suzana's belly. Leisurely, he removed what there was of his clothing. Eyeing his cock, Suzana unwittingly pushed the handle a bit deeper and shallowly penetrated herself. Her groan was unstoppable.

"That's it." He took his cock in his hand, eyes trained on her pussy. "Make yourself come."

She squeaked. "Myself...?"

"Yes."

Her eyes dropped hungrily to his cock. "But..."

"Make yourself come first." He continued to stroke himself, that maddening smile on his too-handsome face.

The flogger was such a wonderful black. If she squinted, it almost looked like his cock. It was certainly hard enough, although the leather did not quite have the same feel as him. *Oh, yes!* She watched him watching her, imagined the flogger's handle as his cock. Her pussy swelled and wept. Her hips began to rock. Something coiled just below her belly, aching, wanting, almost... It snapped and she howled her release, furiously rubbing her pulsing cunt with the flogger.

"Very nice," he said when she subsided.

She licked her lips. Yes, it had been. But now she knew what would be even nicer. "Please, my lord."

The left side of his mouth hiked up in a grin. "Please?"

"Please fuck me."

"You learn fast."

She beamed.

"Roll over. Get on your hands and knees."

She didn't ask why. In two days, Krael had shown her nothing but pleasure, even with the whip. She had no reason to doubt him.

"Turn around. Ass facing me."

She laughed and complied.

"What's funny?"

"I -- oh!" His big hands slid over her ass, squeezing her cheeks like ripe melons. "I was laughing at myself for feeling embarrassed."

"Ah." His thumbs trailed down the crack of her ass, delving deep. "You're not embarrassed?"

"I am. But it's silly to be."

His fingers slid around until two of them slipped into her channel. She moaned. "Yes," he agreed, pumping slowly. Once. "It is." Twice. "Silly."

She couldn't agree more, but lost her voice for the words. Her back arched at the sheer ecstasy of having any part of his body penetrating her.

He adjusted, and the fingers left her channel. She groaned at the loss, only to gasp and flinch when his palm cracked against her ass. She froze, staring at the blankets before her. The same hand smoothed over the sting. She had just relaxed when he slapped the other side.

"Ask why."

"Why?"

She squealed when he landed heavily atop her, shoving

her into the blankets. "Because your pleasure is mine to give."

Smothered by his body, Suzana tried to squirm. She gasped when he dug the fingers of one hand into her hair and yanked her head back. Lips brushed her cheek. All at once, Suzana's body tightened and trembled. "My lord!" she moaned.

"Yes," he hissed, pushing back. "Back on your knees."

She scrambled to comply, crying out when he spanked her again. Not stopping. Not until her backside was aflame. Then, with a harsh cry of his own, he slammed his cock deep into her dripping depths. She screamed, the pleasure-pain far too intense to contain. Instantly her body convulsed, her mouth gaping as she struggled to gulp breath as he filled her. This position put a whole new meaning to deep! She fell to her elbows, pressing her forehead against the blankets as she adjusted to the impossible fill of his invasion.

"Gods!" she gasped, clutching and panting. "Lir, yes. More, please!" It hurt, but oh, what a hurt! "Yes!"

He pulled out, then thrust hard back in. She couldn't stay still. Her hips canted to the side, finding a delicious angle where he rubbed her in another new spot. The next time he shoved forward, she threw her hips back at him. They both gasped as she managed to take just a little bit more of him.

"Fuck," he muttered, pressing his forehead to her spine. She shoved back again, and he growled, catching her hips. "Stop moving. I'll come."

"Yes!" she cried, pushing back again.

"Goddess!" He reared back, and she chanced a glance

over her shoulder, just to watch that hair slide behind him, his eyes closed, his face tight in concentration. He caught a firm grip of her hips and set the motion, almost fucking himself using her body. And she was a more than willing tool. She spread her thighs and pushed back, furiously matching his rhythm.

She spiked with a scream, and he growled, fucking her through her convulsions so that the orgasm never *quite* ended. She cried and clutched and moaned, quite sure she was in agony but feeling nothing but ecstasy!

When she could almost take no more, he came, filling her with wet warmth.

He wasn't finished. Propelling her forward with a push, he fell atop her. Eagerly, he pushed her long hair aside to devour the sensitive skin at her neck. She shuddered, the wash of pleasure a surprise after such a great release. He lapped and nipped at every inch of her back, down to the cheeks of her ass. She wiggled when he bit her there, groaned when he slapped her.

Why did that feel good?

She buried her face in the pillow. Yelped when he fell heavily beside her and flipped her body so that she was cradled in the curve of his. He tucked her top thigh onto his hip, spreading her, then guided his cock back inside her. Again he drove her until she sobbed with release.

He lay back a moment to catch his breath, then rose to retrieve water and cloths to wipe her clean. Her smile, though tired, hurt her mouth it was so wide.

When he finally crawled onto the blankets beside her, she snuggled against his side. Her cheek pressed to the hard muscle of his chest, her shoulder tucked neatly under his arm. Her breasts pressed against him and her leg thrown over his, she'd never felt more at peace. More at home.

"I love you," she murmured as sleep took her.

Chapter Eleven

The door opened. Suzana muttered in her sleep but remained snugly tucked against Krael's side.

Rhon dipped his head through the doorway. "Nalfien sent for you, Captain."

"Tell him not today," Krael muttered, sliding his hands through Suzana's hair, which lay in thick curls across his chest and belly. The shining black nearly disappeared against his skin.

"But..."

"Tell him not today. He can come after me if he dares."

"Yes, Captain."

Krael sucked in a breath and let it out slowly as he rubbed his cheek against the top of her head. Why bother? Valanth wanted Suzana. He would have her. Krael's time with her was precious. Why should he waste it with the sorcerers?

"I love you."

She'd said the words. Why? She could not be in love with him! It didn't happen that way. Besides, what did he need with a truemate? He had never felt a particular need to breed and had always enjoyed many women. Why would he want one teeny little one?

She sighed, rubbing her cheek against his chest. Her breath lightly caressed his nipple. The damned thing hardened just from that! As for his cock? Unless he'd just pulled it out of her -- and not always then -- it had been constantly hard the last few days.

He felt her smile against his skin. Watched her hand extend from its adorable curl on his sternum to flatten against his ribs. Delicately, she traced his muscles, finding a few old scars that were barely noticeable unless seen up close.

"Do you say 'good morning' here, my lord?" she asked, the sleepy rasp to her voice yanking at his lower spine.

"Not generally, no."

Her hand trailed down his belly. "How do you greet someone when you wake?"

His cock jumped when she extended one elegant finger to trace the very tip. "If we wake in bed with someone, usually we fuck."

She raised her head, shocked. "No!"

He smiled. "That's what we were created for."

"But...*every* morning? What if you're ill? Or out of sorts? Or...?"

He reached for the hair behind her ear. Used it to pull her face toward his. "Then greetings are rarely in order."

He kissed her, amused when her attention wandered from her question to their tongue-tangle.

She protested when he pulled away. Dragging her eyes open, her heart leapt to see the wicked amusement in his clear blue eyes.

"Next lesson."

She blinked. *Oh!*

Quite easily, he pushed her neck and shoulders, nudging her down his body until she was face-to-cock. It was so big! How in the wide ocean did she fit *that* inside her body?!

He released her hair and, while she stared, positioned a pillow behind his shoulders to prop him up. "Suck it."

She turned wide eyes on him. "Suck it?"

His half-lidded eyes burned. "Yes. Lick your lips, then take as much as you can into your mouth."

Unsure, she did as he commanded. She had to get up on her hands and knees, her head bent over his lap. She took the long column of hard muscle into both hands, barely able to span the width. Expanding her lips wide, she slid the head into her mouth.

"Mmmm," she hummed, finding his taste delicious. The width of him was difficult to manage, but the natural oil that seeped from his skin proved to be quite spicy.

He groaned, and she chanced a quick glance up to find his eyes shut, head dipped back. What a sight! The wide, long landscape of his belly and chest shone in the firelight. That glorious hair framed his face, fanning out to cover quite a bit of the bed to either side of him. The design on his face glinted alive in the flickering light.

She drew him out and lapped at the pleasing taste just under the plum head. He bucked, breath catching.

Experimentally, she did it again, delighted when he squirmed, clutching the blankets beside them. Oh, what fun! Wetting her tongue, she traced the entire head, squeezing the shaft with her hands.

"Yes." His hands found hers to show her how to squeeze. How to slide up and down. When and where to apply pressure. She learned her lesson, all the while keeping the tip of his cock wet with her tongue.

"Goddess! Suza, suck it. Suck it hard!"

She obeyed, her cheeks caving in. She gagged when he abruptly thrust up, but recovered quickly. She used her hands, realizing that she needed to make a pussy of her hands and mouth to give him full enjoyment.

Nine torments of Rhae! How could one little innocent drive him wild like this? She barely knew what to do, but the touch of her hands and the feel of her tiny little mouth, those teeth scraping his sensitive skin as she struggled to get as much of him into as possible... Sweet mother of night, he was lost!

"Suza, stop!"

She didn't listen. He had to lean forward and yank her head up with one hand, using the other atop her fingers to pump his seed from his cock. She watched, bewildered, her tongue caught between her teeth, and he came harder just at that sight. Roughly, he yanked that gorgeous mouth to his, fucking it with his tongue the way he'd just fucked it with his cock. Until he was drained. And drenched.

Groaning, he fell back in the pillows, needing a moment.

On her knees beside him, Suzana surveyed his body.

Then, quietly, she got up and went to the privy. This time it was she who returned with bowl and water to wipe him clean. If he was any judge, she took great delight in wiping him down. He made a mental note to let her bathe him. Oh, yes, she'd love to wash his hair.

After returning the bowl and cloth, she climbed onto the bed and onto his body. He enfolded her in his arms as she spread herself across his chest, her head tucked beneath his chin. For long moments, they lay quiet -- she toying with a lock of his hair, he stroking her hair and back.

Bliss.

"I love you, Krael."

He stiffened. Suzana held her breath. He'd heard her words. She knew it. "My lord…"

"Shhhh, Suzana."

She shook her head, pushing up to brace on her arms above him. It wasn't easy to span his width, but she managed. She met his blue-eyed gaze straight on, wanting no mistake. "I love you."

One black lip lifted in a snarl. Her heart stopped. Abruptly, he lifted her away and left the bed.

"My lord…"

"Suzana, you can't love me."

She sat on the bed, watching him pace before her. "But I do."

"No!" He stopped, the wave of his hair swishing forward before settling about his naked body. Oh, what a body?! She wanted to run her hands over that beautiful expanse rather than argue, but the words must be said. "You don't. It's infatuation, nothing more."

She frowned, then carefully erased it from her face. "I'm not a child, my lord. I've been infatuated. I know the difference."

"No. You don't. Humans can't help but want us. It's part of what we are. Part of what Rhae made us. You might have strong feelings for me now. But I'm the first one you've been with. There will be others."

Panic burbled in her chest, but she struggled to suppress it. "No."

"Yes."

"I don't *want* anyone else."

He shrugged, holding himself very still. "Now, perhaps."

"Never!"

He snarled, pacing away from her. "We have nine days together. That's it. If you're not pregnant by then, you'll go to another."

"What if I *am* pregnant?" She touched a tentative hand to her belly.

He blew a blast of air through his lips, an exasperated sound. "Suzana, I told you. It doesn't happen all at once. It takes time for the sorcerers to find the right match for you."

What was that flash of emotion she saw pass over his stern features? No matter. As fast as she saw it, it was gone, lost as he turned his head and that wonderful fall of hair obscured his face.

She tried a new tactic. "Does this mean that you don't love me?"

He spared her an angry glance before retrieving a cup from the side table. "Didn't anyone explain truebonding to you?" He opened a bottle of wine and poured.

He didn't say no. She took heart in that. "Yes, my lord."

"Then you know that we can't be."

"Why can't you be my truemate?" She knew she was repeating herself, knew she was making him angry, but she struggled to find the truth. She *knew* they were destined to be together.

He shook his head, downing his drink. "It doesn't happen the first time."

"Why not?"

"It never has."

She ignored the cold thrill that threatened her heart. "Never?"

"Not that I know of." Pacing again. The sweet, round mounds of his bottom peeking through the silver white of his hair, his cock swinging before him, both thoroughly distracting her.

"*Can't* it happen the first time?"

"No."

She frowned again. He didn't sound sure. But she hesitated to press him.

She felt the tears coming. There was nothing to do to stop them, though she tried. There was a very real possibility that she would be separated from Krael. When she *knew* he was her match. Her truemate. Her people didn't share the label, but she knew the concept. She had seen soul-mating within her own family, between her own parents. She knew love could and did happen instantly. Why couldn't Krael believe her?

Staring at her knees, she gave up the fight and let the tears rain down her cheeks, dripping onto her breasts.

"Suza." His voice was stern. She didn't look up. Couldn't bear the sight.

When his gleaming dark thighs came into view, the tears came harder. His hand caught her shoulders, and she went limply into his embrace.

"Don't cry."

That prompted the sobs. Miserable, she wrapped her arms as far as she could about his brawny torso, buried her face against his neck.

"I only want you."

"Now. I'm the only one you've known."

"I don't need a comparison to know!"

He grunted, sitting back in the pillows.

She sniffed. He grabbed up a corner of one blanket, and she used it to wipe her eyes and nose, carefully balling it up and tossing it to the side. She remained within his embrace, at home like she'd never been before.

She pressed her lips just above his nipple. *I love you*, she thought. Swiping her tongue over his nipple, she thrilled at the way his body jerked. *I* do *love you*, she insisted silently, closing her lips about the hard little nub and sucking. His hands bunched in her hair, one of them trailing down to cup her buttocks. Her own hair was silk against her back, but it wasn't the silk she wanted to feel. She pulled back to readjust until she was straddling him. As he slouched, her pussy was pressed to the hard ridges on his abdomen. She shoved her hands in the hair to either side of his face and pulled him into a kiss.

He was *hers!* She'd never felt so possessive about anything before, but this she knew.

"Fuck me. Please!" she begged, lips still pressed to his, sharing his breath. "Take me, any way you want me."

"Mmm," he rumbled, the vibrations tantalizing her pussy. "You fuck me."

Her attack had lowered him in the pillows until he lay near prone. His cock lightly tapped her ass. Eagerly, she wiggled back until the head prodded her dripping opening. She lowered her hand to position him, then abruptly slammed her whole body back to impale herself.

He hissed, fingers digging into her hips. "Yes!" she shouted, clutching her hands on his chest, scratching him. She lifted, then dropped, crying out when his length bumped her womb, but she loved it! Wild, she writhed atop him.

When it came, her climax clenched her entire body, so violent that it took Krael by surprise and wrenched away his control. Her quivering body sucked him dry, then continued to clutch him inside.

Chapter Twelve

Suzana plucked the harp lightly, producing a sweet, haunting lullaby that she accompanied with loving words. The ballad was a favorite among her people, a traditional song sung by a maid to her true love.

Suzana's true love lay back among the pillows of their bed, his eyes closed and big hands folded sedately over his muscled abdomen. His lush white hair spanned the bed about him, a silken blanket among the other blankets. Suzana watched him carefully, waiting to see if he recognized the intent of her words. She'd consciously chosen the commonspeak version of the ballad to sing, wanting him to hear the love in her voice.

She used only a touch of her empathetic powers, just letting them flow lightly over him. Calm him. Warm his blood a touch. Judging by the calm look on his face and the half-erect state of his cock, she decided she was doing well.

The words of the ballad ended, followed soon by the last few strains of the music. She remained still at her corner of the bed, watching him intently.

His eyelids lifted halfway. "Did you place a spell on me?"

he asked calmly.

"No, my lord."

He quirked a snowy brow. She lowered her gaze a bit. "It's not really a spell, my lord. I only sought to calm you."

"Was I not calm?" His voice was far too sedate for her liking.

She swallowed. "I'm sorry, my lord."

"What have you to be sorry about?"

She raised her gaze to his, heart rate kicking up a notch. What was he thinking? "I…"

He tilted his head to the side. "You weren't trying to make me love you?"

A lump clogged her throat. It took two tries to swallow it away so she could speak. "I would not do that, my lord. I *can*not. It's not in my power." She met his gaze full-on and said bravely, "Though I wish that I could."

His face fell, and for one brief second she thought she saw pain. But then the calm mask was back.

She watched silently as he rose from the bed. He crossed the room to one of the tables. Her heart leapt to her throat when she saw him pick up the whip. Not the flogger, the whip.

He turned, his blue eyes smoldering. "Get up."

"My lord, please. I didn't…"

"Get up."

She scrambled to obey. After carefully setting her harp on the floor, she planted her feet on the rug beside the bed, pressing her back against one of the solid posts at the corner of the mattress. Krael tossed the whip on the blankets, then stood before her. His cock now stood at attention, but he ignored it.

"Turn around."

She did.

"Gather your hair in front of you."

Hastily, she reached back to pull all of her nearly knee-length hair over one shoulder so that it draped before her.

"Put your arms up and grasp the pole."

She obeyed, trembling. He stepped into, pressing that cock against her back as he reached up to tie her hands to the post. He must have picked up the leather strap when he picked up the whip. Shaking, she pressed her forehead to the post as he stepped away. Out of the corner of her eye, she saw him take the whip from its nest among the blankets.

She jumped when he nudged the small of her back. As he dragged up, she realized it was the first part of the whip, the stiff piece just off the handle, with which he caressed her skin. The leather smoothed up her spine, over her bare shoulder. He stepped in and pushed it under her chin, using the taut curve to lift her chin and turn her head up and back so she could see him.

"I can't have you, Suzana," he said, voice flat, at odds with the fire in his eyes. "Know that. Not forever and not for my own. Not if you don't carry my child."

When she opened her mouth to protest, he shoved the whip at her, just enough to close her jaw. Some of the fire leaked from his eyes, causing his brow to furrow slightly and his nostrils to flare.

"I don't want you to hope for something that can't

happen."

Tears welled in her eyes, and he used his free thumb to smear them away.

"The *rhaeja* himself has declared that he will be your next lover. And what the *rhaeja* wants, the *rhaeja* usually gets."

Was that it, then? Was that why he denied even the possibility that they could be truemates? Because Rhae's chosen had declared he wanted her?

"The *rhaeja* enjoys pain, Suzana," he said in that dark molasses voice. The whip left her chin to slide back down her back. "As do I. I've prepared many women for him." He leaned in toward her ear. "I like it."

Despite her distress, she squirmed. The whip, like the flogger, began to seem like an extension of his hand. Another part of him to touch her with.

She gasped when he nipped at the bare side of her neck. "I want to watch you dance." His free hand closed over one cheek of her bottom, squeezing. "I want to mark your ass and your back. My marks!"

She cried out at the vehemence in his voice, still so close to her ear. That hand slid between her thighs from behind, finding her wet center.

"I'm going to mark you, Suzana." Her pussy clenched around his invading fingers. "I'm going to mark you, and I'm going to fuck you, and I'm going to *make* you my own, if only for a time."

She cried out, completely in agreement with all but the last of his statement. She pushed against his fingers, struggling against the strap that bound her to the bed.

He took her mouth, shoving a harsh tongue into her willing mouth as he drove his fingers deep into her channel. She writhed, aching to get more of him, frustrated that she couldn't.

Then he was gone, her ragged cry following him. She heard the swish of the whip. Knew what it meant. Knew it would hurt. Why did that make her hotter?!

"Scream, Suzana." The whip cracked, not on her flesh but in the air somewhere behind her. "I want to hear you scream."

Thwack!

She screamed. Even before the burning pain blossomed on her right buttock. She screamed for him. At him. Anything for him.

"Yes!" *Shtack!*

Another scream. *Lir, that hurt!* She pressed the bedpost between her breasts, wrapping her arms as best she could around the sturdy post. Using it as a lifeline as her world centered on the exploding pain in her back.

In rapid succession, the whip laid into her back and buttocks. Tears streamed down her face, into her screaming mouth. She danced like he'd said she would, unable to remain still. She writhed for him, knowing he watched. She took every lash, absorbing the pain as best she could as she gloried that he branded her as his very own.

His own! Even through the pain, the very thought flushed her sex.

The *swish-crack* stopped. Suzana clutched the bedpost, sobbing. Her back and buttocks were one solid flame.

Strong hands quickly released the thong securing her hands, but she continued to clutch the post. Her death grip was all that kept her from melting into a puddle of agony on the rug. The same hands picked her up bodily, forcing her to release the post. She fell face-first into the blankets, her legs dangling over the edge of the bed. She screamed when Krael covered her with his body, pressing his chest into the burn on her back, his belly crushing her buttocks.

"Mine!" She heard him even though he growled.

"Yours," she cried, alive with the need for him to take her, to complete the possession. Her very womb wept for him.

Her legs parted and he shoved home. She shrieked, unable to distinguish between the white-hot flames searing her back and the succulent torch of his cock sliding into the clutching depth of her body.

"Krael!" she screamed, slamming back into him with all her might.

He shoved hard, his huge cock stretching her, the hurt from within blending with the hurt from without until she couldn't tell pain from pleasure, agony from ecstasy. Her orgasm exploded as fiery magma, bursting from her soul to ooze icy hot from every last inch of her.

Krael was seconds behind her, clutching her tight as he filled her to overflowing with wave after wave of liquid love.

She blinked to semi-consciousness as he held her, the oil from his chest smeared into the welts on her back. "I love you, Suzana," he murmured.

Chapter Thirteen

"It doesn't matter."

"Why?"

Suzana lay on her belly, her cheek nestled in a soft pillow. Krael sat beside her, within her sight, tenderly rubbing salve into the welts on her back.

She didn't question the whipping. After it was done, she'd known somehow that it was necessary. For him. To truly have her, he had to mark her. It was a sign of ownership. She would gladly endure it again if and when he felt the need. She was astounded to have actually *enjoyed* it on some level. And the warmth in his eyes kindled a spreading warmth that tingled throughout her body.

But that was not her question. "I don't understand. Doesn't love mean you are truemates?"

His beautiful eyes watched his hand on her back. The other hand lay on his thigh, holding a small bowl of the salve that smelled of eucalyptus.

"Usually. But not always."

"No?"

He shook his head. "I've seen truemated couples who aren't in love."

"How awful."

He shrugged. "They learn to cope. Most times they develop a relationship with others, either separately or together."

"What does that mean?"

He smiled. "She may find another man to be with during the times she's not in heat. Or she may find a woman."

"A woman?"

That produced a chuckle. "Have you never heard of such a relationship?"

In truth, she had, but she had never witnessed it. She didn't quite believe that such a thing could last. After all, what did they do? Now that she knew sex, she couldn't imagine it not involving a man and his cock.

Her eyes drifted to Krael's cock, watching it nudge slightly as he moved, loving how it seemed to snuggle up against his balls.

She shut her eyes as the urge to cry tried to take her. "I can't live without you, Krael."

He sighed softly. Leaning forward, he placed the salve on the table beside the bed. He remained seated beside her, seemingly unable to take his eyes from the marks on her back. She watched him, and her heart swelled. The love, the possessiveness, was now easy to read, even in his stern face.

Slowly, she drew to her knees. He watched, bemused, as she crawled before him. His hands readily aided her when she eased herself onto his lap, straddling him. She winced when his hands squeezed the marks on her buttocks as he snuggled her against him. She wrapped her arms about his neck, digging her fingers into the hair at the nape of his neck.

"I don't want anyone but you."

"I don't want to give you up," he admitted, voice low.

"Truly?"

"Truly."

"Kill me."

He stiffened. "*What?*"

"I won't live in some other man's embrace. I won't be truemated to a man who doesn't hold my heart."

"Suza…"

"Kill me."

"And if you're pregnant?"

He admitted the possibility! She swallowed. "After the test. If I'm not pregnant, kill me."

He scowled, the content of their conversation truly hitting him. "You're talking insanity."

"No, my lord. I am yours. I know this with every part of my being. My heart and body are yours to use or abuse as you will. I cannot be with another. Especially the *rhaeja*. I do not wish to become like that woman who was with him the night of the contest."

Krael's eyes widened slightly. Did he think she hadn't noticed? Did he think her too stupid to put two and two together?

"And I will not be handed to man after man when I know I am yours."

Krael stared in horrified fascination at the woman curled in his lap. She was absolutely serious, of that he had no doubt. Utter conviction shone in those violet eyes. There were no tears. No protestations. He had been the subject of desire before, had lived through the wiles of women who wailed and moaned to get their way. This was not the case with Suzana. Dry-eyed, she simply asked him to end her life if she could not be his.

And damned if a large piece of his soul didn't sing for it! Yes! She was right. If she couldn't be his, she would be no one's.

She leaned in to kiss the hard muscle just above his nipple. Pressed her lips there to taste the pounding of his heart. "I love you, my one and only lord." He shuddered.

He smoothed his hand in her hair, holding her face to his chest. "And I love you," he murmured, astounded by how easily the words spilled from his lips.

"Then, if I can't be yours, kill me."

His snarl returned. Gripping her hair, he snapped her head back to meet her shining gaze. "Because I love you, you ask me to take your life?"

"Among my people, it's a matter of honor. A man's love is his own. He would never allow her to be sullied by another man."

"So he would kill her?"

"Yes."

He grimaced. "Your people sound overdramatic and suicidal."

Hurt, she tried to push back from him, pulled up short when he refused to relinquish his hold on her hair. "Love is sacred," she said, voice laced with anger she had not yet shown him. On her, it looked odd. Out of place. "Without it, life has no meaning. I've had everything ripped away from me. My home, my family, my freedom. Now you've taken my heart. If you deny me, if I'm not yours, I *have* nothing to live for."

He caught her up against him despite her struggles to escape. He dug his hands into her buttocks, purposely reminding her of his marks. She subsided, sullen. "Shhh. I insulted your people. For that, I'm sorry."

"Only for that?" she muttered against his chest.

"Suzana, you can't ask me to kill you. It's not our way."

"Is it your way to pass me to a man who will make me into a blank-eyed sex slave?"

He pulled back, shocked. She speared him with her gaze.

"It's true, isn't it? He did that to her."

He could only frown. Certainly he couldn't deny it.

"Could you give me over to him? To that? My lord?"

Staring into her beautiful round face, he saw the truth of her words. What kind of man would he be if he handed her into that?

Slowly, he nodded. "No. I can't. I won't." He pulled her against his chest again, and this time she didn't resist. "I won't let you go, Suzana. Even if you're not mine, I'll kill you before I see you taken away from me."

Chapter Fourteen

Suzana lay within the warm, tiny world created by the bed beneath her and the man above her. Krael's whole body surrounded her, his thighs folded beneath hers, his elbows braced to either side of her. His hair completely shrouded them from anything outside their two joined bodies. Slowly, his hips rolled back and forth, tunneling his cock deep within her, then withdrawing slowly so she could feel every ridge and bump on the way out. His hands supported her shoulders, wrapped around them from beneath to brace her. She pressed her forehead to his chest, breathing heavily around the pain in her heart.

Even as her body climbed toward climax, a part of her counted every passing moment. It was day nine, and sometime soon they would come to test her. Sometime soon, they might try to take her away from Krael.

She could not let that happen. She had decided days ago, not long after his heartfelt promise to her, that she would devise a way to take her own life. Just in case he failed her. She wasn't stupid. She knew he might balk. Even among her own people, where such practice was accepted, it was often difficult for the loved one to complete the actual act. She had yet to decide between hanging herself with one of the thick cords that tied back the curtains on the window, or throwing herself headfirst from the same window. But she was sure either one would do.

"Suza," Krael groaned, his lips pressed to the top of her head.

Such ragged emotion. Shutting her eyes hard against impending tears, Suzana reached down to clutch both muscular cheeks of Krael's ass, pulling him closer, demanding more of him even though he already filled her to the brim and beyond. He picked up the pace, stroking faster to spike her arousal. She squirmed, glorying in the way his big body trembled, how his breath caught when she twisted and managed to squeeze him just a bit harder.

"Krael," she moaned, released into her climax.

"Goddess," he cursed, joining her.

Neither orgasm was the explosive release she'd come to expect. She didn't scream; it didn't hurt. But the heady warmth and spreading ecstasy opened the floodgates of her emotions. She could no longer deny the sobs that threatened. Mortified, she subsided from shakes of pleasure to body-wracking sobs.

Krael pressed his lips to her forehead, his hands clutching her shoulders. "Suzana, don't cry."

She tried. But she couldn't stop. Desperately, she clung to him, her arms wrapped about his middle as far as she was able. When he tried gently to pull her away, she clutched harder.

"I love you," she breathed, uttering the words for the

first time in days.

"Suzana…" he began, voice stern.

But he was cut off by the sound of the door opening. Suzana didn't look. She didn't want to. She didn't want to see the man who would come to remove her from Krael. She clung like a baby monkey when Krael pushed to kneel and face the newcomers.

"Oh, you have marked her! How very nice."

She froze. The *rhaeja?*

"My lord." Krael's voice rumbled through her skin. "I'm honored by your presence."

"I'm sure you are. Have you trained *my* little mage well?"

Suzana let him unlock her arms from his waist, knowing she was embarrassing him. She didn't want to cause him grief, but neither did she want to be away from the touch of his skin. She clutched his hand when he would have removed it.

"I have, my lord."

She peeked through her heavy fall of hair toward the door. The *rhaeja* stood, thankfully clothed in a pure white robe, just inside the doorway. She was relieved to see that Radin was also present, standing in the doorway itself.

"She's needy, isn't she?" Valanth observed.

Krael failed to answer.

Suzana watched the white robe blend with Valanth's loose white hair as he approached the bed. "Very well. Let's get this over with."

"My lord, are you testing her?"

"Yes."

"Again, my lord," said Radin, stepping into the room, "I must protest. A third party should test her."

"Do you doubt my word, *boy?*" Valanth snarled, rounding on Radin.

"No, my lord, but think how it will look. Everyone knows you've declared Suzana for yourself. Shouldn't someone else test her?"

Valanth's glare narrowed. "Could it be that you just want to taste my little mage?"

Radin smiled cheekily. "Do you blame me, my lord?"

Taste? What did they mean? Suzana watched the exchange with a bleeding heart, not really wanting either man to touch her. As they argued, Krael tugged her toward him. She went willingly and allowed him to arrange her between his spread legs, her marked back to his chest. He scooted forward until both of their legs draped over the side of the bed. With one arm wrapped about her middle, he settled the other with his big hand at the base of her neck. It took a slight squeeze that barely threatened her breath for her to realize. He'd put her in a position where he could throttle her. Or, just by raising the other hand, snap her neck like a twig. She closed her eyes. He intended to keep his promise!

Krael watched the bickering sorcerers warily. He was thankful for Radin's presence. Without, Krael had no doubts Valanth would simply take Suzana without bothering to test her. But Krael needed that test. It was the one tiny ray of hope that might keep both he and Suzana alive.

But he didn't count on it. As soon as she was pronounced not pregnant, he'd snap her neck. The moment he did, his life was forfeit. Not only would Valanth be enraged that Krael denied him his "little mage," but the deliberate taking of a potentially fertile female's life was cause for death. Valanth was the only known exception to this rule, and that was only because no one could prove he'd killed his truemate or any of the others.

Rhon now stood in the doorway, the boy's eyes wide in surprise. Krael guessed that it was more the boy's presence than anything else that caused Valanth to subside. "Oh, very well." Valanth spread a hand toward Krael and Suza, eyes glued on Radin. "Test her."

Radin smiled, that mischievous grin that won him so many friends. "With pleasure, my lord."

Suzana squirmed, and Krael bent his head to her ear. "Radin is going to taste that sweet cunt of yours, Suza," he murmured. "Spread your legs for him."

She complied, despite the unsure frown on her lips.

Radin knelt, smiling up at Suza. Something he saw made the smile falter slightly, and Radin darted a glance at Krael. Krael gave him nothing. Without Valanth's hovering presence, he might have said something. But, then again, maybe not. Radin would no more approve of Krael's plan than anyone else. He might, in fact, be less understanding.

Radin's gaze narrowed, but as Valanth's presence kept Krael quiet, so, too, it kept Radin's thoughts within his head. With visible effort, he regained his smile, aiming it at Suza. "Be at ease, Suzana." His hands slid over her bare thighs, fingers dipping between to graze her moist pussy.

Krael would be helpful. Perhaps, in doing so, Rhae would bless him with a miracle. He rubbed his cheek against the satin of Suzana's hair, lifting his hand from her belly to her breast to playfully tweak a nipple.

"Get on with it!" Valanth snapped, causing all three of them to jump.

"Yes, my lord," said Radin, almost a sigh but not quite. Crouching down, he bent until his lips grazed the curly hair guarding her mound. Inhaling deeply, he nuzzled further. His lips parted, and his tongue extended to search out her clit. He did not seem to mind one bit that she was still moist with Krael's come.

Suzana shuddered, her body sinking deeper into Krael's embrace as Radin pressed forward, sealing his lips over the apex of her sex so he could suck her into his mouth.

"Let him taste you, Suza," Krael murmured, nuzzling her ear. "I want to see his face all wet from your come. I want him to taste what I've tasted."

She moaned, writhing. He tightened the hand he kept at her neck, reminding her of his promise. His promise that she was his and no one else's, even if he did share her for a brief time. Her hand crawled up over her head, into his hair. She took a healthy handful, bracing herself with it as she ground her body toward Radin.

"Look at him, Suza," he commanded, taking his hand from her breast to sink his fingers into Radin's hair. He pulled some of the silk over Radin's shoulder, letting it dribble over her hip. Radin glanced up but didn't protest the move, adjusting his arm below Suzana's thigh to make more room for Krael's plans with his hair. "Shove your tongue into her, Radin. That's what she wants."

Instantly, Radin complied, and instantly Suzana shattered. Radin held her hips, securing his mouth on her sex. Krael's grip tightened on Radin's head, pressing the man even closer.

"He's not done," Krael told her when he knew she heard him again. "He'll make you come again, lapping up that sweet honey that only you taste like."

She bit her lip, and again he squeezed her throat. The reminder sent her over the edge again, and she yanked hard on his hair, the pain nearly bringing tears to his eyes. He growled, bending to bite her neck, knowing she loved both the sound and the action.

Suzana couldn't catch her breath. Couldn't find her sanity. Her body writhed between the two men, orgasms bouncing between them in one long, unfathomable stream. Each time she thought she'd had enough, Krael would growl, or tell Radin what to do to her, or he'd squeeze that hand on her throat to remind her that he had her life in his hands. Tears streamed from her blind eyes as she pushed into Radin's talented tongue.

With one last agonized quake, her body dropped. Radin continued to lick and suck, and Krael continued to croon, but she was spent. It felt good, but she could simply no longer respond.

She struggled to open bleary eyes as Radin sat back. His face did, indeed, glisten with her juices. He raised one elegant hand to wipe his chin and cheeks clean, languorously licking his palms afterward.

Smug, he turned a grin to Krael. "Did you want to be a father, my friend?"

Beneath her, Krael froze. The hand at her neck tightened, just enough to threaten the breath that she held in shock.

"*What?*" This from Valanth, whose presence she had all but forgotten. He loomed behind Radin, who turned on his knees to face him.

"It's true, my lord. She's pregnant."

"What?" It was her turn to demand, although in a far more quiet and feeble manner. But Radin heard. He turned to her. "Yes, lady," he said, his voice soft, his gaze warm. "It seems you've done what no other woman has and found your truemate in your first nine days."

She stared, so shocked that she didn't cringe when Valanth swooped over her. None of them realized his intent until three of his fingers were buried deep in her pussy. She cried out, flinching before she could stop herself. Angrily, he twisted, ignoring Radin's shocked protest. Almost as quickly as he was in, Valanth pulled his fingers out and stuck them in his mouth. They watched him roll her taste on his tongue.

"Impossible," he muttered, withdrawing them. "No woman finds her truemate the first time. Even less so a virgin."

No one said anything. Valanth stared hungrily at Suzana, his orange gaze raking her still-heaving breasts, curved belly, and the wet hair guarding her sex. He snarled slightly, then lifted that gaze to Krael.

"I congratulate you, Captain," he said, voice dangerously blank. "I suggest you take good care of her."

Suzana held her breath as he twirled, then stalked out, nearly running over Rhon in the process.

Only when he was gone did Radin stand. For a moment, he stared down at Suzana and Krael, who still remained frozen in shock. "Would you really have killed her, Krael?" he asked softly.

Krael's hand transferred instantly from her neck to her far shoulder, pressing her tighter against his chest. Softly, he growled.

Radin met her gaze briefly, then again looked to Krael. Shortly, he nodded. "It would seem to be a moot point." His grin returned. "Allow me to add my congratulations." He bowed and turned to go.

"Radin." Krael's voice stopped him at the door. The sorcerer turned, his earrings glinting in the firelight. "It's true, isn't it?"

Radin's jaw dropped, even if a slight smile remained. "Are you implying that I might lie about such a thing?"

Suzana froze. Such a thought hadn't occurred to her.

"Yes." Obviously, it had to Krael.

"And how do you propose I planned to get away with that? Within a cycle he'd know if she wasn't pregnant."

Krael's breath-crushing hold on her relented slightly. "So it *is* true?"

Radin rolled his eyes, waving a disgusted hand at them. "Suzana, I pity you the thick-headed lout you've bonded with." He grinned at her. "I hope he's worth it."

It finally all dawned on Suzana. It was over. She was Krael's. If she understood correctly, in the eyes of their society and in the judgment of their goddess, she and Krael were the same as married. More so. And she was pregnant!

In due time, she would give birth to Krael's son.

A grin split her face, and she clutched Krael's hand where it lay on her shoulder. "He is," she assured the smirking sorcerer. "He most definitely is."

 THE END

Jet Mykles

Jet's been writing sex stories back as far as junior high. Back then, the stories involved her favorite pop icons of the time but she soon extended beyond that realm into making up characters of her own. To this day, she hasn't stopped writing sex, although her knowledge on the subject has vastly improved.

An ardent fan of fantasy and science fiction sagas, Jet prefers to live in a world of imagination where dragons are real, elves are commonplace, vampires are just people with special diets and lycanthropes live next door In her own mind, she's the spunky heroine who gets the best of everyone and always attracts the lean, muscular lads. She aids this fantasy with visuals created through her other obsession: 3D graphic art. In this area, as in writing, Jet's self-taught and thoroughly entranced, and now occasionally uses this art to illustrate her stories, or her stories to expand upon her art.

In real life, Jet is a self-proclaimed hermit, living in southern California with her life partner. She has a bachelor's degree in acting, but her loathing of auditions has kept her out of the limelight. So she turned to computers and currently works in product management for a software company, because even in real life, she can't help but want to create something out of nothing.

ANTHOLOGIES AVAILABLE In Print from Loose Id®

HARD CANDY
Angela Knight, Sheri Gilmore & Morgan Hawke

HOWL
Jet Mykles, Raine Weaver & Jeigh Lynn

RATED: X-MAS
Rachel Bo, Barbara Karmazin & Jet Mykles

ROMANCE AT THE EDGE: IN OTHER WORLDS
MaryJanice Davidson, Angela Knight & Camille Anthony

THE BITE BEORE CHRISTMAS
Laura Baumbach, Sedonia Guillone & Kit Tunstall

WILD WISHES
Stephanie Burke, Lena Matthews & Eve Vaughn

Publisher's Note: The print titles listed above were previously released in e-book format by Loose Id®.

Non-fiction from Loose Id®

PASSIONATE INK
ANGELA KNIGHT

OTHER TITLES AVAILABLE In Print from Loose Id®

ALPHA
Treva Harte

COURTESAN
Louisa Trent

DANGEROUS CRAVINGS
Evangeline Anderson

DINAH'S DARK DESIRE
Mechele Armstrong

HEAVEN SENT: HELL & PURGATORY
Jet Mykles

HEAVEN SENT 2
Jet Mykles

LEASHED: MORE THAN A BARGAIN
Jet Mykles

INTERSTELLAR SERVICE & DISCIPLINE: VICTORIOUS STAR
Morgan Hawke

THE TIN STAR

J. L. Langley

STRENGTH IN NUMBERS

Rachel Bo

THE TIN STAR

J. L. Langley

THE BROKEN H

J. L. Langley

THE COMPLETENESS OF CELIA FLYNN

Sedonia Guillone

THE PRENDARIAN CHRONICLES

Doreen DeSalvo

THE SYNDICATE: VOLUMES 1 & 2

Jules Jones & Alex Woolgrave

VIRTUAL MURDER

Jennifer Macaire

WHY ME?

Treva Harte

Publisher's Note: The print titles listed above were previously released in
e-book format by Loose Id®.

LaVergne, TN USA
08 January 2010
169292LV00002B/5/P